Contents

Acknowledgement

There are many people to thank for helping me get this book written and published. While it sometimes feels a bit lonely writing, turning my musings into an actual novel has involved a lot of help at home and from a network of other amazingly supportive authors.

Mr Parker has kept everything else running during those times I have hidden away in the office, furiously typing or going through feedback notes or reading How-To tomes. I couldn't have done this without him. Also my friend Breffni and her partner Greg who have both been hugely supportive.

Then there are the other authors who have critiqued or beta-read for me. Kristin Lance—you were the first and are an inspiration. Others include: Anne S. who kept pulling me up on *Show Not Tell*; Melissa McTernan who writes the loveliest adult Fairytale stories; Esther Star, another amazing author who helped shape the book; and Megan Black whose influence significantly improved my MS. I can't thank you all enough for the time you spent.

Finally, my ray of sunshine, Aron, who kept me entertained with his stories while I wrote and helped me with a male reader perspective on some of 'those' scenes.

Chapter One

Rosie

The door to Sid's office closed behind me with a hushed click and I victory-danced, fist-pumping the air.

Sid Bramwell, agent extraordinaire for Rosie Byrne and her Trio had finally come up with the goods and secured us a booking for that very night at Café Paradiso, one of London's most prestigious live music venues.

Okay, it was a cancellation rescue booking, but what the heck—a booking was a booking. And it was at Café Paradiso: business executives and the social elite, fine dining accompanied by classy live music (that would be us).

We had finally hit the big time.

Well… maybe not the big time, but this was undoubtedly a huge step forward and could open the door to decently paid gigs in the *better* venues. Sid usually placed us in one of the jazz-café type pubs. However, our bookings always resulted in repeats and the last time he came to see us, he had been suitably impressed at our development over the past year. I had been on his case ever since. That, and all the hard work we put into honing our sets, was finally paying off.

Suddenly aware this floor was all glass-partitioned offices and that I was highly visible to the office workers in them, I stopped, straightened up and lifted my chin. Floating at least six inches off the ground, I headed back to the lifts.

Sid's office was on the ninth floor of a modern, glass-walled block in Central London, high enough that sunlight was streaming unhindered through the windows of the offices as I exuberantly strode down the glass corridor.

Today was shaping up to be a good—possibly great—day.

As I reached the lifts and stood back to see which of the three would arrive first, I fired off a text to the band:

<<Gig tonight at Café Paradiso. Will call later with details and timings. 😎

I caught my reflection in the highly polished lift doors and realised I was grinning like the proverbial Cheshire Cat. I giggled as the doors in front of me swished open, and took one step forward, only to be floored as I gazed up into the most gorgeous eyes I had ever seen; the colour of melted chocolate, they were fully rimmed with long, dark lashes.

As I took in more of his face, my breath caught in my throat. Sweet Jesus, he was absolutely stunning. A lush head of almost black hair, swept back and curling at the neck, framed his face. Whatever the smattering of salt and pepper at the edges suggested, I couldn't guess his age; there were no giveaways on his perfectly symmetrical features.

Straight off the cover of a GQ Magazine, his full lips opened slightly as I stared. I could already imagine those lips kissing mine as my fingers scrubbed across his perfect, two-day-growth designer stubble.

I couldn't help but check out the rest of this Adonis, and, since he didn't move, maybe he wanted me to.

This was surely an athlete: long, lean, broad-shouldered, clothed (more's the pity, I thought) in a beautiful Savile Row, black three-piece, clearly tailored to fit closely enough to hint at defined biceps and thigh muscles.

Showoff.

His shirt and tie were also black, the latter slightly loosened, revealing an undone top button. Black was definitely this guy's colour.

His shoes looked like they might be hand-made. And his hands were large but perfectly proportioned, unadorned and a little rough around the edges of his nails. I have a thing about big hands.

I imagined straddling his narrow, chiselled hips, those amazing hands on my body.

Bloody hell, you perv... I was now checking out his package.

I quickly raised my eyes to that gorgeous visage in time to see something flash behind those dreamy eyes. A lazy, bemused smile spread across his face as his head tilted slightly to one side. His eyebrows arched as he appeared to be inviting me to... something.

His den of iniquity for hours of pleasure?

Oh God! What must I look like?

The Cheshire Cat grin frozen on my face, I had brazenly checked him out and was standing like a lemon at the lift door, seemingly rooted to the spot. The door nudged at my foot, spurring me into action. He was leaning against the railing at the back, the only one in there, leaving me plenty of room to sweep in and immediately turn to face the doors as they slid shut, hiding the hot flush climbing up my cheeks.

I rolled my eyes, annoyed at trashing my Rule One: *Never let a guy know what you are thinking.*

I breathed in deeply through my nose, then out through my mouth, becoming aware of his scent, a masculine, spicy but fresh, citrus and peppery scent that set my senses jangling.

Then he started humming. He actually started humming! In a lift!

I soon realised what it was. An old Frank Sinatra number, 'Strangers in the Night'.

Oh, hilarious.

He obviously thought he was a comedian. Full of himself or what?

Well, it wasn't night, and we certainly wouldn't be sharing love before the night was through—or any other time for that matter. Sex: all-night-long hot and sweaty sex maybe; he *was* bloody drop-dead gorgeous. But love was not on the table. Not now. Not ever.

There was definitely something, though…

I could feel his eyes on the back of my head, a soft caress. My temperature rose, and I slowly started to suffocate. I didn't want feelings like this stirred up. I prayed the lift would shoot to the ground floor and let me escape.

No such luck.

At the next floor down, the doors opened onto a crowd of milling, twenty-somethings who moved into the lift almost as one cartoon blob, forcing me to take a couple of steps backwards. I stumbled against those Size Elevens and would have lost my balance but for a pair of strong hands grasping my elbows and stopping me from toppling over.

The rough stubble of his cheek brushed against my ear, and

a low, rumbling voice murmured, 'You're okay—I gotcha,' in a sexy, drawling Southern States accent that sent shivers up my spine.

Something shifted in my chest as my lungs seized up. I was about to twist my head around to say—I don't know what—something like, 'Thanks', when the guy standing in front of me stepped back and toppled me off balance again.

I fell against Dixie Adonis, and the back of my head made contact with a firm, muscled chest while the small of my back pressed hard against... a solid erection. That substantial bulge grew as I wriggled against it. I couldn't believe I did that but, Hot Damn!—I couldn't help it.

My body's reaction was instant and extreme; I honestly thought everyone in the lift must surely see the heated flush that surged through me, and hear my gasp as I struggled to breathe. Dixie Adonis could hardly not notice as I was pressed so tightly against him. An insistent throb pulsing at the junction of my thighs, in my now-damp knickers, I closed my eyes for a few seconds, wallowing in thoughts of the deliciously hard cock that twitched discernibly against my back.

Shit!

What the hell was going on with me? I couldn't remember any guy affecting me like that so suddenly.

Get a grip, Rosie.

After what felt like an eternity, the lift stopped at the third floor where—as the sign and distinctive aroma informed us—the Coffee Shop was situated. The horde poured out, leaving me, for no good reason now, still pressed against his gloriously hot body, strong hands still wrapped around my elbows.

I hesitated for a moment longer, then stepped forward, his hands simultaneously releasing me. I turned around to find him looking down at me, his face inches from mine, his gaze searing into me, his lips slightly parted and his breathing jagged.

Holy Moly! To see the effect I was having on him was intoxicating.

I was drawn from his eyes to his lips. God, I wanted to taste those lips. I looked back into his eyes as his lids slowly closed. He breathed in deeply and straightened up as that slow, languid smile once more lit up his face. His now open eyes twinkled—I swear that's what they did. My whole body tingled as I bathed in the warmth of that smile.

He leaned forward again and murmured into my ear, in that deliciously husky drawl, 'I can only apologise for my… erm… friend. He seems to like you.'

As another wave of euphoria threatened to reduce me to a quivering mess, I repeated over and over in my head: *Rule Two: Seize control. Always be the one calling the shots.*

As the lift doors finally opened onto the ground floor, I shot back what I hoped was my most sultry, fuck-me smile. 'You'll have to introduce me to him sometime,' I purred. I flashed my eyes at him and immediately turned and walked away, swinging my hips. Once I'd cleared his line of vision, I raced around the corner to where I knew the pristine, marbled Ladies' Toilet was situated.

As the door clicked shut behind me, I slumped against it.

What the hell was that? I had no idea who this stranger was. So why had I wanted so badly to feel his arms around me? And why the hell had I walked off without exchanging so much as a contact number? The chances were I'd never clap eyes on him again.

I felt strangely bereft. Hell, I didn't even know his name.

I soon came to my senses. What would I want with someone who could so easily provoke a reaction like that from me? How would I keep control of a relationship when all I could think of was drowning in those beautiful, fathomless eyes, wrapped in those comfortingly masculine arms?

Yes, my physical reaction had been extreme, deliciously so. But what shocked me was that amazing feeling of warmth and security when he'd caught my arms and said, 'You're okay—I've gotcha.' That smooth, sexy drawl that had dampened my knickers and sent shivers running up and down my spine. I could hear it again in my mind; I played it over and over.

It really wouldn't do.

I walked over to the basins and ran some cold water to splash over my face. I looked at my reflection in the mirror.

No.

Feelings like that can only lead to betrayal and heartache, and I've had enough of those to last a lifetime. Yes, he's a hot guy, but I have my life sorted out. I've got my three Fuck Buddies and the rules they stick to. This is good and how it should be, how it must be. And right now, I've got to organise my band for our most prestigious gig to date.

I pulled myself together.

Eventually, I left the Ladies and handed my ID tag to one of the two women on the reception desk who barely even looked my way, so immersed were they in an animated conversation. I caught the words, 'Did you see…?', '…dreamy eyes…', '… arse…' and, 'OMG….' and surmised that they were probably discussing their latest crush.

As I left the shade of the building, I had to shield my eyes. The glare of the city streets at lunchtime can be punishing, the sun high in a clear cobalt blue sky casting minimal shadows, reflecting off the pavement and all the glass and steel and windscreens.

The street was a roiling mass of office workers on their lunch breaks separated by the relentless stream of city traffic, choking the air and kicking up the dust that suddenly seemed to appear from nowhere as soon as the dry spell hit.

I loved it. I loved living in the city. I loved the constant noise and movement, the 'busyness' of it. In the beating heart of London, I was constantly caught up in the life and energy of it all—no time to dwell on the past.

I set off home, the list of *Things to Do* forming in my mind.

Nathan

What the fuck was that all about?

I watched her sashay out of sight, grinning at her adorable, Audrey Hepburn-like *very proper English lady* accent.

I already knew I was going to have sleepless nights thinking about what her petite, beautiful little body would look like naked, the feel of her against my cock, the sight of her breasts rising and falling in time with her panting, those sparkling eyes and those quivering, parted lips; I knew these things were going to haunt me along with the delicious scent of her.

Oh, I wanted to introduce her to my dick all right and make sure she never forgot him. She had taken my breath away with that parting shot, not to mention leaving me with a raging hard-on.

There had been something else going on—something I couldn't quite put my finger on—something that unnerved me.

As soon as I regained my senses, I left the elevator and marched through the milling business suits and sensible heels, past the scrutiny of the sheepishly grinning receptionists. I pushed my way through the exit barrier, slipped through the outer door, raced down the steps and winced as everything hit me at once.

The sun was blazing, reflecting off the glass windows and stainless-steel cladding of the buildings surrounding me and even bouncing off the sidewalk, blinding me. The traffic was relentless and noisy, and the sidewalk was crowded with people hurrying to and fro. I shielded my eyes and searched up and down the street, but couldn't catch sight of her.

I turned back to recheck the reception area. Maybe I'd passed her without realising. It took a couple of minutes for my eyes to adjust to the comparative dark in there again. But... nothing. I pinched the bridge of my nose, berating myself for letting her go like that.

I left the building and wandered aimlessly up the street, trying to analyse what had just happened. I passed my favourite coffee shop and went in to get a caffeine hit and my shit together.

I got a double espresso for the kick and sat down on one of the vacant love-seats in the window. This place was snug, welcoming and quirky: dark, softened floorboards, comfortable seats and sofas with those cushions all over that women can't seem to live without and men don't understand at all. They have old jazz-gig posters in frames adorning the walls along with the familiar 1958 photo, 'A Great Day in

Harlem', and they play jazz music, loud enough to hear but not so loud that you can't hear yourself think.

I replayed the events of the day in my mind.

My first meeting had been with Sid Bramwell, the music agent who procured most of the artists for our live music venues. The artist booked for Café Paradiso that very evening had cancelled because of emergency surgery and Sid had asked to see me about a substitute. His offices are in the same building as Connor and McQueen, our family business's UK arm, so I'd dropped in on my way up.

Overseeing details at this level is not usually my thing. Finding the right person for the job, identifying someone I believe has the right skills, and then empowering and delegating—that's my talent. But Café Paradiso was my baby, and live music one of my passions; identifying the right music acts for it was one element I was keeping for myself for the moment.

Sid, a chunky, balding fellow who looked and sounded like a caricature cockney character from a Guy Ritchie London gangster movie was, of course, convinced he had just the right band to take the slot. Given that it was too last minute to secure a well-known act, and it was a school night so the customers weren't ticketed for a particular concert, it was at least a good opportunity to try out an up-and-coming.

'I know you've been talking about getting a resident act, somefing that could be a signature style for the club. You're lookin' for somefing classy and distinctive. Great musicians but wiv the glam factor—so somefing for the guys or gals to focus on.

'I might just 'ave wot you're lookin' for, somefing right up your street.

'I've got an unknown but bleedin' class act. They are gonna make a name for 'emselves on the jazz circuit, I don't doubt it.'

I felt scepticism creeping up on me. What was he gonna try and sell me here? But he went on.

'They are a jazz, swing and blues ensemble, four of 'em at present, but they could expand and bring in some 'orns given the right opportunities. Free exceptional musicians and a singer at'll knock yer bleedin' socks orf.'

Okay, so he had got my full attention again.

He went on. 'Alf-pint size pretty brunette—tiny little fing, but when she lets rip, man can she silence a room wiv 'er velvety voice. An' they can turn their 'ands to uver styles as well. Perfick opportunity to give 'em a try out I'm finkin.'

'Sounds like a plan, Sid,' I said.

'I'll be along to come and check on 'em,' he told me. So I invited him to join me there for dinner.

'Great stuff. Love to.' His phone rang. 'D'you mind?' he asked. I could hardly object, I had dropped in on him unscheduled.

I waited while he took his phone call, scanning the photos and posters plastered on the free-standing screens set about the place. Pictures of Sid with a string of A-list chart-toppers and other performers decorated them.

A shot of Sid with a tribute Rat Pack group sitting beneath a black-and-white of the actual Rat Pack caught my eye, and Frank Sinatra stared back at me, setting off a melody in my mind, one I knew would annoyingly be on repeat for the rest of the day until I'd want to take a hammer to my head.

My second meeting had been three floors up in my own offices, with Mason Williams, my capable PA, Rhys Evans, the Executive Manager of several of our venues, including Café

Paradiso, and the contracted Project Manager who would be responsible for the fit-out and decoration of a venue in Manchester's Northern Quarter that we were in the process of securing.

That meeting had gone well. The Project Manager we had contracted was turning out to be a find and had given us a first, brief sight of designs that looked terrific.

I had left them to thrash out other details, going off for a swim and workout.

There I was, daydreaming in the empty, peacefully quiet elevator when the doors had opened, and I had found myself gazing down, locking into the most seductive, beautiful, dark green eyes I have ever seen.

I watched her checking me out and liking what she saw, her exploration of my body like a feather tickling my skin. Then her eyes dropped.

I certainly liked what *I* saw and, much to my chagrin, my cock duly responded.

Maybe it was her pert little nose or the adorable dimples in her cheeks when she was smiling that captivated me. Wispy dark glossy curls framed her pretty little face with the rest of her hair pulled back. Sexy, petite but curvy—something about her was utterly compelling.

Hot and amusing as it had been watching her check me out, when her eyes locked onto mine for the second time, I got a fleeting glimpse of something melancholic. Don't ask me why but that's the moment I fell under her spell. Hard. And her reaction wasn't lost on me either; the attraction between us was palpable, crackling in the air.

She'd flounced in and immediately turned her back on me, embarrassed, I guessed, at being caught ogling. Not that I minded. She could ogle me all day and night if it meant I could gaze into those sexy eyes. I couldn't help but notice the breathtaking shape of her ass in the tight blue jeans she was wearing.

I started humming. It's an involuntary thing for me, especially if I'm feeling a bit uncomfortable. If I've got something running through my brain, like a Frank Sinatra song I've just heard, I can't help but start humming it.

Then fate intervened.

The lift filled up, and she fell against me—ended up with her back pressed hard against me in a way that could leave her in no doubt about how I was responding to the situation. Jeez, it was so fucking hot, looking down at the top of her head and feeling her pressed against my dick.

Compelled to say something when we found ourselves alone again, I thought myself quite the clever guy, coming up with my line. But her response was a killer, and I can't deny I nearly shot my load. I had to fight for control, by which time she'd flown.

We'd barely exchanged three sentences but, already, this was a woman I wanted to know better, a whole lot better, and that was unusual for me. It had been seven years since betrayal turned my heart to stone, seven long years since I had wanted to have more than sex and superficial conversation with a date or a pick-up.

Right then, though, I needed to get back to my apartment.

I would have to come back the next day to find out who my mystery woman was.

Chapter Two

Rosie

I arrived back at my flat, made a coffee and sat down to make the calls. Sid had given me a number for the event manager at Café Paradiso, who would provide details for the gig.

Not only did this place have what sounded like a state-of-the-art PA system and everything that went with it, the woman explained that they also had their own audio technician. He usually worked with a band to ensure that what they wanted from the system is what happened.

Pacing the floor now, I rang and passed on the details to the band. I knew that if they were already booked with any of their other ensembles, they'd sort out a *dep*—a deputy who could step in for them. The Café Paradiso booking was critically important for our quartet.

Pete, our Double Bass player, the guy we all call the *Daddy* of our band, would swing by and pick me up in the van. Adam, our fantastic jazz pianist, and Annie—the same age as me and the youngest female jazz drummer I've ever seen—were both bubbling with excitement. We'd all meet at the venue at 6pm, prompt.

CHAPTER TWO

The day was getting better and better.

Well... apart from the Dixie Adonis episode, which kept playing through my mind every time I wasn't focused. And every time, it left me with the same breathless, heady feeling that had overwhelmed me in the bloody lift.

It occurred to me that I could always go back to Sid's office block and see if I could track down where Dixie had been and what his real name was. It shouldn't be too difficult, right? A striking American like him would stand out in a London office block.

I wasn't sure how I might go about enquiring and how creepy or weird it might come across. There had been two women on reception—I could ask them, they'd get it. I mean, who wouldn't have noticed those chocolate brown eyes and that sexy Southern drawl? The one that had me imagining chocolate being poured on my tingling body and having it licked off... slowly...

Shit!

That would have to wait til the next day. I had to focus on making the gig perfect.

Putting a show together is no five-minute job. It takes hours to work out what songs to include and in what order, to ensure a spread of styles and different solos. And then there's making sure they fit to make each set forty-five minutes long, ensuring every song choice will contribute to a performance that will impress the hell out of everybody.

I grabbed an apple and bit into it as I selected a range of songs that comprised a wide variety of styles: jazz, swing, some American Songbook numbers, some bluesy numbers and some modern songs given a jazz or bossa treatment. All songs that would show us off, each in our own right.

I went over and over the lists until I had settled on twenty first-choice numbers with six reserves just in case—way too many, but it would give us options if needed. I had made sure every member of the band's favourites were in there too. Bye, Bye Blackbird and Fever for Pete, Adam's take on Cheek to Cheek and Moondance, and Annie's favourite, Every Step You Take—she loves modern songs turned into jazz. As for me, I love the bluesy stuff—At Last, I Put a Spell On You and Angel Eyes.

I winged the setlists and spares off to the guys to challenge if they wanted to and then make sure they had the right charts in the right key on their tablets.

And when that was all done, I had to start prepping myself and take time to pick my stage outfits.

An unwelcome but not unexpected fluttering started in my stomach. Would I be good enough? Am I good enough? My mouth went dry, and I grabbed a pint glass of water from my kitchen.

Would they think I have what it takes to hold an audience in a place like this?

With a longer-term goal of making a name in the British jazz scene and hopefully securing a recording contract, getting attention at venues like this one was pretty critical.

I had to shake off the nerves.

I looked through my wardrobe, pulling things out, scrutinising then discarding them until I had chosen two outfits to take with me, one for the first set and one for the second. I hung them over the door, ready to go in my dress carrier.

I had a sudden thought: if tonight went well, I would be buzzing later. I ought to phone Matt or Liam or Jamie, my current regular Fuck Buddies, and have one of them waiting for me when I got home. I'd want to celebrate, and uncomplicated sex would be on the cards.

I decided I'd do it later when I'd sorted a few other things out.

I had another sudden thought: I should take my just-in-case outfit—my Lexi Farah Champagne dress. I took it out of my wardrobe and hooked the hanger over the top of the door to look at its entire length. I loved this dress—how it made me feel when I was wearing it.

I had to have this long gown significantly and expensively altered to accommodate my lack of height, without it losing its shape; an ultra-thin strap that looped over one shoulder, and a split that reached up to the top of my right thigh, this dress draped over my body leaving very little to the imagination while still looking incredibly classy.

I scrabbled through the hoard of shoes in the bottom of my wardrobe until I found the pair of cheap nude strappy sandals, which perfectly matched the colour of the dress. I looked a million dollars in that get-up. Okay—I *felt* a million dollars in that get-up. I would only wear it tonight if my performance needed a bit of a boost; after all, I wanted to save it for when I found Dixie.

Dixie...

I held my breath, closed my eyes and imagined his gazing intensely into mine while one of those huge hands wrapped itself around my exposed thigh and moved gently upwards. My heart thudded as I imagined his other hand cupping my face, rubbing his thumb across my lips and pushing it gently into my mouth for me to lick and suck, all the while pinned by his intense, dark chocolate eyes.

I sat down on my bed as a vision of him materialised beside

me. He leaned in and kissed me, pushing me back to lie across my grey and pale pink duvet. I felt that rock-solid shaft again, this time against my belly as he lay on top of me.

My hands—his hands pushed my shirt up and kneaded my breasts, the nipples hardening against my—his touch. I visualised his pulsing cock, and imagined him easing the tip into me.

I slipped my hand into my knickers and circled my swollen and oh-so-wet clitoris with my fingers. I breathed in hard, held my breath, and then let it out with a gasp. I did it again. My orgasm didn't for an instant blot out the image of that face and those compelling eyes.

Shit! SHIT! I try not to do eye-to-eye sex. Too intimate.

I needed to get this guy out of my head. He'd probably got an ex-debutante wife or a model girlfriend or even kids. He must be at least early thirties, I speculated. He might be gay? No, don't be ridiculous—not with the reaction he had to me in the lift.

I remembered my disappointment when the gorgeous hunk who is now my bestest friend in the world, Josh, broke it to me that I wasn't his type after I'd been ogling him and making eye contact for over an hour.

'Baby Girl, you are wasting your time and your fabulous assets on me, my dear,' he'd whispered in my ear. I had snorted my drink, out through my nose and all over, then laughed. He'd laughed with me, helped me mop up, and we had been best friends ever since.

Back to the lift—the large, rock-solid shaft I'd felt in my back when I'd fallen against him was pretty strong evidence that Dixie wasn't gay. And that thought had me deep breathing again.

I didn't have time for that.

Leave me alone—I've got things to do. Tomorrow Dixie. I'll track you down tomorrow.

I only had an hour before Pete arrived. I jumped in the shower and washed my hair while going through some vocal exercises to warm up my voice, humming basic scales, the blues scale starting somewhere near C (I'm not pitch-perfect) and moving up the octave. Another, starting as low as I could, sliding my voice up and flinging it as high as I could go, then sliding all the way back down again—this one always sounded awful!

I decided to wear my hair loose rather than trying to put it up or curling it.

I made lemon tea with honey to soothe and smooth my vocal chords and started in with the hairdryer.

Nathan

So, smart casual. I showered, close-shaved and gelled my hair into place. It had a mind of its own and flopped all over the place if I didn't stick it down. I thought about leaving the beard to grow a bit more, but it would get irritating. Besides, I'd have the stubble back within a couple of days.

I dressed in dark blue slacks, jacket and signature matching dark blue shirt. Then I looked for what shoes to wear.

I own a couple of pairs of Italian, handmade leather shoes that my daddy got me when I finished travelling, and I'd kept them looking good.

I smiled remembering his words when he took me to be measured for them. 'Son,' he'd said, 'you can tell a lot about a man from his choice of shoes and the shine on them. If they are good quality and looked after, this is a man who respects himself and, therefore, others.' My daddy was full of gems of wisdom and liked nothing more than to share them. I believed he was right and had taken his words to heart. My tan Italian-made wingtips, I reckoned.

If this band, *Somebody and Her Trio,* proved to be as good as Sid seemed to believe, it would show that he had, at least, understood what I was looking for and could help fast-track me finding it. I'd been searching for some time, trawling round live-music venues. The plan was that the right resident band would keep the customers coming back on the nights not featuring a headliner or chart-topper.

Finding the right ensemble isn't that easy—many of the bands I'd seen had been terrific, but none so far had the edge or style I was seeking.

Sid had said the singer was a pretty brunette. A vision of an auburn, elfin bombshell stood before me, eyes sparkling with mischief and lascivious promises, and a dimpled smile that could raise the Titanic.

At that moment, Alexa, who was playing 2Cellos as requested, switched to the live Zagreb concert and Benedictus opened, gently bathing my room in one of the most heavenly pieces ever written for cello, played in the most sensitive, beautiful way. And what could be better than *one* cello playing it? That would be two.

I closed my eyes and saw hers again. I knew she was going to haunt me. From the second I had locked into those beautiful, smoky eyes and seen that momentary flicker of sadness, she had awoken something in me, called to me. I wasn't sure what it was that had awoken or what the message was.

Whatever, I thought, it'd be better put back to sleep. Café Paradiso—that was my passion now and, while it might fail, it wasn't a woman who would wantonly betray me, cut my heart out and cast me aside. Besides, it wasn't going to fail—I'd make sure of that.

As the melody rose, Hauser made that damned cello sing like the most melancholic, hauntingly beautiful voice you ever heard, and I was back staring into those eyes, cupping her face in my hands, raining kisses all over and telling her that everything would be all right now, I had her.

What a schmuck! What the fuck made me think she needed rescuing? Least of all by an emotional train wreck? And what the fuck was I doing indulging in childhood fantasies about a knight in shining armour, charging to the aid of the beautiful princess?

Better to stick to the adult-rated fantasies—after all, I was on a promise, wasn't I? And it wasn't as if that was difficult, imagining myself stroking, licking, probing every inch of her hot little body. Not to mention all the other things I would do to her, like watching her going down on me, looking up at me with those soulful, sad eyes.

Sad eyes? Jeez, that had only been a fraction of a second before the shutters had come crashing down again. I might even have imagined it.

But I hadn't, and beyond logic or rationality, I knew I had to find her.

Chapter Three

Rosie

We all arrived promptly at 6pm as arranged, met up with Stuart the sound guy, and set up on the fabulous stage in Café Paradiso, all crushed velvet curtains and lights.

Shivers ran up and down my spine as I looked out onto a honey-coloured oak floor, populated by dazzling, white-clothed dining tables with dining chairs all faux-leather and wood. They were laid up in twos, fours, sixes and eights with bowls of roses and table lamps adding colour and a touch of class.

A large open space invited dancing, and I could imagine the place packed and pulsing late into the night.

We had half an hour before the bar opened. The drums assembled, the instruments positioned and the microphone and stand set up centre-stage, we sound-checked and hastily tried a few lighting schemes.

As well as sound, Stuart would control the lighting, bathing us in different colours and effects throughout the night. We went through the set list with him, indicating the mood of each song, and agreed to place ourselves in his experienced hands to set up the lighting appropriately.

Our first set would start at 8.30 pm and the second at 9.45 pm. They had an in-house DJ who manned the decks between times and through to 1 am.

Heading through to the backstage area, we were all delighted to be shown the cherry on the cake for us, a real luxury—a dressing room with mirrors, makeup lights, chairs, hanging rails, even curtained booths for getting changed in. I wouldn't be dashing into a grotty little pub loo, questionable stains and smells and all, to get dressed and sort out my makeup. And we'd have somewhere to relax a bit in the break. This was heaven.

Having dumped our stuff in there, we headed back out through the main area.

I noticed the cosy booths down one side wall—wine-coloured leather studded bench seats with tables and facing chairs set up in ones and twos. Along the other side of the room were a series of circular bench booths of dark rose-pink crushed velvet seating around central round tables. I imagined sitting out in the audience here, eyes on the stage, the sounds of cutlery on crockery and the chinking of glasses with a background hum of conversation.

The whole scene was dazzling, gleaming, polished, pristine, and screamed business class. I imagined us working places like this every week. It was a nice fantasy.

First, we had to get through this gig and not let Sid down.

Once we were all set, we had to hang around until we were due to go on. We took ourselves off to the upstairs bar, ordered some drinks—soda water for me, lagers for the others—and sat around going through the set. The guys organised their charts in our final chosen order on their iPads.

We went through each number, reminding ourselves of the structure and what solos went where. In jazz sets, much of the instrumentation is off-the-cuff, based on a chart, a beat usually initiated by the singer, and prior agreement on who was going to do what solos where. Although the overall structure will always be the same—a song will rarely sound exactly the same twice.

When we'd been through everything, I nipped off to the loo—never a good thing having to pee in the middle of a set—and I realised I never did call Matt, Liam or Jamie.

I grabbed my phone deciding on Matt, who had been my first Fuck-Buddy.

I remembered my first sight of him between sets at a corporate thing I was working, a tall, straw-blond, surfer-guy type standing at the bar drinking alone when I went for my pint of soda water. He offered to buy me a drink, which I declined. I usually got complimentary soft drinks in venues I performed in; I'd never drink anything alcoholic until I'd finished my set—too unprofessional.

I'd asked him why a fit guy like him—he certainly was easy on the eye—was drinking alone in a room full of 'beautiful young things'. He told me they all knew better than to 'mess with' him.

Although he hadn't smiled much, there was definite chemistry between us. Proximity with him had my heart thudding against my ribcage and butterflies doing somersaults in my stomach.

I'd asked, 'What if *I* was to try 'messing with' you?'

'That'd be perfectly acceptable for one night, Sweetheart,' he'd answered, suddenly revealing a cheeky, knicker-dropping smile.

After my gig, he bought me a drink at the bar; then we'd moved on for more drinks in a late-night place not far from my flat.

He not only looked delicious, he smelled divine—Hugo Boss he told me when I asked.

We found it easy to talk, probably because, although we felt a connection, neither of us had any expectations of developing it into a romantic relationship. Not that that stopped him from being heat-provokingly tactile—he was finding it as difficult to keep his hands off me as I was him.

We both had reasons for not being interested in romance and for not wanting to go down the route of hooking up with a succession of total strangers. Too risky—certainly for me.

So, we agreed that we'd jump each other's bones that night and, if we liked it, we'd become a go-to for sex for each other.

Through that first night, we'd fucked hard and fast several times, and the freedom I had felt to glory in the physicality of it was breathtaking. At the end of the night, we'd grinned at each other sheepishly and knew this was the start of... something.

Those first few encounters with him were as great—no strings, no emotions, just great sex and a regular test to be on the safe side.

During this time, we came up with the whole Fuck Buddy idea and made up the first set of rules. And to make sure no one got too intimate or close, we introduced a non-exclusivity rule to keep everything grounded.

My rules include the two I've already mentioned that are relevant only to me:

Rule One: Never let a guy know what you are thinking.

Rule Two: Seize control. Always be the one calling the shots.

Those and the others certainly did the job with Liam and Jamie, meaning I now had three guys to call on to keep me happy.

That non-exclusivity rule did the trick. I had no intention of ever getting too close to anyone, of letting my guard down ever again, and that rule kept things very clear for the guys too.

So.

Matt.

He'd be the perfect choice for tonight. Hot lips and stamina to die for, he'd be the one to drive those dreamily gorgeous melting chocolate-brown eyes out of my...

Bugger.

Too late!

Those very eyes, lined with gloriously long black eyelashes, floated in front of me as that beautifully masculine, handsome face and that incredibly hot, firm body I'd fallen against materialised in my mind—not to mention that solid shaft pressed against my back.

I closed my eyes as those huge, warm hands held my elbows again. That oh-so-sexy drawl caressed my ear with, 'You're okay—I've gotcha,' and I saw that flash of his eyes and sharp intake of breath as I'd delivered my killer response to his apology.

I'd given the guy a clear invitation and then flown off before he could take me up on it.

Clearly, though, I did want him to take me up on it.

I wondered whether I had made as much of an impact on him as he'd made on me, whether he would react well to me tracking him down.

Maybe he would; I'd learned that the promise of sex was a

pretty good motivator for men.

Maybe he wouldn't. Perhaps he'd already written me off. It's not as if a guy as hot as him would have any trouble hooking up—he'd have women drooling over him.

But the attraction between us had been almost tangible, like electricity in the air. His gaze had reached deep into me and tugged on something.

I realised that I had lost track of time. I rushed back to the bar where the band were still sitting chatting, and we all headed back downstairs to our dressing room.

I sat in front of one of the brightly lit mirrors and put my stage makeup on; I never overdo it frankly, but some false eyelashes, a bit of colour and a touch of shiny red lipstick are pretty essential under the glare of stage lighting.

I popped into one of the curtained cubicles and slipped on my bright fuchsia-pink sheath dress. Thankfully, I'd had my legs spray-tanned a couple of days before so I could go bare.

I sucked on one of my vocal lozenges, and performed a few last 'lip-bubble' scales, sticking my fingers into my cheeks and vibrating my lips through scales up and down. It sounded delightful—NOT.

That was me—ready to bring the house down.

Yeah right!

YES—I've got this.

We'll see.

Nathan

I arrived at the ground-floor tropical-themed bar to find Sid waiting for me with another guy carrying two cameras.

Sid explained that he would like to use this gig to get some decent promotional shots of the band if that was okay, and introduced me to his photographer.

I'd got us a table booked for 8 pm, the band would be on half an hour later. Leaving the other guy behind, we made our way downstairs, where a doe-eyed hostess escorted us to a table situated to one side of the stage, providing a great up-close view.

Here in the basement, there was a huge bar across the back wall, all mirror, smoky glass, black acrylic and shiny metal, brightly lit by four huge drop lights beneath which tiers of colourful bottles were lined up. Trays of gleaming, polished glasses, twinkling in the lights, were set up in various spots along the bar, waiting to be filled and distributed. It was all sparkle, glitter and colour.

I scanned the room. My plan was for this to become one of the most successful live music dining venues in the capital.

We sat. I had an excellent view of the stage.

We ordered, and I picked out a decent little wine.

'So, Nafen. Is jazz your fing?' Sid asked me.

'I love music, Sid.' I told him. 'My parents introduced me and my brother and sister to all sorts of music.' I smiled, remembering us all dancing around the kitchen or hallway to some Country or Rock' n Roll track.

I continued, 'My parents' parties, which are pretty legendary where I come from, always include a dance session with music from the Rat Pack, Bobby Darin, Nat King Cole, and, of course,

Ella Fitzgerald, Sarah Vaughan and Peggy Lee.

'So, yeah, I've had a lot of exposure, and I would say it's certainly on my list of 'things'.'

The wine arrived, and the waiter immediately brought it to me and poured me a drop; I sniffed it—it was fine, not corked. I nodded at him and he poured us both a glass.

Sid took a slug. 'Well, if you like that stuff, you'll like what you're gonna 'ear tonight. Any partic'lar favourites?' he asked.

I leaned back, rubbing my chin. 'Well, given that the singer tonight is female, I'd say Peggy Lee is probably one I like a lot. I like her laid back, understated style and she has great timing. I have a CD of her with George Shearing, *Beauty and The Beat*—great title, huh?'

'Well, you are gonna jus' luv Rosie then,' Sid said, gesturing at me with his glass. 'If I 'ad to compare 'er, it would be wiv Peggy. I mean, she does all the uver gals' numbers an' sorta makes 'em 'er own. Wiv' Peggy numbers, she pretty much sticks to the original style, ya know? She says ya can't mess wiv' perfection.'

I laughed. 'I like her already.'

Our meals were served. We'd both gone straight for the main course, both chosen the ribeye, rare. I happened to know that the chef there was one of the best steak chefs in town. I should know—I'd hired him.

'Yeah. she's got that lovely deep, rich tone and 'er timin' is fab.' Sid shoved a forkful of steak into his mouth and carried on talking between chews. 'An'... she's got a great band backin' 'er too.... includin' a rarity—a female jazz drummer... about the same age as Rosie. Really good. So, they make quite an impact togever.'

'They've been togever about a year now and are gettin' it

nailed, ya know? I'm startin' to push 'em at the higher-end venues. Tonight could be a great springboard for 'em. They'd be a pretty good signature band, I reckon.'

I was now very much looking forward to hearing them.

The lights dimmed slightly, and a voice announced, 'Ladies and gentlemen, please welcome our guest band tonight, Rosie Byrne and her Trio.'

There was a smattering of applause. Everyone else, like us, was busy eating their meals, and this band was unknown.

I looked to the stage to see a girl climb in behind the drum kit dressed in shorts and sporting a black bob striped with neon blue.

A giant with greying hair grabbed a double base from its stand at the back of the stage. He was a mountain of a man. Wouldn't want to confront him in a back alley.

The last to take the stage was another diminutive woman in a short dress, her hair a riot of waves. I couldn't see her face because her back was still to me but something niggled in the back of my mind—there was something vaguely familiar about her. She placed a large glass into the holder on the mic stand, turned to the two others, lifted her left arm in the air and started clicking her fingers to set the timing of the beat of their first song.

As the double bass sounded, I understood why the pianist hadn't taken his position yet—this was the start of the song *Fever*, one of my favourite Peggy Lee numbers, and they were going to perform it with just the double bass and drums.

The three of them were bathed in soft lighting as the singer turned to the front and eased into the opening line in a gloriously deep, rich, dark, velvety voice.

Holy Fuck! I nearly choked on my steak.

Standing there on the stage, dressed in a little bright-pink number that showed off a perfect curvy shape and smooth, silky, bare legs and arms, was my mystery woman from the elevator.

I had to gulp down some wine to stop from choking aloud. Sid looked at me, eyebrows drawn down; I glanced at him long enough to wave away his concern before my eyes shot back to the stage.

Of course.

Now it made sense.

She'd got into the elevator on the floor his office was on—she'd obviously been in to see Sid.

And that was the last rational thought I had for the next couple of minutes as I drowned in the sight of her beautiful, elfin face, her incredibly hot little body and the hypnotic sound of her husky, sexy voice.

She was working the room with those fabulous eyes. When I could force myself to drag my eyes away and look around, I could see guys with forks suspended in mid-air, mouths hanging open, and women with unmistakable 'WOW' looks written on their faces. The room around us had fallen quiet as the audience became hostage to the allure of her sensual vocals.

She swept her gaze around to the right as she got to an instrumental verse and our eyes locked, her face a mask of professionalism.

Her eyes flicked between Sid and me, a million questions written in them. I tried my most reassuring smile, and something lurched in my chest as her eyes lit up and her lips curled into a subtle smirk.

Not dropping a beat, she glided straight back into the song, glancing away from me and back around the room to keep everyone engaged.

She turned that intense gaze back to me as she sang the final words of the song—those repeated hints at sizzling and burning setting my blood on fire.

Her eyes never left mine and what I saw in them told me, in no uncertain terms, that I was still on a promise.

The last note hung in the air, fading into a heavy momentary silence. Then, as if the spell had been broken, the room erupted in applause. I was on my feet with everyone else, clapping and whistling. She was sensational.

I looked over at Sid. He was staring at me speculatively.

'They are terrific, Sid, you were absolutely right,' I yelled at him over the noise.

'Yeah,' he said, 'they are very, very good, mate. An' you seem to 'ave made a connection, huh?' he said, his eyebrows dancing suggestively.

He'd obviously seen the looks that had passed between Rosie and me. As the noise abated we sat down, and he carried on.

'If you want some advice, I'd be cautious wiv that one,' he said. 'Our Rosie is, undoubtedly, a gorgeous gal, but they reckon she's a ball breaker. Rumour' 'as it, she only sees guys for sex.' He grinned from ear to ear. 'Now I'm not sayin' there's anyfing wrong wiv that. Given the chance, I would. Well, if I wasn't an 'appily married man, that is, who didn't want 'is balls chopped off.'

I grinned and shrugged at him. *Well, uncomplicated sex is always my favourite kind.* I was intrigued.

'Well, Sid, if that opening number is any indication of what's to come for the rest of the evening, this little band of yours will certainly be high up on my list of potentials.'

'Yeah,' he said, 'these guys are definitely gonna make a name for 'emselves.'

The next number began, so I turned back to watch the show unfold. The pianist had joined the band now and hammered out a catchy riff as a very different intro to a well-known tune. I sat back to hear what they were going to do with this number and I wasn't disappointed, I'd never heard Cheek to Cheek performed like that—it was superb.

This was getting better and better. Rosie was too professional to allow what was going on between us to interfere with her performance. She'd given me an unmistakable message, and now she was focused on the show.

All too soon, she announced they would take a thirty-minute break, and the band left the stage to the sound of thunderous applause, but not before she looked over to me and held my gaze for a few seconds. She beamed that breathtaking smile, all sparkling eyes and dimples. Then, she was gone.

I became aware that Sid was saying my name. I turned and looked at him.

'An' 'e's back in the room,' he announced. 'Man, you 'ave got it bad. Where were ya? Lost in some fantasy, huh? Tell me, did it involve bangin' the brains out of a half-pint songstress by any chance?' He threw his hand up, palm facing me in a *Stop* gesture... 'No, don't tell me, I might fink twice about the wisdom of promotin' this band to you.

'So, do you want me to introduce you to the team now or do you wanna suspend judgement 'til you've seen the 'ole set? Or maybe you'd be too star-struck and go all gaga on me,' he chuckled.

'Hey, I'm sold,' I replied, 'and business is business. This band has shot to the top of my list so, yeah, I would like to meet 'em.

But, Sid—for the moment, I'm just a guy interested in possibly booking the band, okay?'

'You're the boss.'

Rosie

I came off stage floating.

OMG. He's here. Dixie. And he wants me—it's written all over his face. What's he doing with Sid? Oh, who cares? He's here!

OMG. Listen to that applause! We are smashing this. We've just gotta keep it going through the next set.

I didn't know what to think about first. Everything was so overwhelming; I could hardly breathe.

I got to the dressing room and, unable to hold our excitement in, we all performed a victory dance around the room, whooping and leaping about. I barely heard the knock on the door and, as I was closest, flung it open to find Sid standing there grinning at me like an idiot.

I threw myself into his arms, still whooping and laughing. He lifted me off my feet, laughing with me, and spun me around. He set me back down on my feet and started speaking.

'Hey guys, that was absol…'

I heard no more. My head was suddenly full of sirens and mush.

Standing beside Sid, smiling down at me, his eyes burning into me, was my Dixie Adonis.

Head to foot in midnight blue, my insides liquefied at the sight threatening to turn me into a gibbering, drooling mess. He looked absolutely gorgeous. Smooth cheeks my fingers twitched to touch made him look younger.

His smile widened. God. It was as if he could see what I was thinking.

Get a grip! I told myself and forced the turmoil to calm in time to hear Sid saying, 'Boys and girls. Rosie? ROSIE!' I snapped my gaze back to Sid.

He glared at me. 'Boys and girls, I'd like you to meet Nafen Connor. 'E's lookin' for bands to feature in fairly regular slots,' he shot a look at Nathan, 'and quite liked what 'e heard out there.'

Quite liked? Quite *liked? What the hell was that supposed to mean? Hey, don't fall over yourself with praise,* I fumed internally, shooting a deadpan Gorgon glare at Dixie that I hoped would wither his balls.

Nathan responded, holding both hands up in surrender. 'Let's be clear, I thought you were terrific out there.' I saw the guys' eyes widen when they heard his swoon-inducing, Southern American drawl.

That languid, lop-sided grin flipped my stomach again. Then he winked at me and a surge of heat engulfed me.

Bloody hell. This was ridiculous. I didn't like it. I felt like I wasn't in control of my feelings. And yet, at the same time, the tingles washing over me were wonderfully intoxicating.

Sid went on, 'Nafen, this is Pete Gallagher.'

Nathan moved further into the dressing room to save Pete having to get up from where he'd flopped down onto one of the chairs in front of the brightly lit mirrors. They shook hands and Nathan lazily drawled, 'Nice to meetcha Pete. That's a mean double bass you play. That solo in Bye, Bye Blackbird was outstanding, man.'

'Jazz pianist, Adam Laidlaw.' Nathan turned to shake hands with Adam.

'Hey, Adam. Was it you who came up with that rolling riff in Cheek to Cheek?' he asked. Adam nodded, smiling broadly. 'Loved it.'

'Nafen Connor, meet Annie Carling.'

'Annie, this is a real pleasure,' Nathan purred, taking Annie's hand in his and raising it to his lips. 'Not so many women in your game. You may be one of the best drummers I've seen in the flesh, so to speak.' He grinned and Annie, shuffling about on her feet, tugged at the hem of her shorts. She slowly flushed scarlet, a sight rarely seen; clearly, his effect on women wasn't confined to me.

I felt a slight prickle of something in my gut. Jealousy? Surely not. Definitely. Not.

'And, um, the band's vocalist, Rosie Byrne. Why do I get the feelin' you've met before?'

'Oh, we *met* each other in the elevator near your office earlier today, Sid. But we weren't... *introduced*...' He pinned me again with that searing gaze. 'Of course, that was before I knew Rosie was the singer you were telling me about. Ms Byrne.'

He moved closer so that he was standing over me, tilting his head so that his face was just inches from mine. 'So nice to be... *introduced* to you,' he drawled, his eyes flashing with hidden meaning and lingering long enough over the word 'introduced' to have my libido shoot flashes all over my body. He held his hand out to me, palm up as if he was also going to raise my hand to his lips when I laid my fingers on it.

My parting shot earlier suggesting that he 'introduce' me to his cock sometime had flummoxed him momentarily; I needed something equally disarming now.

With my back to the others, I deliberately swept my eyes down to his fly, lingered, then licked and nibbled my bottom lip as I raised them back up to meet his. I trailed my fingers gently across his outstretched hand until my hand was completely engulfed in his.

'The pleasure's all mine,' I purred, watching his eyes darken and his breath hitch. He muttered something under his breath—too low to hear, but I could have sworn it was 'Touché.'

He turned back to the others, dropping my hand, regret shooting through me that I hadn't simply given it to him and felt those lips brushing the back of it.

'I'd like to buy y'all a drink at the bar after,' he offered. He flashed one last smile around the group, saving me for last. His eyes darkened once again, and he shot me such a hot, intense look, I nearly melted on the spot. He smirked to himself as he turned to go and strode off down the corridor.

Sid brushed past me and muttered in my ear, 'I 'ope you know what you're doin', Rosie. Don't screw this up. Screw him, or blow him for all I care, but don't blow the potential deal we might 'ave 'ere.'

'Sid!' I cried in a mock hurt tone. 'How could you doubt me? You know I always have everything under control,' I shot at him.

'I 'ope so Rosie, I 'ope so,' he said and hurried after Nathan Connor, aka Dixie Adonis.

Chapter Four

As Nathan and Sid disappeared back down the corridor, I turned to the others. It was time to prepare for the second set.

'Hey guys, honestly, you were amazing out there. I'm sorry I messed up the lyrics in Angel Eyes—sang the same verse twice—and I completely screwed up the second key change in Fever.' My internal self-doubter and harsh critic jumping in as ever, never happier than when putting me down, although I tried hard to ignore her and not be needy.

'Oh, here we go again,' said Adam rolling his eyes. 'Rosie, you were brilliant. Did you not hear that applause? That was for all of us.' he said, indicating quite clearly that I hadn't succeeded.

'No one noticed,' said Pete, quietly. 'You're listening far more closely than anyone else in the whole damn place, and you have a natural ear so, even if it's not what's written, you pretty much always sing something that sounds right. You sounded great out there, Rosie. You know you did—well, part of you knows you did. Shut the other voice off; tell it to go to hell.'

'Well, the audience is fuckin' loving it!' whooped Annie. 'Have you ever heard Sid so fuckin' hyped? And that tall Yank, he seemed pretty fuckin' blown away, if you ask me.'

She does have a way with words, our Annie.

Just get out there and give it your all. You know you can do this.

Of course, it wouldn't hurt to give my image a little boost. I might be short and not exactly slender, but I knew the Lexi Farah dress, with only a pair of tiny silk knickers underneath, was slimming and looked classy. And it was so revealing, I was sure it would have Dixie drooling. I would put it on, have him eating out of my hand, and begging for mercy. Men are so predictable!

Decision made. I touched up my make-up, then popped into one of the curtain cubicles once more, slipped the dress on and strapped on the matching sandals. Momentarily calm and collected, I was ready for the second set.

He's out there.

And, I was floating again; the same heady euphoria that had swept over me when I saw him in the audience—when our eyes had locked and his had burned—grabbed me once more.

I played back the visit to the dressing room, the intense, heated gazes, innuendos that made my knickers damp, and my hand cocooned in his. And that last look.

Oh God, I want to drown in those eyes. And I want him. I want those hands kneading my breasts, caressing my body, those fingers inside, stroking, stretching me, his mouth demanding, his lips soft, hot…

'Rosie! Are you ready? It's time!'

Nathan

I poured out the last of the wine. Neither of us was drinking quickly. I had decided to keep my wits about me now I knew she was here and that I was going to have her before the night was out.

She wanted me. If I'd had any doubts about that after the elevator incident, she had just swept them clean away. And, you know what? I liked that she was so assured, enough to be that forward; she should be with a body and face like hers—talk about launching a thousand ships. I know women find me attractive, but one look from her made me feel like I could conquer the fucking world.

I soon found out why Sid wasn't knocking it back. He leaned across the table. 'Look mate, d'you mind if I leave you to it shortly? I've been neglectin' 'er indoors a bit lately; I wanna try and get 'ome before the witchin' hour tonight if I can.'

'Hey, that's cool,' I replied. I wasn't unhappy that he wouldn't be there when the lovely Rosie and I had our next *encounter*. I'd got the distinct impression he wasn't too amused at the apparent connection we'd made, and I wanted to keep him on-side.

'I'll just stay for the first couple of numbers, check that their second set is goin' down as well as the first, then I'll be off,' he said.

The lights dimmed, and the stage lights came up to reveal the band members taking their places again.

Holy Fuck! I choked again and heard Sid gasp.

Rosie had appeared in a dress that left very little to the imagination, a silky number with the tiniest strap over one shoulder, that clung to her delicious little body revealing the shape of luscious round firm breasts, beautifully rounded hips and had a split up to the top of her thigh.

'Fuckin' 'ell,' said Sid. *My thoughts exactly.* 'She sure knows 'ow to get attention, huh?'

The music started, and that warm, velvet voice told us about the boy from Ipanema while the vision that was Rosie gently swayed her hips to the hypnotic Samba beat. I managed to tear my eyes away from her and check out the audience again. All eyes in the room were glued to the tiny figure on the stage, mesmerised. I doubt there was a limp dick in the whole joint or a woman who didn't wish they had a fraction of her appeal. She. Was. Sensational.

The atmosphere was electric, the tension palpable. And as for me, I was on fire. The audience wanted her, and she wanted me. And, as if to confirm that, she shot me a glance that spoke volumes and had my cock aching to plunge deep into her soft, wet sex.

Then, she broke the spell herself, delivering a slight departure from the original lyrics suggesting that the boy from Ipanema looked at *him* rather than her. The audience smiled—some laughed—and the tension vanished, transmuted into rapturous applause as the song finished.

As they began the second number, the photographer came over and showed Sid the shots he had. He had stayed for the costume change between the two sets but already had enough views of the new dress. Sid got him to show me through the view-finders on the cameras. One shot stood out for me. It was Rosie in that heart-stopping dress, singing soulfully into the mic. It was stunning. I told Sid I'd like a blown-up copy. He looked at me speculatively again but told the photographer to make a note.

As soon as he had left, Sid stood up. 'That's enough for me. Blimey, I need to get 'ome to my missus. It's 'er lucky night, I'll tell ya.'

We shook hands, agreed to keep in touch and he took off, leaving me free to concentrate my whole attention on the luscious Rosie Byrne, who was going to be mine very soon.

That thought came as something of a surprise to me. Mine?

I thought over what Sid had said. I was jumping ahead of myself here, wasn't I? Maybe she would only want me for sex and then would want to move on. Well, I'd happily do that. A couple of dates all culminating in hot sex. That had pretty much been my life since Linnea gutted me and left me to bleed.

I looked back at the stage, where Rosie was in full swing with an upbeat number. She was dancing and loving every minute. The instrumental break started, and she looked over, beaming that infectious smile. Once again, we locked eyes. I sat through the rest of the performance, completely hypnotized by this woman.

The set was coming to a close. The band had played their *last* number and been called back onto the stage for an encore. Rosie belted out a blistering version of *I Put A Spell On You* that had me agreeing—she had indeed put a spell on me.

They finished the number and could not be coaxed back onto the stage for another encore, though the audience was desperate for one. We had a house rule—only one encore.

The lights came up, and I made my way to the bar. I had invited the band for a drink after their performance and wanted to ensure a space for them there while they were packing up and, probably in the case of Rosie, changing. I sat and waited for them to emerge.

Rosie

From the first song, *The Boy from Ipanema*, to the encore, *I Put a Spell on You*, we gave the performance of our lives.

The audience went wild for another encore. I was on Cloud Nine but it was a house rule—one only.

After a round of high fives and quick chat to schedule our next rehearsal—we were all free on Friday afternoon—I said, 'Let's get the drum kit packed up then and go for this drink,' impatient to get out of the dressing room and ultimately into the bar and to my Dixie Adonis.

'Aren't you getting changed?' asked Pete pointedly, still zipping his Double Bass into its huge leather case.

'Look, I know you guys will want to get out of here asap,' I said. 'I can come back and get changed after you've gone, rather than hold you all up now.'

Jake, Annie's other half, poked his head around the dressing room door. Annie squealed and threw herself at him. 'Jakey, baby! I've got a hot date waiting at the bar to buy me a drink,' she announced to him when she came up for air.

Jake laughed. 'Well, why don't you go and claim your drink? I'll pack up the kit, Kitten.' My heart rate doubled as I realised we could go to the bar straight away.

Pete continued our conversation as though there'd been no interruption. 'Uh-huh? And it's not as though you're out to impress anyone in that... nightie, is it? Look, just be careful out there, okay? And as for this guy, please don't cut his balls off if there's a chance we'd get a shot.'

I looked back at Pete full of mock outrage and hurt. 'I don't know what you're talking about,' I said. Inside I was grinning; so, they thought I was a ball-breaker?

'Right,' he said, 'so you'll be wanting me to wait to give you a lift home then, yeah?'

I grinned. 'No, Pete, I'm a big girl; I can make my own way home.'

'Yeah, right.' He collected me up in a big hug and whispered in my ear, 'You be careful girl, you are precious to us you know.' As he put me back down he added, several decibels higher, 'You were on fire tonight, Rosie. I have never heard you sing so well. Brilliant.'

That meant a great deal to me—Pete rarely dished out praise. I'd watched him many times analysing our performances like a critic writing the latest jazz blog entry. I was very touched by his praise, my heart swelling in my chest and somehow threatening to turn the taps on in my tear ducts.

It was definitely time to head for the bar. I knew the others wouldn't stay past one, maybe two drinks wanting to know a bit more about what we might get from Nathan, who he was, and what venues he might work for; they all had reasons to get home. And that would mean I would be left with my Dixie Adonis and the night. Of course, I reasoned, there was always a possibility that he would buy us all a drink and then leave, but there wasn't really a chance of that—he wasn't going anywhere without me. I'd be making sure of it.

As we left the dressing room, I thought about him flashing those intense dark brown eyes at me, melting my insides and making me wet with anticipation.

And that is what you want this guy for, remember, you'll have to have 'the talk' with him before you take this further than tonight, I thought.

Well... that's interesting... so you're already thinking beyond tonight?

We arrived at the bar. Nathan had secured a space and a couple of bar stools for us, and he ordered us all the drinks we requested. My performance over, I was now free to indulge in my favourite drink of the moment, an Espresso Martini. I claimed one of the bar stools and sat, slightly facing the bar. 'Thank you, Dixie,' I said.

He looked at me, tilted his head slightly forward as his eyebrows went up and up. 'Dixie?' he said. 'Uh-huh? Okay. Well, if you wanna be more precise—and maybe a bit more PC—it's Bluegrass.'

'Kentuckian,' I observed.

'Indeed—that's my family home. My momma is English though, so technically, I'm dual nationality.'

'Gosh,' said Annie. 'Does that make only half of you a blue-collar, red-hat, Bible-thumping hick?'

Oh my God! That girl has no filters. Pete, Adam and I just held our breath in horror.

Nathan tipped his head back and roared with laughter. 'Yeah!' he came back with. 'And only half a supercilious, pompous colonialist with bad teeth!'

Annie regarded him for a couple of moments, then cracked up with laughter herself. 'Okay, you'll do. I like you,' she announced. 'How did your mum and dad meet? How have you ended up here in London?'

We breathed a collective sigh of relief, and I sat quiet for a while listening to the conversation, drinking in the sight of him and luxuriating in the sound of his voice and the lilt of his accent.

'Well, my daddy was a pilot in the US Air Force, stationed at Lakenheath in Suffolk. He and his best buddy married English sisters. My daddy took his family home to Kentucky when he left the military. The other two, my aunt and uncle settled in England, in London, which is pretty much how I ended up here when I visited them and decided to stick around.

'How about you, Annie, what got you into jazz? And how come drums?'

It wasn't lost on me that he singled out Annie to chat to first. He threw a glance, in my direction then focused his attention on her as she spoke, leaning in and tilting his head to be sure he could hear everything she was saying.

I was mesmerised watching as his eyes told Annie that she was the centre of his universe for those few moments, that the tale she was unfolding was the most fascinating thing he'd ever heard.

'Uh-huh? Well, go Annie.' I heard him say, watching her straighten up and puff out her chest like a preening flamingo.

He turned his attention to Adam, and I watched him do the very same thing, Adam positively glowing under his attentive gaze.

Every now and then, in between talking to one or another, he'd flash me a glance, even winking at me once or twice, just to make sure I knew he was still thinking about me. And every time he did, I pretty much melted on the spot.

Two couples made their way over to the bar and stood in front of me.

'Oh my God, you were soooo good. You were all fantastic,' oozed one of the women, casting her glance around the group, 'but I love your voice; you are amazing,' she directed at me. The others in her group nodded vigorously and smiled. 'Will you be coming back here? This is one of our favourite spots, so we're here once a month-ish, but we would come in to see you if you were on. Wouldn't we?' Again, lots of vigorous nodding and muttered yeses.

'Well, thank you, that's very kind of you. It's our first time here, and we'd love to play it again wouldn't we guys?' I drew the rest of the band in.

'Really glad you liked it,' Pete threw in.

'Yeah. Def get us back here,' Annie chipped, bobbing up and down.

Even Adam, our man-of-few-words managed, 'Enjoyed playing this place—great to have such an appreciative audience.' We all turned and looked at him in amazement.

I turned back to our newly-found fans. 'So it would be great if you could tell the management you'd like us back.'

'Oh, we definitely will and put reviews on their website and Facebook and anywhere else we can find. It's *Rosie Byrne and her Trio*?'

'Yeah—that's right, B-y-r-n-e, and that would be cool. Thank you so much.'

'Thank you,' our new fan bubbled, 'you've made our night.' They made their way off in a cloud of 'Thank you's and 'Fantastic night's.

'Well, that's your adoring public, eh?' Nathan said admiringly.

The others soon took their opportunity to thank Nathan for the drinks and departed, leaving me with my Dixie Adonis and the night.

He stared at me for what seemed like an eternity. Serious. Calculating. Sizing me up. Despite my heart rate playing skipping games in my chest, I resisted the urge to say anything and waited for him to make the first move.

He took a deep breath in. I could see every tiny muscle movement on his face, hear the air being pulled into his lungs as though it was the only sound in the room. I waited for him to speak—it looked as though he were about to.

Then he laced his hands together, turned them out and stretched them up over his head, the muscles in his chest perceptibly rippling under his shirt. He separated his hands and let them drop, then tilted his head to stretch his neck, first one way, then the other, never taking his eyes off me for a second.

He moved like a big cat, oh so controlled but oh so languid. The whole show had me rooted to my seat, utterly spellbound.

Then he nodded as if he'd come to a decision about something. He leaned over to me and brushed my ear with his lips as he murmured, 'So, Ms Byrne, tell me, don't you usually change out of your stage gear before you start drinkin' at the bar?'

It sounded more like a challenge than a question.

'I knew the guys would want to get off home, so I decided not to make them wait while I changed before we came to take you up on your kind invitation,' I shot back at him.

That slow grin spread across his face. 'Uh-huh? If you say so.'

He held his hand out to me to help me off the bar stool. Not a word was said, but I found myself taking his hand, stepping down from the stool and standing there looking up at him.

He stepped back, his smouldering eyes taking in every inch of my body. And every inch of my body lit up in a mass of tingling goosebumps under his gaze. I struggled to breathe.

As he leaned in towards me again, his lips ghosted over my ear sending electric pulses feathering over my scalp and straight down to my lady bits. 'Now. Rosie. Tell me the truth. Did you keep that dress on for me?' he purred.

Spontaneous combustion! The insistent throbbing in my crotch had just leapt even higher. The phrase *gagging for it* leapt into my mind. I was. Oh God was I. Gagging for it, for him. I leaned slightly in towards him, breathing in that wonderful, heady aroma again—bergamot, sandalwood. I'd have to find out what the hell that was. He tilted his head to bring his face closer to mine.

'Why, Mr Connor, of course I did.' I smiled coyly at him. 'You weren't able to take your eyes off it for nearly the whole of my second set.'

'Oh, it wasn't the dress I was lookin' at, Rosie,' he said, running his tongue across his bottom lip and not releasing me from his eyes even for a moment, 'it was what's underneath it I was studyin'.'

I felt the silky touch of my dress go taut as my nipples hardened. His eyes dropped for a heartbeat then returned to mine, darkening; his irises now entirely black.

'And what did you conclude from your studies?' I asked him breathlessly.

'They confirmed what I had already surmised earlier in the day, Rosie,' the tenderness in his voice as he said my name making my knees go weak. I was trembling now, and he could obviously see it because he took my hand again to steady me.

'And what was that Mr Connor?' I whispered, gripping his hand for support, not at all sure that I could remain standing when he answered.

He moved closer, his lips caressing my ear again as he put his arm around my waist and pulled me to him. 'That you are, beyond question, the most astonishingly beautiful woman I have ever set eyes on,' he breathed. 'That I want you more than I have ever wanted anything. That I have to have you, or

I might just stop breathing.'

Something lurched in my chest; my legs nearly went out from under me, and I clung to him, feeling the warmth and the firmness of his body through his shirt and trousers, wanting to melt into him. He had taken me entirely by surprise.

I had been expecting something superficial, something graphic about what he wanted to do to me, and his declaration had taken me unawares, not the least because it described perfectly how I was feeling about him.

He moved me slightly back so he could scan my face for my reaction. I must have been grinning like an idiot because he smiled at my expression, and then a deep, rumbling chuckle sounded in his chest. The whole episode had been so intense that, now the tension had snapped, we were in danger of leaping on each other, completely forgetting that we were, not only in a public place but that I was an object of attention and would be being scrutinised.

I looked away from him and saw a couple of guys along the bar watching us with apparent interest. 'We should get out of here,' I muttered. He nodded back at me. 'We need to talk, somewhere we won't be under scrutiny,' I added.

'We need to talk?' He looked taken aback and then smirked again. 'Talkin's good. For starters anyhow,' he suggested.

I couldn't help but smile. 'I need to get changed and get my stuff from the dressing room,' I continued, 'Why don't you come and help me; we'll decide what happens next.' I flashed a loaded look at him.

He nodded his assent with a strange smirk on his face. He was so tantalising—every move he made, every expression in his eyes, so provocative. My hand still firmly held in his, I set off, threading my way through the tables as I headed for the door beside the stage that would take us back to the dressing room.

As we passed tables, people kept stopping me to say how much they'd enjoyed the show, how great the band was, how much they loved my singing—I glowed in the praise.

'They surely loved you, didn't they?' Nathan purred at me.

'People are kind,' I replied, 'it's lovely of them to be so sweet.'

'Kind? Sweet?' he said. 'Rosie, they love you because you're amazing. You have a wonderful voice. You're a terrific singer. They're not being *kind*.'

I laughed, feeling embarrassed and self-conscious but, at the same time, delighted that this sexy, beautiful man had just called me amazing, wonderful and terrific. I pushed through the door into the corridor as my libido kicked up again at the thought of what was about to happen.

Chapter Five

Nathan

I couldn't wait any longer to taste her.

As we entered the corridor and the door to the restaurant area closed behind us, I pulled her back to me. Taking hold of her chin, I leaned down to touch her lips with mine. I kissed her gently and she melted into my body. She kissed me back so gently, the softness of her mouth yielding to the dominance of mine. I licked her bottom lip and explored her mouth with my tongue and I could feel hesitation in the way her tongue gently caressed mine.

Suddenly, she pulled back, piercing me with an intense glare. There was something in her eyes. Fear? Anger?

She was shaking her head as if denying me. Then, like some crazed jungle cat, she threw herself back at me. Our lips crashed together as she thrust her tongue into my mouth, demanding I push back at her. It was desperate, almost brutal, but so hot.

Then she broke with me, grabbed my hand again and pulled me down the corridor to the dressing room. She fumbled with the key card to unlock it, and we swept into the room.

I wanted to make her feel special and knew I had to take control. If I didn't, this would completely get away from me, and I'd just take her—a compulsion that was new to me. I was always up for sex with a beautiful woman, but I couldn't remember experiencing this need to hold someone.

As we entered the room, I closed the door behind me and turned the lock. Spotting a wooden chair, I swept her up in my arms and stood her on it, her chin now barely above my head. She was looking down on me, quizzically. I answered her bewilderment by sliding my hand through the split in her dress and gently stroking the skin of her inner thigh with my thumb.

She moaned, chewed her lower lip, gazed intently at me, and grabbed two handfuls of my hair to hold on. I moved my hand slowly upwards, circling and stroking with my thumb, all the while holding her eyes with mine.

As my hand was approaching her pussy, I slowly pulled the top of her dress down, revealing a full and firm breast, her dark pink bud of a nipple standing hard. I looked up into her face and her eyes pleaded with me. I reached her sex, her silk panties barring me from direct contact. I pulled them swiftly down, slightly lifting her and whisking them from under her feet. I looked up into her eyes while I buried my nose in them, the scent of her making me groan.

She watched me, fascinated. I began again at her knee trailing my thumbnail up her inner thigh until I reached her slick and silky folds. I ran my thumb up and down her split, teasing over her clitoris. She was warm and so deliciously wet, I had to taste. I covered my thumb in her pussy juice, then put it into my mouth and sucked. She tasted so fucking good that I nearly lost it.

She still had her hands laced through my hair, and she pulled my head towards her breast. I needed no more prompting—I took that delicious little bud into my mouth and nibbled and licked and sucked, using my thumb again to flick, stroke and circle her clit.

Now she was writhing, making small mewling sounds, panting through parted lips, her hips moving in rhythm with my thumb. I looked up at her, her eyes closed and her head thrown back. She was magnificent. My cock was throbbing and straining against my pants, but there was a kind of ecstasy in that. This was for her.

Gently, I exposed her other breast and went to work on that with my lips, tongue and teeth. Her panting became deeper, and one hand dropped from my hair to my shoulder where she gripped, her nails digging into me through my shirt. I could feel the tension building in her.

I brought my forefinger into play, nipping at her clit and stroking her wet opening. Then I slid a finger inside her. She gasped, her eyes flew open and she pleaded with me. 'Oh, Nathan! Oh, God! Yes, please do that! Oh! Oh!' Then her eyes were closed, her fingers threatening to sink right into my flesh, her internal muscles gripping at my finger and her panting and groaning becoming deeper and louder.

I found her sweet spot with my finger and, using that and my thumb on her clitoris, and my teeth nibbling on her nipple, brought her to a shuddering climax. I threw my arm around her to steady her and keep her safe, then continued, watching, mesmerised as waves of multiple orgasms rocked her.

It was the hottest thing I'd ever witnessed—the writhing of her body and the sounds she made. She let out a long, shuddering moan, and I stopped as she collapsed into my arms. I lifted her down and engulfed her, raining kisses on her face until she buried it in my chest, clutching the front of my shirt with one hand and the back with her other.

I held her like that until she stopped trembling. She pulled slightly away, enough to look up at me. 'Oh my God,' she moaned, 'that was...' she breathed in and out deeply, regaining her equilibrium, 'very adequate.' She giggled, then flashed me that blinding smile—the one that was all dimples and sparkly eyes. It was so irresistibly infectious, I was soon grinning back down at her.

'Oh, we strive for *adequate*, baby,' I said, raising an eyebrow. 'That was for being sensational out there tonight.'

'My reward?'

I nodded. 'So deserved, my little songbird.'

'And how do I thank you?' she said, her eyes searching my face. She smiled a knowing little smile, then following it with her eyes, trailed a finger from my collar down my chest, slowly down over my stomach and heading towards my aching cock. I grabbed her hand before she could touch me, knowing I would be lost if she did and thinking we should probably be out of there by now. The CCTV in the corridor outside would have clocked us coming into the dressing room—I knew for a fact that it didn't cover the area just inside of the door from the main room, but it would have captured us coming in here. We should be making a move very soon to avoid the security staff speculating.

As if reading my mind, she looked at the clock on the wall. 'Bugger. I need to get changed and we need to get out,' she said. 'I bet they don't even realise we're still in here.'

Laughing, she turned back to the mirror, and I watched in fascination as she peeled off her false eyelashes. Her make-up was still spread out in front of the mirror and she applied some pink to her cheeks, something dark to her eyelids, mascara to her eyelashes and some pink lipstick.

'That'll have to do,' she exclaimed, looking adorable.

Then she stood up and peeled her dress off over her head. I groaned. This was my first sight of her completely naked. I had to use that word again: 'Magnificent!'

She laughed and held out her hand. I reached out to take hold of it, only to have her bat my hand out of the way. Again, she held her hand out and looked at me pointedly. I caught on.

I fished into my pocket where I had stuffed her little silk panties. I held them to my face and breathed in deeply one last time before handing them over. Her eyes danced, her smile dimpled and she laughed again. And the floor beneath my feet vanished, leaving me falling...

On the bench, she located a bra, some jeans and a little pink checked shirt and proceeded to dress. She slipped on a dainty pair of blue boat shoes; her feet were as tiny as the rest of her. Then she straightened and hung up her dress. She enclosed it in the cover and zipped it up. Stuffing her heels into her kit bag, she hunted around for everything else and stuffed it all into the bag.

'So, what happens now, Ms Byrne?' I asked her. She looked at me, speculatively.

'Well, I guess that depends on what you have in mind, Mr Connor. I mean, if we are looking at a hook-up here, I guess we need to decide where we're going for that?'

Oh, I had just the place for that—my go-to pad. I can't really say why I hesitated, why that somehow didn't feel right.

'And if we are thinking maybe a little bit beyond a one-off

hook-up, maybe?' I ventured.

She studied me for a few moments. 'Then we really do need to talk,' she said, nodding her head as if she was making her mind up about something. 'We can go to my flat—maybe pick up a couple of bottles of wine? Then we talk first, okay?'

'You're the boss,' I answered.

What she said had set alarm bells ringing in my head. *'We really do need to talk.'* That sounded ominous. Of course I wanted to talk to her—she was fascinating, funny, engaging and I loved her accent—but the way she said that made it sound somehow threatening.

She zipped up her kit bag. 'Okay, we'll get a cab to mine. There's a little supermarket around the corner from me stays open late—they sell wine.'

'That sounds good to me,' I said. I picked up her bag and the clothes off the hanging rail and said, 'Lead on, m'lady.'

I had known this woman for less than twelve hours, and yet I already knew that I wanted more than a one-time hook-up. I was intrigued about what this *talk* might mean.

I needed to protect myself. Linnea's face floated before me, and gut-wrenching hurt threatened to engulf me. I couldn't ever go through what Linnea did to me again. I had avoided involvement since then for that very reason. And yet, there I was, feeling involved up to my eyeballs with a total stranger.

I would hear her out, and if I didn't like what I heard, I needed to be sensible and get out while the going was good.

Chapter Six

Rosie

Nathan, such a gentleman, had picked up all my stuff for me. We walked up the stairs and to the front door, where a doorman greeted him with, 'Good evening, Mr Connor,' and hailed us a cab. He was apparently a regular here.

I floated on air. I am not a novice when it comes to sex, but I can't remember ever feeling the way he made me feel when he stood me on that chair and did what he did to me. The intensity of it. This beautiful, hot, sexy man had made me the centre of his whole world and making me come the most important thing to him.

When he'd slipped my knickers off and then pressed them to his face as if to breathe me in, it was so erotic, amplifying the tingling that was already permeating my whole body.

I'd had men go down on me, happy to oblige. I'd always thought they regarded it as a bit of a chore, though, a necessary evil to endure if they wanted a quid-pro-quo. I wondered what it would be like to have this man's face between my legs. The way he'd savoured my taste on his thumb, I think he would revel in tasting me first-hand, and that thought made me feel weak at the knees.

The whole episode in the dressing room had been so sensual, I couldn't wait to see what would come next.

But we did need to talk. I had to let him know what he was letting himself in for and he had to agree to my terms before we could take this beyond a one-night stand. I had no doubt about what was definitely on the cards—the night wasn't going to end any other way. But to take it any further, I had to have my safety net in place.

Did I, though? This was so different from anything I'd ever felt—he was so different from anyone else I'd met.

Yes, I did!

I could not—would not—take the risk of letting anyone, even someone as apparently amazing as this guy, be in a position to use or hurt me. It had to be my way or the highway.

Hmmm. A sharp, lancing pain stopped my heartbeat momentarily. I didn't like that, didn't like it at all.

In the cab, the journey to my flat on Greek Street was silent, both of us lost in our own thoughts. I looked unseeing out into the bustling, well-lit London night streets, reliving those moments in the dressing room. The whole episode had been so delightful, my heart was skipping beats every time I thought about what would come next.

As the cab pulled over, Nathan reached for his wallet and pulled out some notes.

'I can pay my way!' I exclaimed, maybe a bit too indignantly.

He looked at me reproachfully. 'I don't doubt that. Force of habit. You can pay next time.'

I had heard clearly, hadn't I? He had said, 'Next time,' hadn't he? *NEXT time!*

We got out of the cab, and Nathan piled my things on me.

'You take these in, I'll get the wine. Point me to it. Red okay for you?'

I gave him directions to the shop, pointed at the door pad on the front door to my block and told him to press Flat 3. I'd release the latch and then he should take the lift to the third floor. There was only one flat on each floor from the first to the third and mine was on the top floor.

I let myself in, hung my things up noticing, with relief, that I had made my bed earlier. I raced madly around the flat, tidying and spraying my favourite, if bloody expensive, Neom room spray everywhere.

I checked the bathroom—no tell-tale signs of any other guys in there. None of my FBuds stayed here overnight, but things got left sometimes. And there was always Josh—he did stay in the spare room sometimes. He even slept in my bed with me on occasion if we'd had one of our heart-to-hearts deep into the night and one of us—usually him—needed comfort-cuddling. I smiled at the thought of telling Josh all about this night.

The door buzzer sounded, and my heart flipped. I pushed the key button, heard the door open and close then listened for the lift. I was alight with anticipation; this was like building up to your first time. And that thought nearly swamped me in a sudden flashback of melancholia.

I reminded myself that my *Rules* would mean never having to go through anything like that again. No one would use me again—not unless it was clearly understood to be mutual.

A small knot of dread formed in the pit of my stomach as I thought of *the talk*. What if he didn't like my terms and wouldn't play ball?

Well then, you'd better make the most of tonight. I felt sure there would be a *tonight* even if this wasn't going anywhere afterwards. So far it had been all about me; I didn't think there was a chance he would leave without some reciprocation—he is a man after all.

Oh, God. The thought of what I could do with him sent thrills of anticipation through my veins.

My doorbell rang. *Shit!* I hadn't meant to shut him out. I rushed to the door, dispelling my previous thoughts, and flung it open to find a flopped-hair Nathan standing there looking like he'd stepped straight off the front page of GQ. He was grinning at me, the most sensationally gorgeous man I have ever looked at, and I wanted to eat him.

He stepped into the lounge, his eyes sweeping the room. I watched him take it all in: my subtle sage, rose-pink and calico colour scheme, lingering momentarily on the art prints on my walls. The furniture and décor in my flat are not pretentious, but they are quality. I guessed he must be wondering how a struggling singer could afford a place like this, but he didn't ask the question. Instead, he gestured to the bottles of wine in his hands. 'Corkscrew? Glasses? Kitchen?'

I led him to my small but perfectly adequate kitchen, all mottled light-grey granite surfaces and dust-grey cupboard doors and drawers. He eyed the counter and then put the bottles down. I opened a drawer, and he fished out the corkscrew while I opened one of the wall cupboards and brought out two bulbous wine glasses.

That tension and crackling were back in the air, emanating from him as much as from me.

He poured a measure of wine into each of the glasses, handed me one, picked up the other, smouldered at me seriously and said, 'So. This *talk*? Shall we get it over with?'

My mouth dried up and, for a minute, I wished that my Rules didn't exist, that I could simply throw myself at this beautiful guy and get lost in him. And that I didn't have to risk somehow turning him off me.

I gulped a mouthful of wine. 'Let's sit,' I said and moved back into the lounge.

This was very odd. I tried to analyse what the hell was happening to my usual resolve. I could understand feeling a little apprehensive when I first started down this road, with one of the earlier *talks*. But the last couple of times, I'd been absolutely fine—confident and in control.

I needed to bite the bullet and get on with it.

I sat on the edge of my leather three-seater sofa; he sat on the matching two-seater, facing me. He took a sip of wine, then put his glass down on the coffee table and looked at me expectantly, waiting.

'Well, the thing is, Nathan, the thing is…' I took a deep breath and launched into my speech.

'Okay, so… I have issues. Issues that mean I don't get involved. I don't have romantic relationships. I have to protect myself. I can't… be hurt. I have to make sure of that. I won't be used. This is not about you, Nathan—I'm sure you're a perfectly nice guy and all that. It's about me, and I—I just don't go there.'

My words hung in the air for a couple of minutes.

'Okaaaaaayyyyyyy,' he drawled, quietly and slowly. 'So, what are we doing here, Rosie?' he questioned, his eyebrows arching up, eyes boring into mine.

'Sex!' I blurted out. 'This is about sex.'

His expression didn't alter; he sat so still, like that big cat again, this time waiting to pounce.

So where the hell had my *ball-breaker* temptress disappeared to? Frustration and a well of totally unexpected feelings threatened to engulf me. I needed to grab control back here. Channelling my seductress, I attempted to re-establish the higher ground.

'Nathan. You are the most gorgeous, sexiest man I have ever met. I haven't stopped thinking about you since those lift doors opened. And I want you. And you've already said you want me.' I tried the smoulder.

His expression remained deadpan. No acknowledgement, no reaction whatsoever. He waited. Once again, I was knocked off-kilter.

'So… I need to put my shields up—you know, like in Star-Trek? 'Shields up, Mr Sulu'…? Do you watch the old Star Trek episodes? They're great; I love them ………' I realised I was babbling.

He waited.

'I have rules, a set of rules. You have to agree to them.'

There. I'd done it. I'd managed to introduce the Rules.

'I see,' he nodded, but his expression still didn't change. 'And if I don't agree to these… *Rules*, what happens then, Rosie?'

'Well, we can discuss them. You might even have your own you want to add in that I've got to agree to…'

Still nothing. I couldn't gauge his response at all.

'So, if I agree to the *Rules* then…?'

'Then we can have a relationship based on sex. We can keep seeing each other and have a wild time?'

Why did this suddenly sound so lame? My other Fuck Buddies, Liam and Jamie, had lapped it up—made it so easy.

'And if I don't… if we don't come to an agreement?'

'We can have tonight, Nathan. And then we go our separate

ways, nothing lost.'

'Nothing lost,' he echoed.

He reached for his glass and took another sip of wine. 'Well then Rosie, you'd better tell me what these *Rules* are.' Still nothing in his expression gave me any indication of what he might be thinking.

I leapt up. He looked at me startled.

'I have them... they're written down...'

'You've got these rules all written down, huh?' His eyebrows did that thing again where they arch up.

'I'll get them,' I said and fled the room.

It was awful. It wasn't how it was supposed to be. He was supposed to agree that a relationship based on sex sounded like a good idea, the mature thing to do. Instead, I felt like a school kid having to explain some naughty behaviour to a stern Head.

It also occurred to me that I needed to tread a little carefully here. After all, Nathan had been introduced to us as someone who could put work our way. If this didn't work out, I needed to make sure the door was kept open for a professional relationship. I had to hope that he would be able to separate the outcome of tonight from the outcome of his seeing and wanting the band for his venues.

I picked up two copies of the Rules from my printer in the spare room and made my way back to the lounge. He was standing at the window, his glass in his hand, gazing down into the street below. 'Busy street,' he said. 'Noisy.'

'Yeah, there's always plenty of life around here, even at the weekends,' I gabbled, relieved to have something to distract us from the conversation still to conclude.

He looked at the papers I was carrying and held his hand

out, his eyes not meeting mine. I gave him a copy and then read through mine as if for the first time too.

ROSIE'S RULES

1. Protected sex only. No exceptions. Both parties to make sure a supply of condoms is available.
2. Absolute cleanliness is a requirement. Always shower first.
3. No overnight stays.
4. No BDSM
5. No vanilla sex.
6. No anal sex.
7. Exclusivity is <u>not</u> a requirement.

He sat back down and read through them several times.

Still nothing.

This was excruciating.

Finally, he looked up, piercing me with his eyes. I struggled to maintain eye contact.

'Hmmm, you don't rule out erotic-asphyxiation?' he asked, expression still deadpan, looking me straight in the eye.

'The *No BDSM* rule covers that, doesn't it?' I replied. 'Doesn't it?'

He didn't look convinced. 'You're not into that, are you?' I rasped, horrified at the thought he might be.

'I can live without it,' he drawled, infuriatingly not answering the question. 'No anal sex?'

I nodded. 'I'm not into that,' I said, trying to sound confident.

'Y'ever tried it?'

'No. And I don't want to!' I exclaimed.

'Okay, okay. Only asking,' he said. 'Can you clarify what you mean by *vanilla sex*? As in *No vanilla sex*? I mean, this is different things to different people. Do you mean you only want sex that involves something kinky or toys or stuff?'

'Erm... well no—erm... I mean... well, it's about the missionary position,' I explained.

'Uh-huh? So it should say: Missionary position not allowed, huh? Shame. One of my favourites. May I ask why that one is barred?'

Shit! I could hardly give my usual stock answer, *Because it's boring,* when he'd said it was one of his favourites

I reached for my glass and took a large swig of wine.

'Well, I'm not into a lot of eye contact and romantic intimacy during sex,' I replied, 'and that position tends to enable lots, and it's a bit too intimate... erm... Yep. That's it really.'

Once again, he pinned me with his eyes. 'You have the most beautiful eyes I have ever made *eye contact* with,' he said. 'I think I could spend a lifetime just gazing into your eyes.'

He tore his gaze away and looked back at the paper. 'I think you might wanna think about re-wording Rule Six to make it clearer what you mean here.

'Okay, what now? We start the negotiation?'

'Well, erm, erm... do you have any, um... rules you would, um... want added to the list?' I stammered out.

'Uh-huh,' he said, 'honesty.' He studied the paper again. 'Complete honesty is a requirement,' he intoned, then pinned me again. 'As in... we are completely honest with each other—about what we like, what we don't like, what we want. *You* ask *me* a question, I answer honestly. *I* ask *you* a question, you have to be honest with me.'

I nodded. Damn. That should already be on the list. 'Okay. Done.' I said wanting him to be okay with all of this. 'So, what do you think?'

'You mean, do I agree to all of this?' he asked. Before I could answer, he went on. 'I can live with most of these. There's just the one I don't buy.'

I held my breath. I already knew what was coming.

'I'm afraid exclusivity *is* one of my requirements if this is more than a one-off, Rosie, even in a sex-only relationship. I don't share.'

Chapter Seven

He may as well have punched me in the stomach. I wasn't prepared for this, for resistance, and it unnerved me. I was momentarily speechless. I felt sick.

Finally, I regained some of my equilibrium.

I slugged back the last of the wine in my glass and stood up to pour myself another—a large one. I gestured to him with the bottle, but he shook his head.

'You have to agree to it. It's one of the main rules. All my Fuck Buddies agree to it,' I explained, my chest tightening. 'I erm I…'

He interrupted. '*All* your *Fuck Buddies*?' He sat there looking at me in disbelief or shock—I wasn't sure which. I gazed back at him, panicking inside. Would this chase him off? He was clearly rattled by it in a way none of the other guys had been.

His tone when he'd said, 'Fuck Buddies', gave me pause for thought as I saw the concept through a different lens. One I didn't like, that made me feel defensive. I didn't know what to say, so I decided it was best to say nothing until I did. The silence stretched on. It was excruciating.

Eventually, he broke the impasse.

'Rosie,' he began, still holding me with his eyes, 'remembering *my* rule mmm? Total honesty? Rosie, why this rule?

Why *non*-exclusivity? And *Fuck Buddies*? How many are we talking?' He sounded pissed off.

'Because,' I whispered, 'because then you can't cheat on me. You can't hurt me or betray me. Not if it's all agreed in advance.' I steeled myself and looked him in the eye. 'And I can keep control. I can get in first if I want to.'

Damn it. What was I saying? I had just met this guy? How was it possible that he had somehow incited me to expose such vulnerability.

It was not how this was supposed to go; where had all this unwelcome emotion come from? I stared at him angrily—angry with myself—my breathing ragged and hitching.

As he continued to gaze into my eyes, something shifted in his. He stood up and before I knew it, gathered me up in his strong, muscular arms, nuzzling my hair and stroking my shoulder with his thumb.

He spoke quietly and evenly. 'Rosie, if we were to do this, take this further than one night, I can't guarantee that one of us wouldn't get *hurt* when it ends. No-one can. That's just life. But this sounds like you *expect* me to cheat, like I'm on trial with an already 'Presumed Guilty' verdict. I don't cheat, Rosie, and I wouldn't *betray* you. That's what my honesty rule is all about. I would expect the same from you.'

He held me for a few minutes. It was soothing, being cuddled like that. My breathing evened out as I managed to get my emotions back under control.

Nathan gently sat me back down and moved back towards the window, turning to pin me with his eyes once more. '*Fuck Buddies?*'

And I was back on a precipice again. This was like a rollercoaster ride; every time I thought things were calming, I was thrown again.

'Yes. Fuck Buddies. I have... three Fuck Buddies... I call one of them, or one of them calls me, and we have sex,' I stammered out, hating that I sounded so defensive, that I *felt* so defensive. Why should I? I was being *honest*. There was nothing wrong in my *arrangements*—all parties were aware and consenting. Why did telling Nathan make me feel so uncomfortable?

I took another large gulp of wine.

I could appreciate that Nathan's way of dealing with insecurity might be to seek the sanctuary of exclusivity, but for me, my Fuck Buddies were my safety net. They meant I wasn't out there putting myself at risk with total strangers. My Rules were my shields, my guard—they were what stopped anyone getting too involved. They were what had kept me in control and prevented anyone from hurting me. I wasn't about to let my guard down—no way.

Nathan's nostrils flared. I could see his fists tightening and his knuckles turning white as he tore his gaze away and stared out of the window into the street below.

'Uh-huh. I see.' He looked at me again, the sparkle and warmth gone from his eyes. He crossed his arms over his chest, took a deep breath in and blew it out again.

'Look, Rosie, this is a lot to process. Maybe I should go now... call you when I've had time to think...?'

No no no no no! I had to think fast.

I didn't want him to leave. I hadn't realised how badly I wanted him to stay until this moment, my chest tightening and threatening to suffocate me. I hadn't properly thought through what I would do if he didn't agree to the rules. I had assumed it would be straightforward. You know: my-way-or-the-highway-but-let's-have-tonight-anyway. Now I was anxious at the thought that he would take the highway.

He wanted exclusivity. Should I feel good about that? Should I, maybe, think about giving that a go? But wouldn't that be letting my guard down? Perhaps I should simply let *him* go—that would be the sensible thing to do, wouldn't it?

Sensible or not, there was something about him, something that made part of me want to tear the Rules up and beg him to stay—agree to anything as long as he stayed.

But I was stronger than that. I would not resort to begging any man.

Maybe there was a way to get him to stay tonight without jeopardising my tidy, organised little world. He'd said he wanted me, hadn't he? Well, he could have me tonight without any terms to consider—that *one-off* he'd mentioned earlier. After all, the Rules were about taking this beyond one night.

'I don't... I don't...' I stammered.

Nathan looked at me expectantly for a few moments. 'You don't... what?' he asked me quietly.

'I don't want you to go, Nathan,' I finally managed to get out.

'What does that... mean? What about these rules?' he asked me, still speaking quietly, hesitantly.

'Look, the rules are about what happens if we want to take this further than tonight. We can still have tonight, though, whatever you decide. We've got unfinished business... haven't we? I thought... In the dressing room, you wanted me,' I said.

I stood and moved to stand in front of him, looking up into his eyes, inviting him to take hold of me, to take what he wanted.

His eyes softened as he took my face between his hands and stroked my cheek. 'Oh, I want you, my smart, talented, beautiful Rosie. Don't be in any doubt about that. I already told you I've never wanted anything as much as I want you. But that's the thing, Darlin'. I already know I want more than tonight with you, and for me, that means I want you to be all mine. For the duration anyways. Your *Rules* are one thing, but you're telling me I gotta share you with a bunch of other guys. That I gotta be just one of a bunch of guys.'

He paused, thinking. Suddenly he completely changed tack. 'Are you gigging tomorrow night?'

'No. No gigs until Friday when I've got rehearsals in the afternoon and a gig in the evening—a pub in Shoreditch,' I told him.

He spoke again. 'I'll pick you up at seven then. We'll go for dinner.' He let go of me, took out his wallet and plucked a card from it. 'Seven pm sharp. Be ready. You'd better have this,' he said, handing me the card. 'These are my contact details. Put my number in your phone, then give me a call straight away so that I have *your* number in *my* phone, okay? You need anything, you call me, huh?'

He put his wallet back in his pocket and before I had a chance to say anything, he took my face in both hands again and kissed me gently.

Then he left.

Chapter Eight

I collapsed back on my sofa, unable to move or even think for several minutes.

I relived moments from the night. How it felt singing on that stage. Nathan kissing me in the corridor to the dressing room and how scared I'd felt as I realised I was responding to his tenderness. Nathan standing me on that chair, his hands on me, in me. It had all been so heady, so incredible.

Utterly deflated, I couldn't believe I'd let him leave. Worse—I'd somehow chased him off.

I shook myself out of it. He'd left telling me he'd pick me up for dinner the following night. He hadn't even waited for my assent, so sure he was that I'd be waiting for him. Or maybe that's why he gave me his number, so I could call it off.

So, what would it be? Call it off or simply acquiesce? The latter was so not me—not any more...

I fed the details from Nathan's business card into my iPhone. The company name said Connor and McQueen Ltd. I now had his work phone number, mobile number and email address.

I put his mobile number into my favourites and mulled over, for several minutes, where to place it. I flipped it one down from the top of the list.

Martin Barlow is at the top of my list, the trustee for my

trust fund. He is a lawyer by qualification and was my dad's friend and business partner in the investment company they'd made their money from—a considerable amount of money. He had always looked after me, made sure I had anything and everything I needed without allowing me to become profligate. On my twenty-fifth birthday I'd get full control of my money—whatever that meant—but I had already asked Martin to continue looking after it—continue looking after me.

Really? This guy was already second only to Martin? No, that wasn't right.

I rearranged the favourites list again, putting Josh back in position after Martin, then the band members, then Matt, Liam, then Jamie, then Sid, then Nathan, then my aunt and uncle.

Seeing the guys' names reminded me of the fact that I'd nearly called one of them to meet me back at the flat. It had gone completely out of my head. What a disaster that might have been.

I read down the list. I went back into it again and put Nathan ahead of Matt, Liam and Jamie. *Hmmmm.* I read through the list several times.

I moved Nathan ahead of the band members.

Happy with that for the moment, I pressed *Call.*

'I said call straight away,' said a stern, drawling, Kentucky accent.

'I cleared up a bit before I sat down to put you into my phone,' I lied. 'What's up? Did you think I wouldn't call and give you my number?'

The voice softened. 'No. I'm just missin' y'already.'

What?

'I'm missing you too,' I said.

What?

'I'm nearly home. I gotta go. I'll see you at seven tomorrow.'

'Hang on!' I cried. 'What do I wear? Jeans and T-shirt okay or should I dress smart? Where are we going?'

'Smart. Maybe a little cocktail dress. I'm takin' you out to a nice restaurant,' he announced. 'Does that sound okay?'

'I'd like that,' I answered, almost coyly.

'Goodnight, Rosie.'

'Goodnight, Nathan.'

What is going on with me?

Nathan

I ran down the stairs so I wouldn't have to wait for the elevator. I couldn't guarantee that, given time to think about it, I wouldn't turn around and go straight back in and sweep her up into my arms. Jeez—who would have believed leaving her, after only knowing her for a few hours, could be so fucking hard?

In the cab home, I sat watching my goddamn phone, waiting for her call. I didn't even realise I was virtually holding my breath until it finally came through.

I thought over the events of the last hour. I don't know what I'd been expecting from *the talk* and then *the Rules. Rosie's Rules*. I remembered the vice around my chest when she'd gone off to get her printed list.

As I'd read through them and thought about what she'd said about *issues*, I had quickly come to understand and had felt a sense of relief. This was no sex-mad ice-queen wanting to dominate men into providing sexual services. This was a young woman full of insecurities, who had been hurt at some point in her past and was trying to protect herself and retain her dignity.

I felt sad. Sad that this beautiful, wonderful young woman had been so badly knocked by something or someone that she felt the need to build such a barrier around herself—as if a set of rules could protect her from being used and abused.

I smiled as I thought about the look on her face as I read them and questioned her. I knew she was squirming under my scrutiny, and I was rather enjoying making her feel so uncomfortable, trying to explain herself. But when it had come to the *non-exclusivity* rule, that was a step too far for me. I had to make it a deal-breaker. Her reaction had shaken me.

Fuck Buddies? Plural? What the fuck?

But then, to see that much pain and hurt in her eyes was too much. I had to hold her. I was even tempted to agree to anything just so she could push that hurt away again.

However, this whole thing was a big deal for me. I could have just taken what was on offer, a damn hot one-night hook-up. With any other woman, that is exactly what I would have done. But like I said to Rosie, I already knew I wanted more. And I could see that she wanted me and more. I had seen the panic in her eyes when she thought I might react badly to what she was saying and not come back.

If she was going to be mine, for however long that might be, there was no way I would be sharing her with anyone. I had to protect *me*. I had to play this whole thing carefully.

'Nothing lost,' my ass.

I thought about the guys with whom she had previously *come to an agreement*—her *Fuck Buddies.*

Maybe she had been lucky, that her instincts had selected out *nice* guys who had bought the crap. Guys who had genuinely regarded her as an equal in the relationship and enabled her to hide her insecurities and bolster her pride and dignity. Guys, though, who couldn't, or didn't want to, see past the bullshit—who couldn't see the fragile, broken wings of this delicate, bruised ego.

Maybe, one, or more, of them had fallen for her and agreed to the rules just to stay in the running, believing that they could win her over into a different kind of *arrangement*. Well, she *was* an extraordinary woman, and that's what *I* was considering doing, wasn't it? Except the actual sharing her part was never going to happen.

I needed a plan.

When I got home, I put on my swim shorts—my jammers, a towelling robe and my beach shoes and headed down to the pool on the basement floor of my apartment complex. I dumped the robe and shoes, dived straight in and pounded my way up and down the pool, going over the options in my head.

I had a busy day lined up: a board meeting at Connor and McQueen, the company that owns the restaurant chain, the bar chain and the Bourbon importing business; a meeting with our Legal and HR teams regarding some serious HR issues we had been having with some of the management in one of the restaurants—that needed careful handling, so I wanted to be involved if only to have my eye on it; then I was seeing Rhys in the afternoon for an operations report.

I needed my Rosie strategy sorted in my head that night because I wouldn't have much time to dedicate to it the next day. In the pool, I could switch to automatic and focus my thinking. A couple of ideas soon took shape.

Rosie

I raced through the day at top speed but, happily, achieved everything I set out to do: a session at the gym, grocery shopping, phone call to Sid for feedback on last night—that had all been very positive, phone calls to the guys to pass on the good news, and some cleaning and tidying to make sure the flat would be presentable.

I was even able to take a bit of time preparing for my dinner date.

That was, after all, what it was—a date.

I started prepping: shower and tidy up with the razor, matching body lotion all over to prolong the effect of my perfume, and then I thought again about this date.

I hadn't done much dating; I'd stuck to liaisons for sex and tried not to blur the lines.

My nights out tended to be centred around the band or Josh. I went to other bands' gigs to check out the competition or simply enjoy and to jazz jams with band members or other musicians. There had been group dinners with the band and partners/friends—I usually asked Josh along to those. Then there was an occasional night out with Josh, gossiping or commiserating—that would be me doing the commiserating when Josh's latest romantic episode ended in tears.

I tackled my hair, blow-drying and curling, wishing he were here to help—he was great with my hair.

I will always love Josh. A warmth spread through my whole body thinking about him. He was my brother, my confidante and my BFF, the only real friend I'd ever had.

I met him at one of The Big Band's open rehearsals. I'd started going along when I first moved to London. He was a gorgeous hunk, no question, so I had been making lots of eye contact with him, checking him out. That's when he'd dropped the disappointment on me that he batted for the other side.

It was Josh who pushed me into asking the bandleader to let me sing a number with them one week when the resident male singer wasn't there.

'Sure, if you can sing something in our pad,' the bandleader had said.

I'd said, 'Moondance?' a song I'd heard the resident singer do with them, so I knew their arrangement was in a key I could manage.

He got me up to sing, and it went from there. They had a female vocalist previously, so had scores for songs in her key. He threw four song titles at me and said, 'If you learn these, I'll get you up again.'

I went back the following week having learned all four and, as luck would have it, their singer had another gig on that day. They got me up to sing all four songs and offered me the job as their resident female vocalist.

The Big Band didn't do much gigging, but I attended the weekly open rehearsals with them quite regularly and sang with them when they had occasional bookings.

Some of the musicians there had put me onto the jazz jams where I'd met the extraordinarily talented musicians who now made up Rosie Byrne and her Trio.

And that is how I was looking at the potential for a real career in singing.

My final bit of prepping was a touch of makeup to lightly even my complexion, pink up my cheeks, darken and emphasize my eyes and eyelashes. I left pinking and shining my lips until after I'd finished dressing so as not to smudge.

I agonised over what underwear to put on, then decided not to. I giggled. I knew that the shape of my unfettered breasts would tantalise Nathan; I know I could do with losing a bit of weight, but they would keep attention away from that. And, I could just imagine his response when I *let slip* that I didn't have any knickers on. I giggled again in anticipation, thinking about how naughty I could be—I would make him agree to anything.

Then, I took out my black ruched dress, a figure-hugger but quite slimming. Although it clung to all my curves, showing the lumpy bits, it was a far more modest dress than the Lexi Farah—round-necked, short-sleeved, knee-length, but so comfortable and easy to wear, I always felt great in it.

I looked at my watch. I had enough time and couldn't wait any longer. I took out my phone to call Josh to tell him all about my latest Fuck-Buddy prospect. And I stopped in my tracks.

Is that what Nathan was? I was trying to put all the pieces into place; we'd agreed that the relationship would be about sex, at least I thought we had.

Somehow, what had happened between us so far seemed in a different league to what I had experienced with any other man. It all seemed somehow *more* with him? More intense, more exciting, just more.

Or was that my imagination? At the end of the day, sex is sex, and an orgasm is an orgasm—nice if you've got another warm body to share it all with but best not to let it get any more complicated than that.

I jumped when the door buzzer went. I checked my watch. Seven pm sharp. I dashed over to pick up the phone and said, 'Shall I come straight down?' assuming that he would have a cab waiting.

'No, Darlin', let me in; I need to drop some stuff off.' There was that word again—*Darlin'*. The way he said it sounded like an endearment—I couldn't take offense. In fact, it sounded like an unconscious caress.

I buzzed him in and waited at the door.

Bloody lifts! The sight of him emerging from this lift turned my insides to mush once more. In all charcoal grey tonight—was there any colour that wasn't this guy's? His eyes held me as that languid smile crept across his face, and then they twinkled at me again. It was mesmerising watching him, and I couldn't help but smile right back at him.

'You look lovely, Rosie. you are so beautiful,' he said and in two strides, had thrown his arm around my waist and lifted me off my feet to plant a kiss on my lips. Not taking his eyes from mine, he lowered me back onto my feet, leaned down to put a bag he was carrying on the ground, then took my face in both his hands and kissed me like he couldn't breathe without it. 'I have been thinking about that kiss since I left you last night.'

I just gazed into his eyes, lost for words.

He eventually broke the spell and picked up the bag he had brought with him, which clinked as he lifted it. He held it up. 'I picked up some more wine. For later,' he said.

Finally, getting the power of speech back, I challenged him with, 'You're making some assumptions there.'

'Indeed I am,' he drawled, tilting his head slightly, so he was piercing me again with his eyes. Licking then biting the side of his bottom lip as he stood back again, he undressed me with his eyes, that sexy smirk curling his lip.

'You like, then?' I enquired.

'Indeed I do,' he said. 'Now, let me dump this and let's get going. Are you gonna be okay walking in those shoes?' he asked, eyeing my black stilettos as he plonked the bag down on the coffee table.

'Yes, within reason,' I answered.

'It's a warm enough night out there; I thought we might take a stroll to the restaurant. It's not too far.'

'Okay, as long as you promise to give me a piggyback if my feet start to hurt,' I demanded.

'You kidding me? I don't know why you women have to wear such ridiculously impractical footwear,' he grumbled.

'Well, for starters, I'm only five foot two, and these add four inches, so I don't look like a munchkin. Secondly, they make me look slimmer, and thirdly they make my legs look longer. That's why!' I retorted.

'Is that so?' he scoffed. 'Well, for starters, every little bit of your five feet and two inches makes me hot and bothered, without adding more. Secondly, you don't need to look any slimmer, or, thirdly, make your legs look any longer than they do. You are perfect in your bare feet in my book. In fact,' he threw in, 'if I had my way, I'd keep you barefoot in the kitchen.' His eyes flashed mirthfully at me.

'You, you, male chauvinist!' I yelled at him, beating on his chest as he pulled me to him.

'Honey,' he murmured in my ear, 'it's the height of the kitchen counter that was on my mind, not any other purpose of the room.'

I gasped. 'You are *so* naughty,' I giggled at him.

'Uh-huh. When I'm thinking about you, I certainly am. And right now, that seems to be every minute of the day. And I intend to be very, very… naughty… later. At least, I'm hoping that to be the case.'

Relief followed by heat flooded my body. Did that mean he was going to agree? It certainly sounded like it.

'But for now, we have to go eat. Are you ready, m'lady?' he asked, stepping back from me and offering his arm.

Glowing with pleasure at taking this man's arm, I pulled the door shut behind me, and we called the lift back.

On the way down, he leaned into me, breathed in and softly murmured, 'I like your perfume, Rosie, very much. You smell of vanilla.'

'Yeah? You don't smell too bad tonight, either,' I shot back at him, grinning. Understatement of the year. He was wearing the same cologne or aftershave or whatever it was as yesterday, and it was intoxicating.

The lift door opened and we set off. I still had no idea where.

Chapter Nine

Nathan

Breath-taking.

At the sight of her, all frustrations of the day melted away. And we'd immediately fallen into our intense Paso Doblé again, our very enjoyable dance that would, hopefully tonight, end up with my cock buried deep inside her. My body was already responding big time to her proximity—she drove me crazy.

But, there was much to do before we got to that. Tonight, I wanted to find out more about her and, of course, resolve the issue hanging over our heads; exclusivity, monogamy, call it what you will—that was the only basis upon which I would agree to continuing this... relationship.

Google had revealed very little about Rosie Byrne, my Rosie Byrne; I found a Facebook page, but it was confined to information about the band and gigs. I tried just *Byrne* and got Gabriel and Ed, David, Jason; I trawled through more pages full of academics, lots of Irish references and a couple of obituaries, but nothing I could link with confidence to my precious little songbird. So, I would have to get her to tell me. I wanted to find out what had so damaged her that she had wrapped herself in this sex-only cloaking device, and that needed careful handling. If she got wind that my interest might be anything other than sex, she might fly.

And was my interest anything other than sex? I hadn't been able to get her out of my mind since those elevator doors opened yesterday. The episode with her in the dressing room had only served to pique my desire for her and leave me wanting, sex and something more than sex.

Less than forty-eight hours since I'd first set eyes on her, and I was contemplating a *relationship*, something I hadn't given a passing thought to in seven years. Her singing talent was an unbelievable bonus—I was absolutely gonna sign this band for Café Paradiso as soon as everything else was in place. Another reason why I had to proceed with caution, although I would hand the business relationship with Sid and the band over to Rhys to avoid any potential conflict of interest occurring.

We reached the street and I turned us left. Clinging to my arm, she certainly handled those needlepoint heels well, placing one tiny foot in front of the other and swaying her hips as she walked.

Of course, I know why women wear heels like that. Because suckers like me go ga-ga at the sight. It somehow changes the way a woman stands, straighter, breasts thrust out, and when they walk, the way they sway their hips—it's hypnotic. I'd wanted to tear that dress off her and leave her standing naked in just those shoes. But Rosie had a real hang-up about her height, and I wanted to let her know that she was perfect as she was—and I had meant every word.

Twenty yards up the street I announced, 'And, here we are,' as I guided her in through the restaurant doors of a popular French brasserie-style place where the food was always superb.

I had booked for two and we were guided to the table I had specified, right in the centre of the large window looking out onto Greek Street. The room was all glittering, ornate mirrors and chandeliers, velvet curtains and furnishings and classic carpets, opulence itself. I could see Rosie was entranced by the place.

'I've lived in that flat for two years, but never been in here,' she whispered to me, all smiles and shining eyes.

'Well, I'm glad to be giving you a first experience of something then,' I whispered back at her and was stunned to see a shadow pass over her face and that sadness I'd witnessed, twice now, hover fleetingly in her eyes. Then she pulled herself up and smiled that Rosie smile—all dimples and dancing eyes.

'This is great. Thank you.'

We ordered drinks, a coffee cocktail for Rosie and a bottle of red wine for me.

When we ordered the meal, Rosie chose the sea bream. I persuaded her to try the speciality here, the snails, as a starter. She told me she'd always had a hankering to try them after watching the film *Pretty Woman* but had never had the opportunity.

Food ordered, drinks started, I began my investigation.

'So, Rosie. Getting to know each other a bit better isn't barred in your Rules, and I would like to know more about you. How about we build each other a profile?'

Yeah, that would be cool,' she replied. So, what do you already know about me?'

'Okay. We'll start with *you*.' I smirked at her.

'Your name is Rosie Byrne, I think. I don't know if that is your full name or a nickname or a stage name or if you have a middle name.

'You are twenty…somethin'?' She held up four fingers. 'Twenty-four?' She nodded.

I continued, 'You live in a very nice little apartment in the heart of Soho.

'You like watchin' TV; you have a large one on your wall and the remote sits on your coffee table.

'You like Science Fiction; you have several Sci-Fi books on a bookcase in your lounge.' She shuffled in her seat. 'And you have watched all the original Star Trek Series. Hmmm, the last bit is a guess.' She giggled, nodding.

'You measure an adorable five feet two in your stocking feet but have hang-ups about your height.' She shuffled some more and sighed loudly.

'You like Japanese art, Kandinski, Monet, and have other pictures and figurines of tall, impossibly slender women with unfeasibly long legs adorning your walls.

'You are a phenomenal singer who has her own trio and a repertoire of jazz and swing and blues numbers that leaves your audience howling for more.

'You like fish and red wine and espresso martinis and you are willing to try foods you've never had before.

'You like real coffee—Italian for the most part?' She nodded again.

'You've seen the film Pretty Woman.

'You have the most gorgeous dark green and hazel eyes in a beautiful face, surrounded by naturally auburn hair.

'You have an exquisite body that looks like it was built for sex, flawless skin, incredible curves and lines.' I loved the way she blushed at this.

'You are bold and forthright and vulnerable and fragile all in one bundle.

'You like sex; and, by the way, you are hot as hell when you are coming.' Now she turned scarlet. I loved it.

'You are seeking sex-only relationships and have a set of rules to keep them that way. Your rules are your safety barrier, putting you firmly in control and protecting you from... something.

'How am I doing?'

'Well,' she breathed, still flushed and now, rattled, 'you certainly take in a lot from one visit. Guilty as charged, I guess. And thank you for the compliments,' she added, quietly.

I reached across the table and took her trembling hand. I gazed into her eyes and smiled, trying to reassure her that there was nothing to fear. I simply wanted to know more about her.

'No compliments, just telling it as it is. Can you fill in the blanks and correct any errors?' I asked her, tentatively. 'Oh and add in a few more details maybe?'

'Where do you want me to start?' she asked, at which point the snails arrived.

Served in shells but already separated, this didn't involve the palaver as portrayed in *Pretty Woman*. She tried them and decided that she liked them. It was enough to break the tension and she relaxed a little.

'I do have a middle name,' she offered. 'It's Ciara. My dad was half Irish, obviously the Byrne half, and very proud of his Irish heritage so he named me Rosaleen Ciara. I would guess that you have some Irish in your ancestry too from your surname, especially spelled like that?'

'I guess. It's not a hugely common surname in Kentucky. We think some way back, a Connor found his way there and settled. We know there's some Native American in our genealogy—probably where my daddy, my brother and I get our eye colour and easy-tan skin. You said your dad *was* half Irish?'

''Yeah. I lost my dad when I was twelve,' she said wistfully. I waited to see if she was going to offer any more but she appeared to be retreating into herself.

I jumped in. 'That must have been hard, to lose your father that young—I can't imagine how tough. What about your Mom? Are you close?' I could tell by the look on her face that that had been the wrong thing to ask her.

'My mother was already an alcoholic when we lost my dad and she just disappeared, even further, into a bottle. I lived with my aunt and uncle—well, they became my legal guardians. I rarely spent time in the same house as them. They travelled abroad a lot. I spent term times at boarding school and holidays in the care of a string of nannies until I was old enough to look after myself.'

She became very quiet again so I decided to try and change the subject, get her onto something she'd find easier to talk about. 'So. London? Have you always lived here?'

She snapped back into the moment. 'No. I was brought up in Sussex. I came to London when I decided I wanted to be a jazz singer.'

'Wow. That was brave. It can't be easy making enough to live on here in the capital,' I observed.

She studied me for a few moments. 'I have... means,' she told me and then immediately jumped to, 'You were right about pretty much everything, including Science Fiction, Italian coffee and sex—especially the sex bit. I have particularly liked the sex with you so far—and I'm hoping there's a lot more where that came from,' she said, her eyes darkening and her voice becoming gruff and husky.

'Well, that makes two of us,' I said, returning her heated gaze.

She suddenly pulled her eyes away from mine. 'Is there anything else you'd like to know?' she bristled.

The snails had gone by now and we were waiting for the main course. I reached across the table and took both her hands in mine this time. 'I guess you have to be pretty strong to come through what you have and get to be the amazing woman I see in front of me now.'

'Yeah, well, everybody's got a story, huh?' She had shared as much as she was willing to and was now, shutting down that line of enquiry.

'There is so much more about you I want to know,' I told her, 'but that's great for starters. We can take our time exploring the rest.'

She visibly relaxed. Then she fixed me with her eyes again and demanded, 'Why?'

'Why? Um er I… why what?' I asked her, at which point our meals arrived and I was able to gather my thoughts and prepare my answer. She didn't take her eyes off me all the time the meal was being placed on the table. The waiter asked if we had everything we needed or if there was anything else he could bring for us. I tore my eyes away from hers to check the table and told him we were fine, thank you very much.

As soon as he left, she repeated, 'Why? Why do you want to know all about me?'

Still holding her gaze, I smiled and said, 'So, *you* don't want to know anything else about *me*?'

She took her time to think, all the while holding my gaze. Then she said very softly, a small frown creasing her brow, 'Yes actually. I do. I do.'

'Then you know why,' I murmured, and she dipped her head very slightly.

I smiled at her. She smiled back, and again, the tension broke and we both started on our meals.

'Is there anything you can't wait til next time to ask?' she offered, softening her stance a fraction.

'Yeah,' I said, 'you haven't talked about any boyfriends? Were there any?'

'Oh yeah,' she replied, and something in her eyes shifted. 'Ex now,' she snapped and shut down again by immediately continuing, 'So. You next. I heard what you were telling the guys last night, about growing up in Kentucky, and your dad being in the bourbon business... tell me more about you and your family.'

'Oh no—not so fast,' I protested, 'you haven't done my profile yet; you have to disclose what you have worked out so far about me before I fill in any gaps.'

'Well, you've got an advantage over me 'cos you've seen my flat—well my living room and kitchen—and got some stuff from that,' she argued.

'We'll take that into consideration. What *have* you learned about me though?' I was curious to see what she had derived from our short time together.

She took a deep breath and commenced. 'Well, your name is Nathan Connor and you are, hmmm, thirty something...'

'Good start,' I interrupted. 'My momma named me after one of her favourite American authors and I share my daddy's middle name, James, and I was thirty-two last birthday.'

'Okay,' she said, grinning. 'Your name is Nathaniel James Connor and you are far too old for me,' she giggled.

'Wow. You got that right,' I told her, ignoring the age

comment for the moment. 'I take it you have read some of his work?'

'Only his book of *Greek Myths and Legend*— it was one my dad used to read to me and I kept going back to. It was what gave me a fascination for myths and legends in general.' Her response told me she'd picked the right author, Nathaniel Hawthorne. She certainly had depths this girl.

'You are from Kentucky, although I don't know whether you were born there 'cos your dad was in the air force and met your mum when he was stationed in the UK. You told the guys he took his *family* home to Kentucky when he left the forces, so that might have included you?' So, she had been paying attention, taking it in. Only interested in sex, huh?

'Yeah, I was born in England but lived in Kentucky from about three.'

'You have family in England, though? Your aunt and uncle? And that's how come you are in London now?' she asked.

'Yeah. They'd built up a couple of chains of bars and restaurants. When they decided it was time to retire and travel some, my daddy bought into their business, and my uncle trained me up to run it on account of me being here and working in their bars already.

'And some of these are live music venues?'

'Well, yeah, they are indeed.'

'Do you get home to Kentucky much?' she asked.

'I get home whenever I can—which is quite a lot given it's four thousand miles away.' I grinned. 'I'm goin' next week for a few days as a matter of fact.'

I caught the flash of Rosie's eyes when I mentioned my trip home but didn't react. We'd have more time to talk about that another day.

'What else do you think you know about me?' I said to distract her.

'You have some knowledge of art,' she offered.

'*Some* knowledge is about right. I know what I like and make it my business to know something about the artist. I'm no expert though, Rosie. I don't know why something is good—or not; I just know I like it.'

'My guess would be that you are doing very well for yourself—you wear high-quality hand-made, tailored suits, hand-made Italian shoes, and the watch I've seen on you is a Patek Phillipe—they're pretty high end?'

Smart girl. Very observant. She had obviously checked me out beyond the looks department.

'So that's it. You're after me for my money,' I joked with her. Her face fell and she suddenly became deadly serious.

'No, no, no, no!' she protested. 'I didn't mean it like that. No! Not at all! I wouldn't!'

'Hey,' I interrupted, trying to calm her. 'I was only kidding, Rosie. Of course I don't think that. After all, it's my hot body you're after. I'm just a sex object to you, huh?' I said, trying to lighten the mood again.

She looked at me, her gaze intense and serious, like she was weighing something up in her head. Then she grinned. 'Hot body, gorgeous face and your performance so far? Yeah—it's definitely the sex I'm in this for,' she laughed.

'How do you know my suits are hand-made and that my shoes are Italian? You seen a lot of these?' I asked her.

'My dad always wore the good stuff—your style reminds me of him so it was a bit of a guess,' she replied. 'Your watch is beautiful; I like it,' she said.

'It was a present from my parents for my thirtieth birthday,'

I told her. 'My other watch, the blue-faced Tag Heuer, that was also a present from them, for my graduation.'

'They're very proud of you,' she stated. It wasn't a question. I smiled in agreement.

'You live in London now,' she started up again, 'when did you leave Kentucky? How long have you lived here?' she asked.

'I left the States seven years ago with an allowance and instructions from my daddy to travel the world and *find myself*. So, I travelled, worked a bit here and there, ended up in London working in my uncle and aunt's bars and restaurants—not for the money—more for something to do with my time. Then, when they decided to retire, my daddy bought in, they trained me up before they took off travelling and I took over running the business here.'

She looked directly at me again and went straight for the jugular. 'So, Nathaniel, why were you sent off to *find yourself*? What happened?'

Chapter Ten

I had kinda guessed this was coming and decided that, if I wanted her to open up to me, I would have to offer her something first. I wasn't sure how this might go. I didn't know if I could talk it through without being overwhelmed by hurt and anger. But, there had to be a first time. Rosie had provided the perfect environment, the sex-only arena within which my motivation for preferring such a relationship could at least appear to be authentic. It would enable me to keep *my* protective barriers, my *shields*, up.

So I told her my sorry tale.

'Linnea, my sister's best friend, was my high-school sweetheart. Together from the age of seventeen and fifteen, we were young, in love and had a brilliant future in front of us. Linnea was accepted into a fashion modelling school and on course for a successful modelling career. I attended college then business school and was on course to join my daddy and my brother in the family business. We became engaged when I was twenty-three and she was twenty-one, and had everything planned out for the wedding the following year. It was the perfect romance.'

'You loved her,' Rosie stated, although I heard the question in her tone.

'Well, I certainly thought I did. I was blissfully happy thinking everything was just fine. She was beautiful, talented and she certainly appeared to love me back.'

'What happened?' Rosie asked.

'A month before the big day, Linnea comes to me, arms the bomb that she 'has met someone else' and detonates it with the demand that I be sworn to secrecy about why we've split; unless I agree to announce a mutual parting of the ways, she will tell everyone she's dumped me for a list of reasons that would paint me in a pretty dim light.'

Rosie gasped. I looked up to find her staring at me open-mouthed.

'Oh that was just the tip of the betrayal iceberg. A few weeks earlier, she'd fallen on the stairs when we'd been at home on our own. She showed me the photos she took of her bruises, the ones she'd tell everyone I gave her if I didn't comply. It would seem she'd been planning this for a while, huh? So much for loving me.'

Rosie's look had turned to one of incredulity.

'You have to understand, Rosie, I was young and stupid, clearly, and thought that all that crap about saving face was important. I agreed to her demands, and we told everyone we'd grown apart and decided to split. Called the wedding off.

'I was pretty miserable, moping about. Then a month later she turns up at a family party with her new man as though they'd recently got together. Turns out to be my best friend—the guy who was supposed to be my best man. The same guy who had been helping me drown my sorrows.

'But here's the best bit—the killer. See my best man was an IT whizz who'd invented some surveillance gadgetry, already built his own development company and had just made his first billion. Now, if you were a cynic, you might think she'd stayed with me because of my financial stability, until a better offer came along…'

I looked up again to find her gazing at me with compassion on her face, her eyes moist, and I realised that she was now holding my hand. 'And then…?' she asked gently.

'You know, I felt kicked and slashed. I'd been betrayed by my girl and my best friend and was pretty focused on my own self-pity. I moped around for months, got drunk a lot, hung out in bars and strip joints.'

'So that's why your dad sent you travelling?'

'Oh yeah. My daddy told me to get my shit together, go and have some adventures, work out what I wanted to do with my life and then come home and do it—or do it somewhere else. He made sure I understood that he and my momma were there whenever I needed them and that, while he hoped I would ultimately make my own way in the world, he would support me all I needed til I got there.'

'What a wonderful father,' Rosie said. 'How amazing to have such a supportive family behind you.'

'Oh yeah, Rosie, I am well aware of all my blessings. I am very lucky to have them. It might have been a very different story without their support.

'So, there we are, and here I am,' I announced. 'And now, I need to use the restroom. Then, we'll order dessert and sort out our… er… unfinished negotiations.'

'That sounds like a good idea. But, really, I've had enough to eat,' she objected.

'You most certainly have not,' I lectured at her. 'I saw you picking over that meal, and I'm telling you, you are gonna need more fuel than that. I have designs on your body tonight for which you are gonna need plenty of stamina. You *will* have dessert.'

'Yes sir,' she replied, grinning as her eyes deepened with intent.

It was all I could do not to run to the restroom. I needed space and air to breathe. Bless Rosie for making that easier than I thought possible. And she'd allowed me to reassert my dignity at the end. It was crazy; I had just confided more to a woman I had barely known for two days, than I have, ever, to anyone else, including my family.

I spent several minutes 'getting my shit together' as my daddy would have put it. I managed to push all the hurt and pain that thinking about that stuff always threatens to overwhelm me with back into its compartment in my mind, and I was ready to face the world again. More importantly, I was ready to pick up where I'd left off with Rosie, to play our wonderfully naughty, intense little games again.

As I re-entered the room, I saw she wasn't at the table. At first, I thought she must have gone to the Ladies' restroom, then I saw her through the window. She was on the other side of the road talking to some tall guy—taller than me I'd hazard a guess and I'm six two. He was bending towards her, his hand resting on the small of her back. Their conversation appeared to be very animated, lots of smiling and laughing. Then, she stretched up and kissed him on the cheek. He put his hand on the back of her head and kissed the top of it. Their intimacy was unmistakable. In fact, I would go as far as to say he clearly loves her.

I was rapidly retreating back out of the room when a soft, feminine voice behind me caught my attention.

'Nathan? Is that you Nathan?'

I turned and came face-to-face with Sigrid Feldt-Jones, the company's legal director. Her face lit up in a smile as she took hold of my arm. 'I thought that was you sitting in the window table with a young woman when we first came in but convinced myself I'd imagined it. Anyway, it's lovely to see you out having some fun.' I took and lifted her hand to my lips and she leaned towards me and planted a kiss on my cheek.

At that moment Rosie came back in through the front door and our eyes met. She looked like a rabbit caught in headlights for a couple of seconds, so I gestured for her to come over. 'It's lovely to see you too, Sigrid,' I replied as Rosie approached us. I reached out and put my arm around her shoulders. 'Sigrid, this is Rosie Byrne, my date. Rosie, this is Sigrid Feldt-Jones, who heads up my legal team.' The two women regarded each other, the difference in their heights emphasized this close together; Sigrid is almost as tall as I am when she wears heels.

Sigrid broke the silence first. 'Rosie. Lovely to meet you,' she said, smiling warmly. 'Look, I'd better get back to Jonathan and the gang. Great to see you here Nathan, perhaps we'll all bump into each other here again sometime.' She looked pointedly at Rosie.

As she walked away, Rosie piped up with, 'I've gotta visit the little room too. Back in a jiffy,' and she dashed off towards the restrooms.

I headed back to our table, grateful for the opportunity to get my thoughts together.

Whatever jealousy or anger might be building up inside of me, it was wholly unjustified. Even if that guy were one of her 'Fuck-Buddies' there was nothing to say she would be jumping into bed with him any time soon—hopefully not after

I downloaded my compromise anyway—not before I went away next week.

You have to let this go for now. Let it go.

She was heading back to the table, smiling, looking so damn hot in that dress.

Focus on that, on what I'm gonna do with her body later.

I looked up and gave her my best smile—although, even I could tell it didn't reach my eyes.

'So, where did you go?' I asked her.

'Oh, I just nipped out—a friend of mine spotted me through the window so I went over to say hi.'

I studied the dessert menu waiting to see if she was going to offer any more information. She didn't.

You have to take her at her word, accept what she has said and move on now before you make an idiot of yourself.

'Uh-huh. So, dessert? I'm gonna have me some ice cream. How about you?'

She picked the White Peach Sorbet—better than nothing I suppose.

The waiter came over to take our order. I gave him Rosie's then asked for ice cream. 'Do you have vanilla?' I enquired.

'Yes, certainly sir, would you like any other flavours with that?'

'No, vanilla is my favourite,' I said, pointedly. It wasn't lost on Rosie. She laughed and nodded her head.

'Isn't it just a *bit* boring?' she said, 'There are so many other flavours to choose from.'

'Mmmm, well we can look into that later,' I grinned at her.

'So... Sigrid?' she asked, although I couldn't tell what she was actually asking me.

'Sigrid? Yeah, as I said, she heads up our legal department.

She's very highly regarded in the world of corporate law. We were very pleased to scoop her up,' I explained.

'She's very… tall.'

'Yup, she is,' I responded. Something was clearly bugging Rosie.

'And slim.'

'Uh-huh?'

'And beautiful. She looks like your type. You two look good together,' she observed.

'She is a lovely-looking woman. What are you trying to ask me, here, Rosie?' I pushed.

'Are you…? Have you…? Is she…? Are you two… having a thing together?' she finally managed to blurt out.

'No. We are not. Not now. Not ever. I don't fuck the staff, Rosie. It's not good business practice. Besides, she is happily married and, quite frankly, I've never thought of her in that way. What is more, if I were 'having a thing' with somebody else, I wouldn't be here with you,' I shot at her, forcefully.

'Oh,' she squeaked, the import of what I had said not lost on her.

'And while we're on that subject, I have a proposition for you. A compromise. But first, I have a question for you…' She looked at me somewhat apprehensively. I took a deep breath and launched into what I hoped would result in a compromise she could accept.

'When I asked you why the non-exclusivity rule, your answer was to do with protecting yourself, putting yourself in a position where no one could cheat on you or hurt you by going behind your back. Yeah?'

'Yes, that's exactly it,' she answered, '*I* can't be blindsided and humiliated.'

'So, it's not that you just like fuckin' around?' I pressed for clarification. 'That you specifically want several partners on the go for… the variety?'

She thought for a few moments. 'No,' she finally confessed, 'I don't do that because I need the variety. It's what sort of stops anything getting too intimate or close.'

I felt a flush of relief and a frisson of hope. 'So, how about suspending the non-exclusivity rule with me but with a built-in option to reinstate it in the event of you feeling at any risk of being 'blindsided' or that things are getting too intimate or close? How would that be?' I pressed her, holding my breath and everything else virtually crossed.

She looked down at the tablecloth, processing, thinking, for what seemed like an age. It took every ounce of restraint I possess to sit and wait for her response.

Finally, 'You know, I think I might be able to do that.' She looked up at me, coyly, but with what looked like a world of hope in her eyes. 'Would that be good enough for you?' she asked me. 'You would still be happy with the rest of the Rules?'

I kept my best poker face on while my heart performed somersaults in my chest. 'Yes, Rosie,' I sighed. 'Just one proviso—that if you are feeling at risk of being blind-sided or that things are getting too close for comfort, you tell me, you give me a chance to fix it before you reinstate the rule. Would you promise me that?'

The waiter turned up with our desserts and set them before us.

I could see she was struggling. 'I need some time, Nathan. I need to think about this and be sure it's the right thing to do—for me.'

Fuck! That cured the somersaults. Now I had to get tough

or risk myself.

'It's a deal-breaker for me, Rosie. I want you. But I will need you to try exclusivity. You have some idea of why.'

She reached across the table for my hand. I gave it to her, waiting.

'I want you too, Nathan.'

'Just try it, Rosie. I'm happy to go with the Rules. Give it a go.'

She nodded, and the somersaults were back.

She lifted her glass. 'Here's to the Rules.'

'And the sex.'

She threw her head back and laughed. 'Oh my God yes. And to the sex.'

Rosie sat there looking intently into my eyes again. Then she gasped slightly, her lips parted, and she began gently panting.

'Rosie Byrne, what are you doing?' I demanded.

She took her hand from under the table and leaned across. She placed her finger on my lips and gently pushed it into my mouth. The aroma and taste of her arousal flooded my senses, my dick stirred, and I groaned. Out of the corner of my eye, I saw the couple on the next table look over curiously. I took her hand from my mouth, kissed the tips of her fingers then leaned across to murmur, 'You are so gonna pay for that later.'

She grinned at me, her eyes sparkling in anticipation. 'Oh goodie,' she purred, 'you do realise I haven't got a stitch of underwear on, don't you?'

Fuck! That hit the target, and I had to adjust my junk.

Her eyes softened. 'Nathan, thank you. For finding us a compromise but also for trusting me enough to tell me your story. I can't imagine it was easy for you, reliving something so painful, and I know you did it for me.'

I couldn't take my eyes from hers, nor could I speak.

'I will share mine with you. I will tell you everything in time, I promise. And Nathan, last night, in the dressing room, was... was wonderful. You have already made the sex more than I have felt before. I can't wait to get home now and see where you are taking me next.'

All I could do was kiss her hands.

How does she do that? How does she take my breath away and leave me speechless like that? Such artless openness. A kiss on the cheek, a kiss on the head, those were innocent gestures. He does love her though, the tall guy, whoever he is.

Chapter Eleven

Rosie

My heart had ached for him as he'd told me his tale. I thought the pain and hurt etched on his face were going to overwhelm him. The thing is, I sensed he was telling me so that I could find a way to open up myself. His courage and generosity touched me very deeply. It was clear now why he wasn't interested in commitment any more than I was, why a friendship based on sex would suit him fine.

I was determined to share my story with him. Not then, the moment had passed, but at the next opportunity. Now, I wanted to make him shout my name.

We walked back to my block and stepped into the lift.

Once in the flat, he disappeared into the kitchen and came back with the bottle of red wine he'd brought with him earlier and two glasses. He filled both glasses and handed me one.

'Now, I seem to recall a conversation in which you invited me to introduce my cock to you. Mmm?' those eyes boring into me again.

My libido hit the roof and instant wetness flooded my nether region—I was so hot for him. I gazed back, heart racing in anticipation.

He held out his hand. I took it.

'How about we start there?' he purred, his eyes darkening with intent. His hand tightened around mine as he seemed to be waiting for something from me.

Consent?

I nodded. He placed his hands gently on my waist.

'This is what's gonna happen now, Rosie. I'm gonna fuck you—hard and fast—it'll be fast I can assure you; I've been thinking about being inside you since those damn elevator doors opened yesterday and I don't think I can hold back. After, well, we'll slow things down again...'

The bulge in his trousers bore testimony to his words.

'Oh. Hold on a minute. Now, don't I recall something about cleanliness in the Rules? Do I have to go have a shower, then wait for you to have one too before we can start?'

'Dixie Adonis,' I growled. 'If you don't fuck me right this minute, I swear I'm gonna explode!'

'Adonis? Okay, I can live with that too. Yes ma'am.' he purred again. 'I am aching for you to touch me.'

I needed no further prompting. I trailed my hand over his fly. He groaned and closed his eyes momentarily. I undid the button on his trousers and slid my hand in feeling the shape of his cock through his silky shorts. Oh my, he was one big boy.

We both groaned. I slid my hand inside his shorts and took the top of his cock in my hand. I couldn't help but notice he was circumcised—that would be a first for me. I gently pulled my hand up and down his member, running my thumb over the tip. He was now breathing hard and deeply.

'Wait,' he commanded, 'raise your arms.' He stepped back,

leaned down and, taking hold of the hem of my dress, pulled it up and off me in one move. He inhaled deeply, feasting his eyes on my naked body.

'Fuck, Rosie. You are so goddamn beautiful.' His fingers found my cleft and he tested for wetness. 'Oh Darlin', you surely do want me, don't you?'

He cupped my buttocks in his hands, lifted me easily and I wrapped my legs around his waist, feeling his pulsing erection against my needy pussy. Then he carried me into the kitchen.

He sat me on the kitchen counter, stepped back slightly and produced a little foil package from somewhere while I slid his trousers and shorts down, releasing his rock-hard cock, the large, exposed head pink and smooth. I wanted to kiss him and lick him, but that would have to wait until we 'slowed things down'.

In a split second, he had rolled a condom over himself, then, he leaned forward and softly kissed my neck, my collarbone and my shoulder, tingles of pleasure radiating from everywhere his luscious lips made tender contact.

He kissed me, running the tip of his tongue over my bottom lip and teasing into my mouth. My sex clenched. God, I wanted him, wanted to feel him inside me. *Now. Right now.*

Raising his head again, he slid his hands under my legs, positioned himself and inserted that lush head in my pussy, once more locking eyes with me.

He pushed into me, slowly, allowing my muscles time to adjust to him until he was all the way in, moaning in pleasure and completely taking my breath away. I could feel my walls stretching and my orgasm starting to build from that first gentle push.

He slowly withdrew, right to the tip again. His eyes flashed, and then he thrust hard into me. I cried out and held on to the edge of the counter to push against him as he thrust rhythmically into me, slowly at first, then faster and faster, harder and harder, all the while holding my gaze, his eyes an intense black now.

Utterly lost in mounting sensation, I closed my eyes and gripped his shoulders. I felt every thrust deep inside me, gasping out to his rhythm. His hands now gripping my hips, I stilled as he continued to crash into me, grunting at each thrust, taking me closer until I plunged over the edge of the abyss.

I clung to him and buried my face in his neck as I cried out. I felt him tensing, emitting guttural groans in time with his, now, ragged thrusts and then he sighed my name. He shuddered, and I pushed every effort I could into moving back and forth for him to keep his orgasm going as long as I could.

Staying inside me, he let go of my hips and wrapped me in his arms, murmuring over and over, 'Rosie. Oh fuck! Rosie.'

Then we were both still, breathing hard and clinging to each other.

After a few minutes, he pulled back from me slightly, looking at me with concern in his eyes. 'I didn't hurt you did I?'

'God no. Far from it.'

He relaxed and smirked. 'Well ma-am, was that, er, adequate?'

Adequate? Jeez, he'd just blown my mind. 'Oh yes. Very… adequate,' I breathed. 'You?' It was suddenly very important to me that he had liked what happened as much as I did.

'Rosie, I have been fantasising all day about doing things to you. And you haven't disappointed. Now, I'm ready for the next course. I have a real yearning for something I got a taste of earlier.'

Still inside me, he looked down at my breasts and moaned, 'God, your tits are amazing. In fact, everything about you is exquisite.' If he hadn't had hold of me, I swear I would have floated up into the air.

He looked down further to where the hilt of his member was still embedded in me. His eyes flashed up to mine and he smirked as he looked down again.

We both watched as he withdrew from me. He pulled the condom off—dispensing with it in the bin—and his trousers back up, then he picked me up and carried me into the bathroom. He set me down and, reaching into the shower, turned it on.

'I'll get more towels,' I said and slipped out of the bathroom. In front of the airing cupboard, I wrapped my arms around my naked self as I experienced a shuddering aftershock. Everything with this man was so intense.

I grabbed a couple of bath towels and hand towels from the cupboard and padded back to the bathroom. His clothes now in a pile on the floor, Nathan was already in the shower letting the water course over him, eyes closed stretching his neck, first to one side, then the other.

His naked body was a sight to behold, lean, rippling, powerful muscle. Dark hair was scattered over his upper chest, and in a line leading from his belly button to a nest of luscious, dense dark curls around the base of his dick.

He stilled and I looked up to see he was watching me through the glass. He slid the door back and held his hand out.

'Join me,' he commanded, and I was compelled to comply.

He took my face in his hands, kissed my eyes, my cheeks

and my lips then moved me back a little again. I was wincing and blinking as the water bounced off his shoulders and into my face. He smiled, turned me around and pulled me into him, sweeping my hair to one side and nuzzling at the back of my neck with the tip of his beautiful, Greek nose.

Soft lips trailed kisses up to my ear and the sensations feathering over my scalp almost turned my legs to jelly. I shivered, feeling his breath against my neck as he nibbled my earlobe, then he bit and a twinge of pain immediately tightened my sex. The velvet texture of his tongue as he licked soothed the spot he had just bitten.

He reached for one of the shower gels in my tray, poured some into his hands gliding them over my skin. I smiled, breathing in; Vanilla and Raspberry, how appropriate.

His hands travelled up my arms, squeezing and kneading my shoulders for a few moments, then he cupped my breasts, rubbing the pads of his thumbs gently over my highly sensitised nipples.

Spreading one hand over my belly, the other still cupping one breast, he pulled me back against him and growled, a deep rumbling I could feel vibrating in his chest against my back.

Then he turned me around and pulled me in close to shield my face. He lathered my back, moving his hands down to cup and knead my buttocks. Everywhere they touched me, his hands left my skin feeling soothed and caressed with silk.

Leaving one hand splayed over the small of my back, he brought his other hand up to massage the back of my neck. I had never before realised that the area at the base of my back was such a powerfully erogenous zone. Heat and tingling radiated from his hand simply resting there and I melted into him.

He kept making appreciative moaning noises. He was worshipping me and it was sublime. He covered me in lather, finally caressing my sex so gently and tenderly, I arched into him, sighing in pleasure, aching for him to enter and claim me again.

But that was not in his plan, and he was clearly the one in control here. I could do nothing but comply.

Nathan swapped our places and poured some gel into my hands. Reaching up, I ran my hands over his shoulders, his chest, lingering to tease his nipples. He smiled and twinkled those eyes at me. I moved my hands lower, covering every inch of his smooth, tanned skin. Then, just as gently as he had touched me, I ran my hands over his semi-rigid cock and heavy balls. He closed his eyes and a moan rumbled deep within his chest again.

I turned him around, got some more gel and went to work. Although it was his broad and beautiful back being washed, I was the one moaning at the feel of his taut muscles beneath my fingers.

I ran my hands slowly up his spine, pressing my thumbs in either side of each vertebra in turn and then down so lightly, he flexed and exhaled through clenched teeth. I ran my hands up to his shoulders and trailed my fingers across the nape of his neck. He stretched his head back and let out a deep sigh. I loved seeing and hearing the effect I was having on him.

I cupped his buttocks in my hands—chiselled doesn't come into it—sculpted and smoothly curved, rock-hard muscle filled my hands. I trailed my fingers between his buttocks then, moved by a sudden impulse, I laid my cheek on his back, put my arms around his waist, and held him tightly. He wrapped his arms over mine and we stood for a few moments like that.

He loosened my grip and turned to face me again, my arms now wrapped around his back. He took my head in one hand and kissed me full on the lips. Then he kissed my forehead, then the top of my head, finally wrapping one arm around me and pressing my cheek to his chest with the other. We stood for what must have been several minutes as the water tumbled over us.

This whole episode had been the most sensual experience I can remember.

My head was completely wet by now, so I reached for my shampoo. Nathan took it out of my hands, stooped to kiss my neck under my jaw, then proceeded to wash my hair. He sought out my conditioner, kissed the other side of my neck and then applied that too. Finally, he stood me under the water as it rinsed all the soap and conditioner off me using his hands to smooth my hair back off my face.

And all of this time, neither of us uttered a word. Everything we said to each other was through our eyes and our hands.

Never before..........

He picked up one of my towels and wrapped me up in it using one of the smaller towels to dry off my hair. A new experience for me, this was better than any pampering at the spa or salon.

He gently dried me. Then, he wrapped me in the towel, sat me down on my laundry box and raised his hand to tell me to stay there. I grabbed a hairbrush and ran it through my damp hair while he dried himself.

I stopped mid-brush to watch him. So delicious, I wanted to lick the glistening droplets from his skin—everywhere. I was mesmerised, following the towel down his arm, across his chest, round the back of his neck.

When he'd dried each of his legs and feet, he wrapped the towel around his waist and stood regarding me.

As if in response to my silent request, he dropped the towel, his eyes deepening in colour as they held mine. I couldn't stop from looking down his body and my breath caught in my throat as his cock filled and hardened. I gasped as it twitched and then I giggled involuntarily, looking back up at his face.

He took my hands and raised me to my feet. Opening my towel up, he devoured my body with his eyes then rasped, 'Can I get you something? Would you like some more wine or some water?'

'Just you,' I sighed. 'You are everything I want.'

As the implications of those words hit me, he swept me up in his arms and snuggled me into him. He walked out of the bathroom and looked at me to tell him which door, then we were in my bedroom, all greys and pinks and dominated by my king-size bed.

Nathan

This was all new for me. I'd never been so taken with the desire to look after, to care for anyone like this.

Even back in the days of Linnea and I, yeah, we made out, had sex, held hands and cuddled. I did feel affection for her. But the overwhelming need to touch and hold and wrap Rosie in my arms? That was something new.

At the age of thirty-two, with a long list of women who I'd fucked, or whose bodies I had played with for pure sexual gratification, this feeling was unfamiliar, alien and totally consuming.

Everything I am doing with this woman is pulling me deeper and deeper into her. It's like gravity: unrelenting, inexorable, inevitable.

I dried off, needing time to process.

I was elated that she had agreed to exclusivity with me. I wanted her to myself. The thought of anyone else touching her, anyone else she might look at the way she looked at me, created a vice around my chest. This was crazy—I'd only just met the woman.

And now, here we were. That mind-blowing fuck and the most sensual shower ever still playing over in my head, I turned back to her. She was sitting there doing that thing again—looking at me like she couldn't get enough.

I had wrapped the towel around my waist but now I let it drop to watch her reaction. She looked up into my eyes and then down to my cock. She licked her lips and bit that bottom one again—not deliberate provocation, I could see it was a genuine response and that was so fucking hot.

My cock duly filled, hardened, then I twitched it making it look like it had sprung to attention. She gasped and giggled and looked up at me again, her eyes deepening in colour. And I wanted to taste her, devour her, make her writhe and plunge into her again. I already craved that feeling of being inside her, only her.

I raised her to her feet. I took hold of the towel encircling her and opened it to gaze again on the most beautiful, provocative body I have ever seen.

Rosie: petite; honey-coloured, smooth, flawless skin; firm, rounded breasts tipped with dusky pink bud-like nipples; a gloriously dark little triangle at the base of a slightly rounded belly. I had no doubt she could inspire artists to paint and sculptors to sculpt.

I broke the silence, barely able to get the words out; 'Can I get you something? Would you like some more wine or some water?'

'Just you,' she sighed. 'You are everything I want.'

I know she didn't realise what she was saying, but my heart lurched in my chest at the thought of being her everything.

I swept her up in my arms again. She was so slight, I loved picking her up and snuggling her into me.

I looked at her to tell me which room to take her into and she indicated the door on the right. I carried her in and laid her gently, diagonally on the bed.

I parted her legs, delighting in the sight of her pretty, pink, luscious pussy, inviting me.

Leaning over her and starting at her soft, wine-flavoured lips, I kissed my way down her neck, over to one pert, perfect breast nibbling and suckling at that bud of a nipple. Across to the other and then I trailed kisses down to her cute little inverted belly button. I buried my face in her soft, pubic hair, the smell of her arousal rising up to me and filling my senses with desire.

Opening her legs a little further, and positioning my body between them, I used my fingers to part her folds then flicked at the tip of her clitoris with my tongue. She jerked, so I went in either side, licking and sucking. Pussy juice appeared at her opening offering me the ecstasy of tasting her nectar. I lifted her buttocks with one hand, licked and lapped at her then pushed my tongue inside her. Her body arched and she moaned my name. Fuck, she tasted so good—rich and creamy.

I returned to her clit, gently caressing the tip with my tongue. She was moaning and writhing; this was fucking divine.

I inserted two fingers into her; she gasped, writhing harder, more urgently. I circled and thrust my fingers into her in rhythm with licking at her clitoris. Her body tensed, and then she arched, letting out a loud, guttural groan. She bucked and cried out—I had to work hard to keep on her and stay with her rhythm.

It was mind-blowing. God, please let me spend my life doing this!

Suddenly, she grabbed my hair. 'Enough. Enough. Oh God, Nathan, I'm going to die in ecstasy if you don't stop!'

Job done. And now, I was going to fuck her, slowly this time, and make her come all over again, all over my cock.

So, if not the missionary position, what position were we going to try? I loved this game. I wanted to die playing this game. With Rosie Byrne.

Rosie

What made it all so hot was not simply what he was doing, but that he was delighting in it so, revelling in it; he couldn't get enough of me. It drove me to the brink of madness; multiple orgasms over and over until I had to cry, 'Enough!'.

As I lay there in the afterglow, I wanted to taste him too, more than anything. I felt him starting to move and knew I had to act before he took control of the next phase.

I rolled over and knelt up. He looked at me. 'Lie back on the bed,' I ordered him, a little apprehensive—what if he didn't like me taking charge? He simply raised one eyebrow then lay back as instructed, head on my pillow, his cock standing up straight. I straddled him and he placed his hands on my hips, expecting, I think, to guide me over and down onto him. In one movement, I slid my knees down the bed and took his crown straight into my mouth. He gasped loudly. Victorious, I knew I had taken him by surprise.

I set about exploring his gloriously big, hard dick with my tongue. I marvelled at the silky, velvety feel of the skin that stretched over a shaft of almost solid steel.

I licked from base to tip then used my tongue and teeth to tease his gorgeous, silky head. I could taste the pre-cum, reminding me of the sea-side—ozone. He trembled, moaning, his buttocks clenching.

I placed my hands under his bum then plunged his cock into my mouth as deeply as I could. I pushed down to take him deeper and deeper in, feeling him at the back of my throat. I'd never done that before. It was making me gag, but I didn't care. I was driven by the desire to please him, to give him everything.

Every breath he exhaled was a ragged sigh, and every sound he made was so erotic, I couldn't stop even though I ached to feel him plunging into my body again. I could wait. He was so totally lost in the ecstasy of it all, I was loving doing that to him.

Then he tensed. 'Rosie, stop, stop. I'm so close and I wanna be inside you again.'

I knelt back up and crawled up the bed until my thighs straddled his waist. I leaned over to my bedside cabinet and struggled to open the drawer so I could find a condom. Nathan's fingers wrapped around my hips, the feel of his strong hands on me making it hard to focus.

Finally, the drawer opened and I rooted about finding what I was seeking. His hands moved making me pause. One had found its way to my lower back and splayed across my newly found zone, goose bumps instantly forming all over my skin. The other cupped my breast and he leaned forward finding my hardened nipple with his lips and teeth making my body tremble in pleasure.

'Fuck. Fuck.' was all I could say between shaking breaths. I slammed the drawer shut with such force, we both jumped. In that moment of surprise, we both looked into each other's eyes and laughed a little.

'Fuck, Rosie. These tits…' he sighed, both his hands now cupping them. Then he was giving my nipples equal treatment, licking, sucking, fluttering with his tongue and sending sparks out 'til my clit was throbbing.

I closed my eyes and remembered him between my legs minutes earlier, that tongue – the waves of pleasure that had rendered me senseless.

Frantic, now, to have him inside me again, I tore at the foil packet with my teeth and pulled away from his mouth so I could roll the silky ring over him. He inhaled sharply as I did, his eyes fastening onto what I was doing with my hands.

'Fuck. Oh fuck.' he closed his eyes fighting for control.

I positioned myself so that the tip of his cock was inside me and plunged downwards, crying out from the sensation that ripped through me. I rode him.

I had begun moving for him, to bring him to orgasm, but soon found that, from this position, I could angle his cock to rub against just the right spot. Now, I was plunging harder and faster as my own began to build. His eyes flew open and he stared at me, a look of pure wonder on his face. 'Rosie, you feel so fuckin' sensational,' he said as he braced his heels to thrust upwards to each of my downward plunges.

Faster, harder we moved until his face tensed and I could see he was fighting to hold back. It was so, so hot, I heard screaming as fireworks ripped through my brain, and as he cried my name out over and over.

Exhausted, I stretched out on top of him, wanting to keep him inside me forever. He wrapped his arms around me and I fell asleep.

Chapter Twelve

Nathan

I awoke looking up at an unfamiliar ceiling and wondered for a minute where the hell I was. Then I remembered, big time, and turned to see a diminutive figure lying next to me, still fast asleep. I rolled, as quietly and carefully as I could, onto my side leaning on my elbow. I lay there watching her breathing.

She slept almost on her front but facing me, her hair spread about the pillow. The grey and pink quilt lay over her as it was over me and I realised that she must have awoken earlier and covered us both up. The quilt didn't quite reach her shoulder and revealed a tantalising glimpse of her breast. I watched it gently rise and fall, wanting to nuzzle in and feel her arms around my head, holding me to her.

How can someone so perfectly exquisite be so unaware of her beauty. Too short, not slim enough, legs not long enough—my ass! I reached out longing to caress her flawless skin, to trace her perfect lines and curves, but held my hand millimetres from actual contact.

I thought about my life at present. I was, what do they call it—*a serial dater,* a womaniser essentially. It made me smile;

there was a part of me that thought that was quite cool. What can I say? I like women. Well… I like *fucking* women and playing with their bodies. Did that make me a dick?

Had I got a *type*? Rosie had said that Sigrid looked like my 'type'. I thought about the women I picked up: models, businesswomen, lawyers (not Sigrid—like I said I don't fuck the staff), career women, more than one or two high-class strippers—pretty much all confident, strong women who knew what they wanted which meant they were sexually self-assured. You don't have to play any games; you both know what you are there for. That's my 'type'. Usually. And, yes, going through the list of most recent, they were pretty much all tall, slim, blonde—although some were redheads, attractive (of course *I'd* think them attractive, I'd been attracted to them).

I'd never analysed myself quite like that before, never bothered taking the time to, and it came as something of a shock. Was I still looking for another Linnea?

The fact was, I wouldn't have been that way if things had been different. Linnea had been my first and, if it hadn't all gone so fucking tits up, I had always thought she'd be my last, my happy ever after. But she had sent it all to hell. I couldn't still be looking for her—she's the last woman I'd want. Maybe I was *fucking her over* again and again? Or had been…

Now this…

Rosie. This tiny, elfin-faerie with broken wings and baggage. My chest tightened.

I took a strand of her silky soft hair in my hand and twirled it around my fingers.

The fact is, what had happened between us last night was so much more than fucking. I've had sex: unconditional, unemotional, gratuitous sex, lots of it. That is not what had happened here. The force of wanting I felt for her and the way she had clung to me and called out my name told a different story. Christ—she'd allowed herself to fall asleep on me, clinging to me, like I somehow made her feel secure.

I had been right after all—he did need rescuing. The question was, would I be the guy to do that? Could I be? Had I healed enough to take my own risk with trust? Right then, I didn't know.

All I did know was that I *wanted* to be that guy; I wanted to be tender, giving. I wanted to make her feel safe. I needed to earn her trust. I had to persuade her to ditch that 'Rule' once and for all before she resorted to it and sent this all to hell.

Rosie was stirring. I watched her stretch, then open her eyes straight into mine. My heart leapt as she smiled at me. 'Mmmmmm, what a sight,' she said. 'Do you know how bad your bed-hair is?'

'Do you know what happens to cheeky little girls?'

'Do tell,' she giggled back at me.

'They get tickled, then they get well and truly spanked!' I roared, grabbing her under the covers and tickling her all over.

'Stop! Stop! I'll wee! I'll wee!' she screamed, giggling uncontrollably.

I held my hands up. 'Okay, okay. Can't have that can we? Disgracing yourself in front of your newest conquest? Go and wee, now.'

She got her giggling fit under control but, before she got up to head off to the bathroom, she looked at me from under the duvet. 'About that spanking…?'

'Hmmmm, I thought BDSM was on the barred list.'

'But you make it sound soooo sexy,' she laughed, then darted out of the bed and the room before I had a chance to grab her.

While she was gone, I found my clothes and got dressed. A tune was worming its way into my ear—the chorus of a Coldplay song. I groaned. I knew I'd be humming this all morning now. I had already started... 'And I will try, To fix you.' I sang as Rosie appeared back in the room wrapped in a fluffy white dressing-gown. She looked me in the eye then saw I was dressing. Her face fell. She looked crest-fallen and then resigned. I rather liked seeing that—she didn't want me to go.

'Do you always do that?' she asked me.

'What? Get dressed?'

'No. Hum stuff out loud. You did that in the lift, you know. I thought you were trying to be funny.'

'Why? What was I humming in the elevator?' I couldn't for the life of me remember.

She laughed. 'Strangers in the Night. You really didn't do it on purpose?' she queried.

'It's kinda involuntary,' I explained. 'Something gets into my head and I'm stuck with it for hours, and I suddenly realise I'm humming aloud.'

'An earworm,' she said.

'An earworm? Yeah, I guess that sounds about right.'

She continued to stand in the doorway watching me. Then she sighed. 'Nathan, thank you. I am glad we... have been able to come to an agreement.'

'Hey. I don't know what you're thanking me for. This is a deal, Rosie, a deal for sex. And I expect you to keep your end of the bargain.

'Darlin', tempting as it is to stay here all day with you, I have things to do that won't wait.' I told her. 'I need to get home, shower and change—sort out my terrible bed hair,' I grinned.

'I've got an important meeting today.'

I pulled her to me and she buried her face in my chest. I stroked her hair and kissed her forehead. 'Are you okay Rosie? After last night?' I murmured into her ear.

'I am very, very 'okay'. I have never, ever been so 'okay',' she purred as her body stretched and flexed in my arms, as though she was luxuriating in the afterglow.

'In that case, I shall endeavour to make sure you remain 'okay' for as long as you want me to.' I kissed her neck and she shivered slightly. I felt my body starting to respond. This closeness to her was... dangerous.

She pulled back. 'And you, Nathan? Was it okay for you? Was I... er did I...?'

'Darlin', you were perfect. You were everything.'

'Are you really my conquest?' she whispered.

'Oh, too right. I am helplessly yours to command, my ravishing little songbird. Your every wish is my command. Ask and it shall be so.'

'Come back this evening?'

'Is that a request or a command?' I challenged.

She drew herself up, stuck her chin out and said, 'It's a command.'

'Then I am compelled to obey.' I leant my face down to hers and kissed her.

'Listen, Rosie,' I continued, 'I'm sorry about breaking your overnight rule. It was a pretty intense day, huh? I guess I was exhausted.' I smiled apologetically.

'We both broke that rule last night, Nathan,' she replied. 'When I woke in the night and saw you so peacefully asleep, I didn't have the heart to wake you.'

'So, you covered me and curled up next to me, huh?'

She smiled and nodded. 'Nathan,' she began.

'Uh-huh?'

'It was so nice waking up to your eyes this morning. I think I could drown in them, they're so beautiful. You're so beautiful.'

I didn't dare speak. I couldn't speak. I just held her tightly, burying my face in her hair. No one, other than my mother and my aunts, has called my eyes 'beautiful' before. In fact, no one has complimented me quite so artlessly as this gorgeous creature. And it touched me deeply.

Rosie

As he left, Nathan said he would call or text me to make arrangements for the evening. I resisted insisting on sorting it then and there; I didn't want him to know how terribly insecure I felt about him calling me. I couldn't let him know how badly I wanted him to want to see me again. I had been worried he'd turn out to be a *Fuck 'em and chuck 'em* guy—only interested in the chase and losing interest as soon as it was over. How humiliated would I feel, especially after agreeing to suspend one of my rules?

And what if that meant he would lose interest in the band as well? There was more at stake here than my wounded pride. I had somehow managed to be stupidly blind to that fact.

Now, I realised I was being stupid, full stop. He wouldn't have left the night before, wouldn't have put any thought into how we could find a solution to that rule that I could live with. He wouldn't have stayed or agreed to see me again, not if he'd already lost interest. He certainly wouldn't have looked at me the way he did before he left...

He had stayed the night. Against my Rules. But I thought about how safe he'd made me feel and how content I'd been lying on top of him, his arms wrapped around me. It had been me who'd fallen asleep.

Not only that but I already knew I would want to break that rule again. Waking up like that, I couldn't have stopped looking into his eyes if I'd wanted to—which I didn't, I really didn't; I wanted to drown in them.

And what the hell was I doing baiting him into spanking me? No man is ever going to have that much power over me—it would require a level of trust I could never give.

I needed to get a grip, get a hold on this relationship and make sure the boundaries were adhered to. Starting right then.

I was in severe danger of spending the day mooning about and daydreaming, so I pulled myself together. I needed to get the bed changed and put the bedding in for a wash. I needed to get to my Aikido class early afternoon, then to my vocal coaching session.

And then, I had to prepare for tonight...

I fired off a quick text to Josh to apologise for the lateness of my text, explaining that Nathan had stayed over, and to let him know all was well and that I would call later. He would worry all day if I didn't keep him updated.

After seeing him last night and telling him I had a new candidate, he would have been on standby just in case I called or texted that I was in trouble. I was lucky he wasn't camped out in my hall, but I had reassured him that Nathan wasn't on the 'suspect' list and that I'd be fine. Not only that, he'd been on his way to a date and had been pretty pumped about it. Fabrizio. I wanted to know how that had gone.

Josh texted straight back:

>> He stayed over!!!!????!!!! OMG He was that good????!!!! Can't wait to hear all about this!

Nathan's text came through before 10 am:

>> Hey Rosie. Do you fancy bar hopping tonight? I often pay flying visits to my bars to check out what's happening business-wise and keep the staff on their toes. We can grab a quick bite at one of them. What do you say? N

That would mean his employees would see him with me – that he wouldn't be embarrassed being seen with me. It also made me realise that I knew so very little about him. I knew that he was looking for acts for venues, that's why he'd come along to see the band. I knew that his father's business employed him to run the UK arm which had some bars and restaurants and imported bourbon. Presumably, these were some of the bars included.

I texted back:

<<Hi Nathan. Sounds good. I'd love to come. What's the dress code?

>> You look good in anything. Maybe something a bit dressy. Shoes you're comfortable in though. Not your stage dress. N

<<Why not?

>> Too much on display. N

<< Spoilsport 😝

>> Yeah, that's me. N

<< OK Want me to meet you at the first one? What time?

>>No I'll pick you up at 6.30. OK? N

<< OK See you then 😘

>> Can't wait. N

Wow. Another date. The thought had my heart racing, and my stomach full of butterflies. And he was particular about me not wearing revealing clothes. That sort of felt good but he'd better not be thinking he could tell me what I could or couldn't wear—or do.

I got through the day somehow.

I was a hopeless case in my Aikido class. I spent most of my time on my arse. I originally joined the class at Josh's insistence to learn some self-defence. I was pretty good at it too—not that you'd have thought so if you'd seen this class.

My vocal coaching session was a bit better. I'd been practising my exercises and singing along to some instrumental stuff quite regularly since my previous session. My coach was training me to sing Scat—the more you do it, the more confident, and therefore better, you get. That's what I found anyway.

I took all of the time in between to decide what I would wear and landed on my bottle-green, bodycon, Bardot dress. I have some patent leather court shoes that match it—they were heels but comfortable ones I knew wouldn't cripple my feet.

Once I had showered and got my face and hair ready, I gave my flat a quick check-over. We'd be coming back here again tonight. I grinned at the thought. Then I realised I hadn't called Josh.

'Hey. Baby Girl. I was beginning to think you'd eloped and left me behind. What gives?'

'Ha ha, very funny. I did have a fantastic time though last night.'

'You must have. He stayed over, huh? What? Were you going at it all night?'

'Not all night, no. We did sleep some.'

Silence...

'Josh? Are you still there?'

'He *slept* over?'

'Yeah. I fell asleep on him.'

Silence…

'Josh?'

'Yes, yes I'm still here—I'm just processing. This is a shock, Baby Girl. You really like this guy.'

'Of course I *like* him Josh. I wouldn't be fucking him if I didn't.'

'No, Rosie. I mean you *really* like him. *Like* him like him.'

'No Josh—don't go reading too much into it. It's not *that* big a deal.'

'Rosie. When was the last time you actually *slept* over with a guy—other than me I mean, of course?'

'Shit! Michael?'

'Exactly. I rather think this is a big deal, girl. So, when are you seeing him again? Has he agreed to the Rules? Are you getting Matt over in between times? Or Liam? Or Jamie?'

'I'm seeing him again tonight, Josh. He's taking me out again. And, um, I won't be seeing any of the guys for a while. Nathan has agreed to the Rules. Well, nearly all the Rules—he's asked for the non-exclusivity one to be suspended.'

'And you agreed to that?'

'Uh-huh.'

Seriously?'

'Yes. I agreed to it.'

'Oh, Baby Girl, you've got it bad. I'm seeing hearts and flowers and rings…'

'Don't be ridiculous, Josh. He wants a sex-only relationship too—but a monogamous one. He said he doesn't share.'

'Where's he taking you tonight? Another swanky restaurant?'

'We're going bar-hopping. His business runs a string of bars and restaurants and he visits them regularly. He's taking me with him to see a few and eat at one of them.'

'So, he's taking you to meet some of his staff? That'll be an interesting introduction: Hey guys, meet Rosie my new Fuck Buddy!'

Silence.

'Rosie?'

Silence.

'Baby Girl?'

Silence.

'Look, just be careful okay? Take it slowly. I'd like to meet him, get a handle on where he's coming from. I'm gonna be away for a few weeks though. I'm being sent out for the annual national audit.'

'Oh No. When do you leave? Can we have a sesh before? Oh—what happened with Fabrizio? I should have asked that first.'

'It went well, I think. Let's put it this way, we laughed... a lot and he stayed over. And he wants to see me again. I like him, Rosie. I need to not screw this one up.'

'Oh Josh. Of course you won't, honey. You've been unlucky is all. It's not you—you simply need to find the right guy.'

'You'll be giggin' over the weekend? Are you free on Tuesday? I leave for Scotland on Wednesday. But I'd like to see you before then?'

'Yes, I'm giggin'. I'll make sure I'm free on Tuesday. Where do you wanna meet?'

'How about Borough Market—usual place? How about I get Fabrizio to join us after we've had a chance to properly catch up? I'd like to introduce you two so that you can meet up for coffee or something while I'm away? Look out for each other a bit? I know you'll like him, Rosie, and he's gonna adore you.'

We said our goodbyes, agreeing to meet up the next Tuesday, and I finished getting ready, putting my dress and shoes on in time for Nathan's arrival.

Chapter Thirteen

The buzzer sounded at 6.30 pm precisely, unnervingly punctual again. As before, he wanted to come up before we set off. I danced around in my doorway, heart in my mouth, waiting to hear the lift start. But it didn't. Then I heard him, running up the three flights of stairs. Fit or what?

He appeared at the foot of the last flight, not looking in the least bit ruffled, in fact, looking cool and yummy. Back in all black tonight—black slacks and a black V-neck sweater under a more casual black jacket. My breath hitching, I wondered whether I would ever get over that rush of seeing him.

He stopped, looking up at me, and suddenly, it was as if the rest of the world fell away leaving him and me locked together with our eyes.

The spell broke and he leapt up the last few stairs, took my face in his hands and kissed me, his mouth covering mine, his tongue probing through my lips, into my mouth, drinking me in like a man dying of thirst. He pulled back, grasped my wrists, pulling my hands above my head and backing me against the wall. He took both wrists in one hand and my head in the other, crashing his lips against me once more.

'Every time, Rosie. Every time I see you, you do this to me,' he gasped out, pushing his hips against me, his erection pressing hard into my stomach. 'I want you, Rosie, right here, right now.'

'Then take me Nathan. We're not on the clock tonight are we?' I was so aroused by his need for me, I wanted him inside me with a vengeance.

I have never, in my whole life, felt so desired, so wanted, so *needed.*

He shook his head, 'No, Rosie, we're not on the clock.'

'Have you got any condoms on you?'

He released my wrists, gently lowering my arms, and dug his hand in his inside jacket pocket and pulled out a foil package.

As he discarded his jacket, dropping it to the floor, I felt under his sweater to find the button on his trousers, undoing it.

He stopped my hands momentarily. 'Are you sure? You drive me mad with wantin' but, you know, just say the word and I'll stop. I'll wait…'

'Take what you want, Nathan. Take what you need from me. I'm all yours.'

He smiled a strange little rueful smile, gazing so deeply into my eyes, I thought he was searching my very soul. Then he released my hands allowing me to continue pulling his zipper down. He lifted my dress and pulled my tiny knickers straight off, tearing them apart and leaving a stinging welt on my hip. 'I'm sorry, Darlin', I'll buy you some new ones. I just… I just…'

'Shut up. Stop talking, Nathan.' I pulled down his slacks and boxers to release his cock, that throbbing, heated rod of steel sheathed in soft silk, and worked him. He tore at the foil strip. I took out the condom and rolled it on in a swift, practiced move.

'Hold onto me, baby, this could get a bit rough,' he told me as he lifted me off the ground by my bum cheeks and braced me against the wall. I threw my arms around his neck and wrapped my legs around him. 'Put me inside you, Rosie. I've gotcha.' I reached down with one hand and guided the tip of his cock into my saturated pussy, crying out as he pushed straight into me, all the way, pain and pleasure colliding to send wild sensation bursting through me.

He buried his face in my neck as he started pounding hard into me, each thrust eliciting a cry from me and a feral grunt from him.

The wall at my back was hard and unforgiving, but his raw, irrefusable need unleashed a passion in me that transcended physical comfort and focused everything in me on our joining, our connection.

Did I orgasm? I don't remember being aware of a build-up and release. All I remember is that waves of ecstasy crashed over me again and again until Nathan, crying out, slumped against me, panting like he'd run an Olympic 100-metre sprint and I started to come down from an incredible high.

As his breathing evened out, he pulled his head back to look at me with a concerned, questioning expression. 'No, Nathan.' I smiled at him. 'You didn't hurt me. Not in a bad way, baby. That was incredible.'

'God, Rosie, you feel so damn good, even with these fuckin' things on. I think we may have moved on from adequate, huh? That was fuckin' awesome.'

'Oh yeah.' I agreed. 'Can we do that again sometime? Only, maybe next time we'll try and get inside the front door?' I know they can't see us from downstairs, but I don't think they could mistake the sound of what was going on here.' I smiled.

No sooner were the words out of my mouth than we heard a

door downstairs open and the sound of people talking as they moved into the hallway. The lift started. We stood there in silence, wrapped up in each other, until we heard the sound of the lift door closing and their chatter cut off. We both started chuckling like schoolkids.

Nathan lifted me off and lowered me to the floor, standing back to pull the condom off trousers. I straightened my dress. Luckily, it was made from the sort of material that didn't crease and it immediately fell into place as I smoothed it down.

Nathan bent down and scooped up my destroyed knickers. He lifted my dress back up to inspect my hip where they'd been pulled off. When he found a fine, red welt there, he traced it gently with his fingers.

'No, this is wrong,' he sighed. 'I shouldn't be marking your flawless skin and hurting you like this. I just seem to lose control when I'm around you.'

'Well, I'd rather you didn't destroy my underwear but, honestly, it didn't hurt much, and that line will disappear in a couple of days. It was so hot. I like that you want me, need me so badly, Nathan. No one has ever wanted me like that. Please don't sweat it. Next time I'll try and get 'em off quick,' I laughed.

We walked into my flat; I headed for the bathroom to clean up and freshen my smudged make-up, he went to the kitchen to dispose of the condom and wash his hands. I ran my fingers through my hair and was good to go. As we headed for the door, he stopped, framed my face in his hands once more and looked intently into my eyes. He breathed in as though he was about to say something, then leant down and kissed me so tenderly, I thought I would melt into him.

We ended up visiting three bars in all, one in The City, one in Belgravia and one in Soho. All called, *The Copper Pipe in ....* with the area finishing off the name. *The Copper Pipe in The City* was where we grabbed our 'quick bite' and I liked it the best of the three. It had quite a sizeable main bar area, several separate private areas and a whole separate function room, all oak and leather and rich dark colours.

I got my first shock of the evening, well, apart from the first mind-blowing shock before we even left home, when we arrived at *The Copper Pipe in The City*. Nathan walked us in with me on his arm, spotted someone, walked us over to him, put his arm around my shoulders and said, 'Rosie, this is Rhys, the best executive bar manager in the business—not to mention he's a Chevalier Sabreur. That means he's qualified to take the top off a Champagne bottle with a sword—how cool is that? Rhys, this is Rosie, the hottest jazz singer in the city (you know, the band at the Café Paradiso I told you about) and my... girlfriend.'

He turned his head and looked me straight in the eye as he said the last bit, challenging me to contradict him. I looked straight back at him, having to work very hard at not revealing the cartwheels my heart was doing in my chest, not to mention wondering why the hell my heart was *doing* cartwheels at all. I tore my eyes from his to look at Rhys as I held out my hand to shake his.

Rhys regarded me wide-eyed, looking at Nathan then back to me several times.

'Rosie. It is a *great* pleasure to meet you. Nathan certainly didn't exaggerate when he told me how gorgeous you are. I can't wait to hear you sing now—he was even more vocal in his praise of your voice and talent.' Rhys pulled me towards him to plant a kiss on my cheek. I could feel Nathan tensing next to me.

Rhys was lovely—a real charmer. Warm eyes, a gorgeous smile and a wonderful sense of humour. He gave off a *boy next door* vibe—an *extremely attractive* boy next door—but you could tell he commanded respect.

He mentioned that he played a bit of guitar himself and that if we stuck around one of the bars one night, he and I could have a little jam together. And yes, one of these days he'd show me how to do the sword and champagne bottle thing.

All through this, he still held my hand and I could feel the tension emanating from Nathan in waves. Was that why he had baulked at the non-exclusivity rule, because he was this possessive? Maybe he was hyper-sensitive after what happened with his ex? Whatever, if he reacted like this when I was just talking to one of his friends, what on earth would he be like if he thought there was more going on?

Rhys finally released my hand, playfully punched Nathan on the shoulder, and left us to take a seat and enjoy our meal as he went back to whatever he had been doing.

'What did he mean, one of the bars? Isn't he the manager of this bar?' I asked Nathan.

'He's an Executive Manager—he's responsible for several bars each of which have an on-site manager to deal with day-to-day stuff.'

'I didn't know there was such a thing,' I told him. 'What's your role then?'

'I run the companies that run the bars and restaurants. That's about making sure they work within the laws and tax systems of the country and ultimately making profits for the share-holders—the owners of the companies.'

I let that sink in and roll around my brain a bit. I began to realise that Nathan had a hugely responsible job and was very powerful within the companies he ran—his family's business.

I sat down in one of the booths and he went over to the bar to get us some drinks and order our food: a handmade burger for him and Welsh Rarebit for me; they claimed to use a traditional recipe with strong beer, mustard and Worcestershire sauce. That would make it one of my favourites, something my dad used to make for me when I was a kid and we'd giggle together about our guilty secret. I have so many wonderful memories like that of my dad, but my main memories of my mum involve atmospheres in the house that you could cut with a knife. I lost myself for a few minutes mulling that over and nearly missed the next shock.

I glanced back at the bar as a pretty, brunette server was placing two glasses of wine in front of Nathan. She chatted away to him, smiling, clearly at ease with serving her boss's boss's boss.

Before he had a chance to pick anything up, a tall, willowy, attractive blonde had sidled up to him. She was impeccably dressed, looking like an executive in a fashion house or something similar—I'd put her in her mid-thirties, a little older than Nathan, maybe. I watched as she said something into his ear—like right up close into his ear. He turned to face her and she put her hands up to grasp his jacket lapels, pulling her body into his and tilting her face forward to kiss him. He moved his head to one side so that her kiss glanced off his cheek and, stepping back, took her hands in his, removing them from his lapels and placing them by her sides.

He turned his head and looked straight into my eyes. He wasn't smiling but he winked at me. He turned back to her and said something and she recoiled as though she had been slapped. She looked over at me and sneered, and by the time she had turned her head back towards Nathan, he had picked up the glasses and set off back to our booth.

She stared at his back then shot a venomous look at me before flouncing off back to the group she had presumably been standing with before.

Chapter Fourteen

I was determined not to be fazed, not to display any reaction to what I'd witnessed, despite my stomach feeling like lead. Nathan put the glasses down, slid into the booth to face me and poured us both some red wine.

He looked into my eyes and started to speak. 'Her name is—' but I interrupted him.

'You don't need to explain anything, Nathan. It seems clear from what I saw that, whoever she is, she's in your past and, therefore, none of my business.' As I said the words, I realised the lead feeling had disappeared. He had made it noticeably clear by his actions that *I* was who mattered to him at that moment, although, what I had said was bravado on my part. Of course I was dying to know who the hell she was.

Nathan nodded but then said, 'If some guy laid hands on you, damn right I would wanna know who he was, Rosie, and what he was to you. *I* would consider that *my* business because *we* have a thing, you and I. Are you sure you don't wanna know anything about her?'

'Well… okay, you got me. I *am* curious. But not because I think you're *having a thing* with her this time,' I grinned. 'I got that message loud and clear last time. Not to mention what I just saw…'

'Well, I'm glad that message has landed.

'I haven't had what you'd call a *relationship*, Rosie, not since Linnea. I've had a lot of hook-ups, quite a few *things* that lasted for say two or three *dates* at most, and a few *things* that have lasted two to three months at most. All of these have been understood, by both parties, to be for sex. The ones that have lasted a little longer have only been those where the lady involved was on the same page and definitely not looking for anything more.

'Gabrielle Harris, the lady in question, here, was one of the latter—it ended over six months ago. I am pretty pissed at her right now because she could see I was with you. Her behaviour was well out of order.

'So... questions?' Nathan asked.

Hell yes.

'You... liked her?'

'I was attracted to her—obviously.'

'You slept with her?'

'Er... no. I never did *sleep* with her.'

'You fucked her, though?'

'Seriously?' He looked at me with his eyebrows raised.

'Why did it end?'

'It was... time. We'd both got out of it what we wanted. We were both ready to move on. We stopped making contact. We've bumped into each other once or twice. In here. She works for an IT company who have offices just up the road. She's usually with other guys but even if she wasn't, I'd have no interest in hooking up again.'

He looked intensely into my eyes. 'An' right now there is only one woman I have eyes for, Rosie. And, in case she still doesn't realise it, she's the woman sitting right in front of me.'

He reached his hand across and cupped my head, running his thumb gently down my cheek. 'The beautiful, talented, smart, sexy woman sitting right in front of me. Did I mention hot as fuck?'

I sat, bathing in the glow of his praise. He made me believe it, if only when I was reflected in his eyes. He made me feel beautiful and sexy—it was addictive.

There was a niggle in the back of my mind though. My chest tightened as I shuffled in my seat. The way Nathan was talking, we were going beyond his two or three dates kind of thing. I guessed, then, that we'd have two to three months then. Well, at least I'd be able to give my guys a timeframe for my being off the FBud list.

He reached into his jacket pocket and held out a familiar-looking small package. 'Hey. If you're gonna tear up every time I pay you a compliment, I'll have to keep plenty of these in my pocket.'

Shit. I hadn't realised that I had teared up. I tried to smile and accepted the pack.

I excused myself, on the pretext of needing the loo and to freshen my eye make-up, and headed to the *Ladies*. I had to pass the group that Gabrielle was with and couldn't miss the Gorgon stare.

I was sitting in my cubicle, as you do, when I heard the main door open and the sound of stilettos crossing the tiled floor to the hand basins. When whoever it was didn't go into the other cubicle, I knew it was her. My guess was she was pissed off that Nathan had blown her off and needed to take it out on someone. I took a couple of extra minutes to gather my wits. Nathan's actions and what he'd told me made it easy to be ready for whatever she had to say.

I left the cubicle and walked over to the sinks to wash my hands. She was touching up her lipstick and, as I looked into the mirror, our eyes met. She snapped her lipstick lid on and spoke.

'Little girl, why don't you go play with the boys and leave the grown-up men to the grown-up women?'

I turned to face her and she turned towards me. She towered over me, sneering but I looked directly into her eyes.

'I think grown-up men are perfectly capable of making their own decisions about who they want to be with, wouldn't you say?' and with that I walked, purposefully, out of the room, thanking heaven I was in comfortable heels that I was less likely to coggle over on. She uttered not a sound as I walked out.

When I got back to the booth, our meals had arrived. 'Thank goodness, I'm starving,' I announced. 'I skipped lunch because I knew we were coming out to eat.' I tucked into my Welsh Rarebit—it was delicious.

'You did say bar-*hopping* didn't you? I'm ready to move on when we've finished eating,' I said, as I was scraping the last mouthful onto my fork.

He grinned at me. 'Okay, so you don't like this place—what are we doing wrong?' he asked me. 'Apart from not barring certain patrons that is?' he added, his grin getting even wider. 'I saw her follow you in, and I saw her come out after you did, looking distinctly shell-shocked. Feisty little thing ain'tcha when you're crossed?' His eyes were shining, full of admiration for me.

'I do like this place, actually.' I answered. 'There's just one thing missing.'

'Oh yeah? What's that?' he came back at me with, as I'd

hoped he would.

'Some live music rather than that piped stuff. I can see you've got a decent sound system in here. You should have a DJ or a band in here on Thursday nights—you'd get a bigger crowd in I reckon.'

He laughed. 'You know, you could be right there, Rosie. We might be a bit too hung up on keeping this template too carbon-copied between the Copper Pipe venues. I might just get my team to look into appropriate licenses for this place. Was that a punt for a booking?'

'Well, now you mention it…' I laughed.

'Don't worry, you're top of my list in every respect,' he said, his eyebrows doing that arched thing again.

I wondered how many other *templates* they had if The Copper Pipe were *this* template and they weren't live music venues at all. I should really do some trawling on the net—find out what I could about Mr Connor and Connor and McQueen.

We finished our meals and the wine and got ready to leave. Rhys came over again to say his goodbyes and check that Nathan was 'still on for tomorrow night'. As we waited for a cab, I asked Nathan what tomorrow night was, and he told me the pair of them were going to work on some plans they were putting together for the new venue.

We went to the Belgravia bar next and finished up in the Soho one which turned out to be not far from my flat. Who knew? Nathan had been this close to my flat many times, but we'd never clapped eyes on each other before.

When we got back to the flat, I had a question for him, about one of the Rules. I didn't want tonight to end with him leaving; I wanted us to be free to do everything we wanted and then stay locked in whatever embrace we finished up in.

There was a risk, of course, that he would say no he had to go at some point. He'd made it clear that he hadn't *slept* with Gabrielle—did that mean he wasn't in the habit of staying over with the women he had sex with?

Stupid bloody rule—it was my own fault for having it in there. To be fair, though, it had never been an issue for me before. I was always quite happy to have my own space back once the festivities had concluded.

Gathering my courage, I blurted it out. 'Nathan, look, there's one of Rosie and Nathan's rules I'd like to um amend, well, delete actually,' I started.

'Rosie and *Nathan's* Rules, huh? We have a set all to ourselves, do we? What did you have in mind?' He pinned me with that serious gaze again, so I had nowhere to hide.

'Um, it's um the *No overnighters* rule. I mean, if you've got all these designs on my body, it seems foolish to have a time constraint, don't you think?'

'Well…?' he sucked air in through his teeth and, looked deadly serious. 'I need to think about that, Rosie. You know, rules are rules and er, we already discarded one yesterday. Are you sure you wanna go that far down this road?'

And there I was again, in the Head's office trying to explain myself. 'Well, it's just that I, um—'

'Hell,' he interrupted me, 'before I know it, you'll be putting anal sex back on the table and then where will we be?' His eyes twinkled, and the corners of his mouth started to twitch.

'You bastard!' I cried, 'You're playing with me.' His hands on my waist pulling me towards him, I was thumping on his chest again. 'You. You.'

When he had pulled me so close I couldn't continue, he leaned down and murmured in my ear, 'Why don't you take a look in my breast pocket, baby?' And there, in his jacket pocket, I found a fold-up travel toothbrush. 'Another of those assumptions I made,' he drawled, grinning that irresistible grin at me. 'You see, Rosie, I also liked waking up this morning to find a beautiful, tiny woman all snuggled up beside me.'

He tilted his head slightly to one side, his eyebrows arching up in that way of his. His eyes softened as he spoke again. 'Are *you* sure about this, though? You *want* me to stay?'

'Yes, Nathan. I'm sure. I want you to stay. I want you...' I whispered.

He continued to hold me with his gaze. His lips twitched into that lopsided smile that made my stomach do somersaults. 'Well, I'd hate to disappoint....'

And so began a night in my flat that saw us fucking in almost every room: I straddled him on my sofa; he bent me over my dining table; he carried me into the kitchen putting the counter to use again; he led me into the shower and lifted me onto him, my back against the tiles, my legs wrapped around him; he dried me gently, tenderly, then picked me up and took me into my bedroom where he laid me, inverted, on top of himself so that I could take him in my mouth again while he buried his face in my sex and, using his tongue, lips, and fingers, had me screaming his name.

And finally, he curled me up, my back to him, wrapping me in his arms and cupping my breasts in his crossed hands. He took me from there, slowly, all the time murmuring into my ear until his breathing became ragged and hitched, his movements more urgent and rapid and he reached down to tease and circle my clitoris, taking us both, crying out, plunging into the abyss.

I had never felt such utter contentment as I did when I

drifted into sleep, still wrapped in his arms, listening to his deep, regular breathing in my ear.

This is heaven.

Chapter Fifteen

Nathan

I awoke the next morning and immediately reached out for Rosie. She wasn't there. I sat bolt upright to look around the room. No sign of her. I felt something slide in my chest.

Then I heard a weird sound like steam escaping from a pipe coming from somewhere else in the apartment, along with the clattering of kitchen utensils. You idiot, I told myself, this is *her* apartment, she's not gonna do a runner from here.

The smell of fresh coffee reached my senses and I started to relax.

Something else shifted in my chest. I thought, *I'm lying here in bed after a night of the most incredible sex I've ever had, with the most beautiful woman I've ever met, and she is making me coffee, after which, I am going to have more incredible sex with her. Does it get better than that?*

I could hear music—something classical—operatic. Was that coming from outside? It sounded like three voices. It was floating, kinda beautiful. Italian. I heard: 'Soave sia il vento, Tranquilla sia l'onda.' Something about breezes being gentle and waves being calm.

It ended. Shame, it was rather lovely. But then, something else started, a male voice—the music more dramatic. Another male voice—then the two were duetting, suddenly launching into such a beautiful melody, I was sure I'd heard before. This time, it was in French: 'Oui, c'est elle! C'est la déesse plus charmante et plus belle.'

The door to the bedroom opened further and the music became louder—it was coming from inside the apartment. Rosie walked into the room carrying two coffee mugs, tears streaming down her face. 'Americano?' she sniffed. 'I sort of guessed you wouldn't be a Latté kind of guy?'

I leapt up out of the bed, and took the mugs out of her hands, putting them down on the bedside table. 'Rosie, what's wrong?' I said, taking her into my arms.

She laughed and sniffed again. 'Nothing's wrong Nathan. Isn't that the loveliest piece—gets me every time,' and I realised she was talking about the music I could hear playing.

'What is it?'

'The Pearl Fishers' Duet. The music was written by Georges Bizet—the guy who wrote Carmen—you will have heard some of that,' she told me. 'Did you know that he died of a heart attack at the age of thirty-seven, believing Carmen was a failure? Unbelievable huh? Just listen to this.' She became still as the two voices launched again into the main theme.

'So who is the beautiful goddess they are both mooning over?' I asked.

'You understand the words?' she asked, looking at me in awe.

'Yeah, I speak French,' I told her.

'Wow,' she said. 'Well, these two friends, after being parted over some daft argument—over a woman I think—vow to be friends for life now and they've sworn that no woman will ever come between them or something. Then they both see this woman—the goddess they are talking about and both fall for her immediately—and you know it can't end well. One of them ends up dying, of course—it's an opera.'

As the piece finished, I asked, 'You like opera?'

'Mmmm, I like bits,' she said. 'I can't listen to a recording of a whole opera, but there are some excerpts that are wonderful. I've never been to one though. I guess it might be different if you are watching it live,' she said, wiping her eyes on a tissue.

'What made you play this?' I asked her.

'Oh, sometimes when I'm feeling mellow, I like to lose myself in some of these pieces. This is one of the CDs my dad used to play before...'

I pulled her in closer and caressed the top of her head with my cheek. I want to tell her that I feel for her losing her daddy so young, but I didn't want her to feel pressured into talking about it—she would when she was ready.

I could smell her hair. Vanilla. It filled my senses.

Mellow? Yeah, that was about right. That was how I felt too.

'And you're feeling mellow now?' I asked her.

'Mmmmmm,' she purred. She turned her face up to me. Her eyes, shining, dropped from my eyes to my mouth and she stretched up bringing her lips so close to mine, I could feel her breathing on them. I bent to kiss her gently and felt her melt into me. She kissed me—really kissed me.

Eventually, she pulled away but continued to gaze into my eyes.

I had to find something to say to break the spell. I was in danger of saying what was in my head. This was too soon to be anything other than honeymoon period infatuation, surely. If I said anything, it might scare her. Hell, it scared me, but what scared me more was the possibility that, if I said too much now, she'd fly, and I'd lose her.

'Americano is fine,' I said.

'What?'

'The coffee? Americano is fine for me,' and pfffft, the spell was broken, we were 'back in the room' to use Sid's phrase. She laughed and beamed that Rosie smile at me.

We grabbed the mugs and sat on the bed.

'You are full of surprises,' I said to her. 'Opera?'

'My dad used to play lots. My dad had a hugely eclectic taste in music: classical, opera, Motown, rock, heavy rock, pop, and he'd play stuff all the time when he was home. And jazz, swing and blues—that's where I got my love of singing them from, I'd sing along to his favourites. Then there were his favourites among the contemporaries of his time, so I was exposed to them too: Robert Palmer. Billy Joel, Michael McDonald—the list goes on...'

I love that she has as an eclectic taste in music, as do I. I could introduce her to my favourites and learn hers over time—something we could share together.

'You're not dashing off again this morning?' she asked me.

'No. I kept the morning free,' I replied.

'End of the week and weekends are our busiest times,' she explained. 'We've got gigs tonight, Saturday night and Sunday night and I've got a Big Band rehearsal Sunday afternoon.'

'Well, that's great to be in demand, huh?'

'Yeah,' she said, sounding unconvinced. 'You could come?'

'Maybe one of those nights. I got a lot to do over the next few days as I'm gonna be away for a few days next week.'

She nodded. 'When do you go?' she asked me very quietly.

'Wednesday. My flight to Chicago leaves Heathrow around midday,' I told her, while a knife shredded my gut again as an image of the tall guy kissing her on the top of her head pushed its way into my thoughts.

'And you get back ...?'

'I'm staying the weekend to visit with family, flying back on the Monday,' I said. 'Look, Rosie, I will keep this Monday night free for sure. If I'm ready, we maybe can have some time on Tuesday, too. Once I'm back, if it all goes to plan, you will be seeing a whole lotta me, I promise you that.'

She nodded her understanding. Then her eyes began smouldering again. 'I guess we'd better make the most of this morning then.'

Rosie

Two nights I'd have to wait to see him again.

Well, maybe it wasn't such a bad idea, I needed a bit of space to get this *thing* into perspective and that was impossible when he was near me.

He wasn't real—he couldn't be. I knew this because he was too damned perfect. Nobody is that perfect.

When I was with him, he made me feel like I was the centre of his universe, like nothing and no one else existed. And when I wasn't with him, I was thinking about him constantly. This had to be somehow chemically induced—I was absorbing some drug he was emitting that was keeping me on a permanent high. It was definitely addictive. But what was going to happen when I came down?

I was going to get the opportunity to find out—he was going to be away for almost a whole week. That should be enough time for this euphoria to wear off and allow me to see clearly again. In the meantime, maybe I should give in to it and enjoy it while it was here, enjoy him while this lasted, while I was still intoxicated. After all, no one could get hurt here. We'd both been clear about the basis of this *relationship*. I couldn't hurt him and he certainly wasn't getting a chance to hurt me—not going to happen.

God, it felt so good to be in his arms.

My morning was a continuation of the dream I had been having the night before, a dream of ecstasy overwhelming me over and over again. Then I had to get back to the real world.

Our rehearsal was very productive. Then, at the venue, everything went according to plan.

This pub had a young clientele. We'd played here before and knew that the modern numbers given the jazz or swing treatment would go down well. Postmodern Jukebox had covered a huge range of songs giving us great inspiration. We included versions of Creep and Seven Nation Army that always went down a storm. I'll always be grateful to Norah Jones for her wonderful version of I Don't Know Why that we used as a base but with our own little spin on it.

Of course, it was back to the pub loo for getting into performance clothes and doing make-up—a bit of a come down after the dressing room in Café Paradiso. Still, this was one of the better ones, a bit more roomy and cleaner than many of the grotty little ones I've had to put up with.

I started wondering about Nathan's other bars—what his live music venues might be like. I was obviously going to find out as he'd made it clear he liked us. I would just have to wait until Sid let us know he'd booked us. I didn't want to compromise the lines between our personal relationship and his business relationship with Sid.

Thinking about all of this, did mean I ended up watching the door and, when I was performing, scanning the bar, hoping to catch the glimpse that would tell me he'd turned up.

He didn't.

By the end of the evening, I couldn't help but feel disappointed. Bloody hell! What was wrong with me, behaving like a love-sick teenager mooning over the latest boy? See that was something I never got much experience of when I *was* a young teenager. There was only ever the one boy—and that didn't go too well… It certainly hadn't involved the butterflies, the pounding heart rate and the crushing anxieties this thing with Nathan was putting me through.

Hah! So much for seizing control and always being the one calling the shots!

Thankfully, it didn't interfere with my performance, and I received the usual round of compliments. As I've said before, people are really kind.

Pete dropped me off and I poured a glass of wine and gave myself a good talking to:

Enough is enough! It's been amazing but let's get our feet back on the ground. Tomorrow morning, you're going to the gym and do your gruelling ninety minute workout—you haven't done that for a while. Then you're going to spend the afternoon starting to learn the two new songs we decided on today. Really looking forward to trying out the Chris Isaak number. And then, you're going to go and give a brilliant performance at tomorrow night's gig—you're going to throw yourself into it and enjoy it, and maybe do a bit more flirting with the audience this time.

I had a shower and went to bed.

I tossed and turned for a while and eventually, I must have drifted off. I groggily became aware that my mobile phone was buzzing on my bedside table; I usually turn the sound off when I go to sleep but, of course it vibrates anyway. I must have been dozing rather than deeply asleep.

I could see it was Nathan. I checked the time, it was 2.34 am.

'Hello?' I rasped incredulously. 'Nathan?'

'Hey baby, where are you?' a quiet, husky voice demanded.

'I'm at home, Nathan. Is something wrong?'

'Wrong? The thing is Rosie, the thing is, I find myself with a burning need to see you. I know, I know you need to, need to sleep honey, you—you got gigs, you need to sleep, I should stay away, but it seems… I ain't getting any sleep… until I see you. You, you can tell me to leave you alone, Sweetheart…?'

'Nathan, where are you?'

'I'm a-a-outside, Rosie. Listen, Darlin', I've had, I've had a few drinks. Rhys and I got working. It got late and, and we just kept drinking to keep going. You know, you know you might wanna tell me to go home and try and sleep it off.'

I pulled on my dressing gown and dashed to the window in the lounge to look out into the street. There, on the other side of the road was a very sheepish Nathan looking up at me, one hand holding his phone to his ear, the other, held out like he was an actor on a stage.

'Come up here, you idiot,' I ordered him. He bowed low and crossed the road. The door buzzer sounded, and I pushed the button to let him in.

I walked out to the lift to wait for him. The lift door opened and there he was, grinning like a fool. His smile was infectious and I was soon grinning back at him.

'An' there she is,' he said, slurring quite significantly. 'Oh God. Rosaleen Ciara Byrne, you have definitely put a shpell, shpell, sssspell on me haven't you. I can't get you outta my head. Take my body, Rosie, take it—it's yours to do with as you please. Take it. I know it's my body you want, baby. Take it. Take it!'

He lurched forwards and put his arm around my shoulders, surprisingly gently given his state of inebriation. He pulled me towards him and kissed me on the head.

I guided him into the lounge, his wonderful Nathan smell increasing my heart rate, but now mixed with the strong aroma of Bourbon.

'I can die happy now, Darlin'. Throw me on the sofa. I won't, I won't be any trouble, I promise.'

'So much for giving me your body, Nathaniel,' I muttered at him. 'Come on, let's get you to bed.'

I guided him into the kitchen first, where I filled a pint glass with water and ordered him to drink—all of it. I refilled the glass then took it and him into my bedroom. I undressed him, down to his boxers, partly standing up and partly after he'd flopped on the bed. I put his clothes on a hanger to keep them reasonable for the next morning.

I took my dressing gown off and climbed in beside him. He immediately pulled me up to the top of the bed so he could snuggle his head on my chest. I couldn't help it, he was irresistible, even this drunk. I put my arms around his head and stroked his hair.

He breathed in, deeply. 'You smell so wonderful, Rosie. You smell of vanilla. Did you know that's my favourite?' he murmured sleepily.

'You may have mentioned it,' I murmured back, smiling.

'Oh Rosie, do you have any idea, any idea how long it's been since I felt this happy? So long. So long. I never thought... You make me... happy. Do you know that Rosie?'

An unexpected surge of pleasure swelled my chest hearing this. You know what they say: 'In vino veritas', In wine, truth—or something like that—although in this case it would be 'In Bourbon veritas'. I loved that I had driven some of his pain away.

I could feel him relaxing, slowly drifting into sleep. 'You make me happy too, baby. Go to sleep,' I told him.

'I do love this. I really do love this. I do love you,' he murmured on, almost imperceptible now.

'Nathan?'

'Uh-huh?'

'You talk too much,' I whispered to him, but he was already asleep, snoring gently in my arms.

I lay listening to him, watching his chest rise and fall in the moonlight and realised this: I was lying in my bed, pinned there by a drunken, incapable man in my arms, who would still be there in the morning, with a sore head, and stinking of night-before whisky, and I felt strangely contented.

And that was the last thought I had as I, too, drifted off into a deep, untroubled sleep.

Chapter Sixteen

Nathan

Fuck! I was dying! My brain had shrivelled in my head and if I moved a muscle, it would bounce against my skull, hurting even more than it did already. Something had crawled into my mouth and died, and every inch of my skin was heated and stretched.

I could see that it was light through my eyelids but didn't dare open them in case I was blinded. The light already hurt enough. I must have left the drapes open last night.

I felt around me—at least I'd made it to my bed—God knows how.

It was so damn noisy! I'd have to complain to the desk – somebody, somewhere was stacking crates of bottles – very loudly.

I could smell something, something good. I realised it was coffee and something else... bacon. Somebody in one of the other apartments had set out to torture me.

Then I could hear somebody singing, a woman. Even in this state of purgatory, it sounded good – she could sing and had such a mellow, velvety voice, it was quite soothing. It was vaguely familiar.

I forced my eyes open and nearly leapt out of my skin – this wasn't my bedroom, or my bed! Where the fuck was I? This was a woman's room.

*Oh Fuck! W*hat had I done?

Then I realised the room looked familiar. I had definitely been here before. The sight of a little pink checked shirt hanging over the back of a chair confirmed for me—this was Rosie's bedroom. Thank God for that!

Oh Fuck! What had I done?

I wracked my brain trying to remember the events of the night before. I had been working with Rhys in the City bar. We had worked into the night, well past closing. I remembered the bottle of Connor's Gold coming out to keep us going. That was on top of all the red wine and beer I'd been drinking earlier. The fact was, since the months after Linnea had dumped me, I wasn't a big drinker. I liked a drink but I was no longer inured to the effects of large quantities of alcohol.

Rhys and I had parted company and I'd gotten a cab to take me home.

All I know is that all day, I'd been thinking of her, about not seeing her, about wanting to see her more than anything. I guess I'd decided I wouldn't sleep easy until I had seen her and, in my drunken stupor, thought it would be fine to go wake her up.

I had no idea what time I must have rocked up here. Bless her, she had clearly taken pity on me and brought me in. But this was not good. I had intruded on her space and heaven only knows what I'd said to her.

I spotted a pint glass of water on the bedside cabinet and downed it. I stumbled out of the room and into the bathroom to take a piss. I washed my hands and face, splashing them in cold water to try and clear my head a bit. I remembered I still had the travel toothbrush in my jacket pocket—where was my jacket? I stumbled back to the bedroom to find my clothes all hanging up neatly. I didn't imagine I was in any fit state to think about doing that the night before—it must have been Rosie.

I found the toothbrush and slipped back to the bathroom. I was brushing away furiously, foam all around my mouth when the door opened behind me and Rosie walked in. My heart leapt in my chest. The sight of her always seems to do that.

She grinned at me. 'Mmm, sexy,' she purred at me. 'That wonderful bed hair and foaming at the mouth. Nothing quite like it to turn a woman on,' she giggled.

Toothbrush stuck in my mouth, I couldn't respond.

'When you're done, come into the lounge,' she said, 'I've got paracetamol, coffee and a bacon and egg sandwich, if you're interested.'

I nodded vigorously, then winced at what it did to my head. She looked at me with a 'What did you expect?' look on her face and off she went. I finished up and tried, without much success, to smooth my hair down.

I walked down the corridor, past the kitchen, where I could hear Rosie moving about, and into the lounge. On the dining table was a place mat, a glass of water with two Tylenol-type tablets next to it and a mug of steaming coffee. I sat in the seat, took the pills and a slug of coffee. Rosie emerged from the kitchen, two plates in hand, one of which she set down in front of me. On it was a sandwich cut in two. I could see bacon sticking out of the sides.

'I hope I did right,' she said, 'I assumed you would prefer tomato ketchup to brown sauce.' She pronounced tomato, tom-ah-toe like they did here in England. It was cute.

'Yeah, tomaydo is good,' I responded and picked up a half sandwich and bit into it. Egg yolk exploded from within and ran down my chin, dripping onto my boxers.

Rosie exploded into laughter. It was a beautiful, tinkling sound and her whole face lit up with mirth.

'I'm so sorry, I should have warned you,' she said, not sounding in the least bit sorry.

'Nobody teach you to break the yolks when frying eggs for sandwiches?' I asked her.

'Ungrateful bastard,' she shot back at me. 'As a matter of fact, my dad showed me how to make bacon and egg sandwiches when I was seven. He used to stand me on a step, back from the hob and show me how he was frying the eggs. He and I would make them every Sunday morning. And every time, he'd say, 'A decent bacon sandwich always has runny egg in it.' And he was right. But you do have to be a bit careful how you bite into it, so I apologise for not giving you a heads up.' She jumped up and got me a table napkin.

I cleaned up, having to admit the combination of runny egg yolk, bacon, bread and tomato ketchup that had made it into my mouth was delicious.

Rosie had half of a sandwich on her plate. 'You start ahead of me?' I asked her.

'Oh no. I don't normally eat breakfast, but I have never been able to resist this—I couldn't have made one for you without doing some for me; it makes me think of Sunday mornings with my dad,' she said wistfully. 'I hope you appreciate my sacrifice,' she laughed. 'I'll have to starve the rest of the day to make up for it.'

'Why would you do that?' I asked her, incredulously.

'I need to be losing weight, not piling it on,' she retorted.

'What are you talking about, Rosie? You don't need to lose an ounce. I've told you, you are perfect—I'm not just saying it... or just being kind.'

'Look, I'm short and still a size 6, sometimes 8, depending upon brand. I should be about a 2 or 4,' she pressed. 'Swedish models are the same dress size as me, I'm sure, and they're mostly six to eight inches taller than me. I look dumpy in comparison.'

An image of Linnea flashed, unbidden, into my head but I pushed it away.

'Now look here, Rosie Byrne, while I'm around, while we have... this... I want you exactly as you are. You are slender and curvy and fucking beautiful. Jeez, one look at you and my dick wants to fuck you into the middle of next week, you're that hot. You hear me?'

'It's mutual,' she said, trying to deflect the conversation. I let her.

I stood up and pulled her up into my arms. 'Listen Rosie, I think I have an apology to make. I am sorry I disturbed you last night. Being drunk and all that. You should have sent me away. Instead, you take me in for the night and then feed me bacon and egg sandwiches with runny yolks. You are some kinda angel, huh? The thing is, I wanted to see you all day, right from since we parted yesterday lunchtime. Seems I can't get enough of you and my drunken instincts were to come find you. I am sorry.'

'I'm not,' she murmured in my ear. 'All that—that's mutual, Nathan. I'm glad you wanted to find me when you were like that, and not go else…' She ran her hand over my chest, twirling her fingers through my chest hair. 'Even with a hangover and bed hair, you are beautiful, you know?' She looked up at me, smiling, with that smoulder in her eye again. 'And Nathan…'

'Uh-huh?'

'Would you tell your dick I'd like that very much,' she said.

Hangover? What hangover? Instant cure.

Rosie

Nathan's hangover certainly didn't impede his performance. He was true to his word, he couldn't get enough of me, nor me him. This would, surely, calm down in time but right then, the intensity and wanting were unremitting.

Before he left the flat, we'd both agreed that, as neither of us had plans aside from work—him and gigs—me, whenever either he or I finished what we were doing in the evening, we'd meet back at mine afterwards.

Mine was the easiest option simply because he knew his way around it now and I'd given him the keycodes so he could let himself in if he arrived there first. Of course, I hadn't seen his flat; until this morning I didn't even know he lived in Pimlico. He told me he'd put that right and we'd christen his place as soon as he got back from the States.

Knowing I would see him later meant I was able to focus my full attention on the gig and socialise with the audience without the intrusion of juvenile butterflies and anxieties. It went well and the venue owner told us he'd contact Sid to re-book us. Everything was still on track for us and it felt good.

Pete dropped me off outside my flat as usual. I looked up to see lights flickering in my window. My heart pounded in my chest and butterflies fluttered about in my stomach, knowing Nathan was up there waiting for me. I let myself in the building and took the lift up. My flat door was open, and the lights inside were switched off to reveal the flickering of candles in the darkness. Alexa was playing something very familiar—a Santana song.

The smell of something delicious was emanating from the kitchen, my table was laid out beautifully for two and there were candles and tea lights all around the room. I was dumbstruck. I could hear a lovely rich baritone voice singing along in the kitchen. I called out, 'Nathan?'

My Dixie Adonis emerged from the kitchen wrapped in my pink striped apron, took one look at me and that gorgeous, lazy smile crept over his face—his eyes twinkling at me. 'Gimme your heart, Make it real, Or else forget about it...' he sang at me, along with Rob Thomas.

'Hey Beautiful,' he drawled, opening his arms. How could I resist? I crossed the room and threw myself into them and a dreamy, melting kiss.

When I could, eventually, tear my lips away from his, I said, 'What's going on Nathan?'

'I will be serving dinner in a coupla minutes,' he explained. 'Your timing is impeccable.'

'Nathan, it's nearly midnight,' I exclaimed.

'Uh-huh,' he answered. 'Gotta look after my lady. Now don't get all excited—this ain't my kitchen so I had to make it simple. We have Pasta Carbonara with a side salad, and some garlic ciabatta—shop-bought, I didn't have time to prepare my own.'

'You cook?' was all I could get out.

'Uh-huh. Multi-talented, that's me,' he said, sexily pronouncing multi: mull-tie.

'Now, you go freshen up and I'll serve up. Join me back here in five minutes.' And with that he disappeared back into the kitchen.'

I wasn't entirely sure how I felt about Nathan wanting to look after me – this was uncharted territory. Michael always *professed* to wanting to *look after* me, but the fact of it was, he wanted to *control* me. Of course, I didn't see that until it was over and I had come to my senses and realised the extent to which I ran around after him, catering to his every need.

Nathan was not a controller; I could tell that much. He was genuine and generous and was treating me as equal within the sexual relationship we were enjoying. In fact, if anything, it was unequal in that he was more giving than taking.

So, when he popped his head round the bathroom door to see how I was doing and presented me with a glass of chilled white wine, 'a decent little single-vineyard Pinot Grigio to go with the Italian meal,' I smiled graciously and settled on enjoying being made a fuss of—he'd made so much effort with the room, the meal and everything.

Michelle Branch was now singing about the game of love as we turned the volume down.

Over the meal, we talked, or rather I talked. Nathan wanted to know why I liked Science Fiction books and films, was I really into space aliens and blaster guns? I tried to explain the finer points of good science fiction. He got me explaining what I found so fascinating about the exploration of artificial intelligence, starting with a history of robotics in fiction, from Capek's *Rossum's Universal Robots*, to Asimov's Positronic Brain, his Three Laws and *The Bi-centennial Man* and finishing with why *Blade Runner* was my favourite movie. He listened, rapt, as I waxed lyrical and he made me feel as though what I was saying was the most fascinating thing he'd ever heard.

After dinner, we cleared up together and then he took me to bed where we had sex: slower, calmer but no less exhilarating. Nathan delighted in playing endlessly with me, taking me over and over until I demanded he come inside me and then, he took us over together, doing everything in his power to hold on and wait for me.

And to finish, he, once again, curled me into him, on my side, my back to him and his arms completely encircling me so he could bury his face in my neck murmuring my name.

He pushed me away from him slightly and ran a hand down my back. The heat from his palm set my skin on fire everywhere he touched me. I craved that touch. Finishing at that spot where just the presence of his hand made me wriggle and tightened my pussy, he spread his fingers out.

'Do you know, Rosie, my hand almost spans your little waist at the back here. Fuck, this body is beautiful. Your skin, your lines and curves, your shape—you are perfect.'

Then he pulled me back to him and reached his hand down the front of my body to where my clitoris was now aching to be touched. He guided himself into me, splayed his other hand across my belly and began that wonderful rhythmic slide. And he kept up such a gentle pace, until he brought me to a shuddering climax and joined me, crying out my name again.

As we lay entwined, Nathan nuzzling my neck, I remembered the night before, a drunken Nathan, almost unconsciously pulling me up the bed so he could bury his face between my breasts. And what he had said: 'I really do love this,' and 'You make me happy, Rosie.'

I slid off him, reaching down and dispensing with the used condom in the bin I'd strategically placed beside the bed. I wriggled through his arms and up the bed, turning to take his head in *my* arms, while kissing his forehead and stroking his hair. Right at that moment I wanted, more than anything in the world, to make this man happy.

He pulled away slightly to look into my eyes with a gaze so intense, I thought he was seeing right into the heart of me. My heart stuttered. I'd been caught out, discovered in a dark secret. Then his eyes softened, and he laid his head back on me saying, 'This feels like home, Rosie.'

As he was drifting off to sleep, pain welled up from inside me and I couldn't stop the tears. I clung to him, desperately trying not to sob too hard and wake him.

This feeling I had for him was getting too strong. It was too much. If I let him in, he could hurt me and I couldn't go through that again. I wouldn't.

I don't know how long I cried because I eventually fell asleep.

Nathan

She moved up the bed, took my head in her arms and showered me with tender affection. I moved to look at her and tell her how I felt, how hard I was falling for her. She looked like a rabbit caught in headlights, so fearful, like she'd been discovered in the act of doing something forbidden, and I realised she wasn't ready to hear it.

I put my head back down and told her as much as I felt she

could accept, that being with her felt like home.

As I was drifting off, my head clasped to her breast, I felt her chest heave and then, she was clinging to me, sobbing but fighting to control it. I knew that I mustn't let her know I was witnessing this. I wanted to wrap her in my arms and tell her how beautiful she was, how much I loved her and how I would never, ever hurt her or allow anyone to hurt her ever again. But I had to resist. If I didn't, I risked losing her, losing everything.

Words wouldn't be enough—I needed to find a way to convince her to trust me through action, not words. In the meantime, I'd have to keep her persuaded that I was in this for the sex so that I didn't frighten her off or force her to reinstate that awful rule and send everything to hell.

Eventually, her sobbing stilled and her breathing slowly became deep and rhythmic. When I was sure she was asleep, I gently pulled away from her. The pillow beneath her was wet and her poor little face was puffy and tear-streaked. She did look peaceful now, though. Very gently I took *her* fully into *my* arms and snuggled her into my chest. I whispered in her ear, 'You're okay, my beautiful Rosie. I gotcha.'

She sighed and, in her sleep, whispered, 'Oh Nathan.'

I thought my heart was going to burst.

Chapter Seventeen

Rosie

Sunday passed.

Nathan was up and away in the morning. I managed to get to the gym, for my gruelling ninety-minute session at last. The Big Band rehearsal went off really well today—all A list players and both vocalists turned out. Our gig went amazingly well and Nathan was waiting for me again when I got back—this time with a Chinese takeaway. It was probably just as well he was going to be away for a week, I would end up the size of a house-end otherwise.

Interestingly, not looking forward to not seeing him for a whole week, I was relieved that he had insisted on the suspension of the non-exclusivity requirement. That surprised me. It had never bothered me with any of my other FBuds. For some reason, the thought of Nathan with another woman, particularly one who might look like Sigrid or Gabrielle, made my hackles rise. Stupid bloody rule.

Actually, scratch that—*any* woman.

Again, I found myself in unfamiliar territory. Even when I'd found out that Michael was cheating, I'd felt betrayed, that it somehow invalidated our relationship, but I hadn't felt jealousy or possessiveness.

One thing I did know: for me, no-one could measure up to Nathan. Sunday night was as amazing as every other night so far. Anyone else would definitely be second best. But I needed to get some perspective.

Nathan couldn't know that I was falling for him. I daren't let him know; I couldn't give him that power. While he believed that I was seeing him for sex, albeit mind-blowing, extraordinary sex, we both knew where we stood and there was safety in that. Besides, he'd been pretty clear about what he was in this for. Knowing I was falling might chase him off.

That night, we would have the whole evening together as well as the night. I was going to prepare dinner—something simple and easy: warm chicken and bacon salad with fresh mango, a honey mustard dressing and sourdough bread, quick, easy and tasty. I'd even bought in some vanilla ice cream—couldn't resist the joke. Another stupid bloody rule but I was not relenting on that one, it was getting ridiculous.

We wouldn't be spending Tuesday night together. It wasn't practical—Nathan would have to be up, packed and at the airport by 10 am on Wednesday morning. It worked for me as I was committed to meeting up with Josh and being introduced to Fabrizio. I was looking forward to that.

Monday night would be our last time together until Nathan got back the following Tuesday. While he would be flying out from Lexington on the Monday, we are five hours ahead, so it would be Tuesday before I would see him.

Nathan

I would be seeing her that night and that would be it until I got back from the States.

After a few hours at the office, I would have Tuesday with Rhys, dotting the i's and crossing the t's on the plans for the new venue, and then spend a night in my own bed for the first time since my first night with Rosie. I needed to get to Heathrow for 10 am—it seemed foolish to risk messing that up.

So that night I was taking the shots and we were gonna get down to some serious disclosure. She needed to unburden and I knew a way that would facilitate her doing that. I had been waiting for the right moment.

Who was I fooling? *I* needed *her* to unburden. I needed to know her story so I could start making some progress on understanding what had caused her so much pain, and learning what I needed to do to earn her trust. I hated that she was hurting so much.

Then I needed to sort me out. I was going crazy thinking about leaving her here to do… whatever. I kept seeing the tall guy, thinking about his hands on her, and worse… Would she keep that rule suspended while I was away? I wouldn't be here for her to talk to if she had misgivings. I had thought I could find a way to deal with this before I went anywhere. But I didn't know how to approach it with her. If I seemed to be getting possessive, would I scare her off? Would it seem like I was looking for more than she was willing to give? If I wasn't careful this would tear me apart.

I knew she felt something for me, I knew it. But that terrified look in her eyes when she thought she'd given herself away—the paralysed rabbit caught in the headlights who would flee the moment the spell was broken—I couldn't lose her. I *wouldn't* lose her. But would I lose me?

Chapter Eighteen

Rosie

Everything was ready, the table was set, the salad made up, the meat cooked and keeping warm in the oven. I'd put some white wine in the fridge earlier but had bought some red in too. I'd made a mental note of what wines Nathan had bought previously to make sure I'd have something he liked. Alexa was playing Pop in Jazz, a collection of pop songs given a jazz treatment—nice background music.

The door buzzer sounded and my heart leapt into my throat, threatening to choke me. Would I ever get over the headrush every time I was about to see him, or the breathless exhilaration—it got me every time.

Although I had given Nathan my keycodes, he wouldn't use them if I was in—he said that would compromise my privacy. I pushed the button to let him in the door to the block, then I opened my own front door and stepped out. One of the benefits of living on the top floor is knowing anyone coming up to it is visiting my apartment.

I listened for the lift, but it didn't move. He was coming up the stairs again. I listened for his footfall and then he turned the last corner, looked up, fixed his eyes on me and took the last flight two stairs at a time. His eyes were burning through me, so full of intent.

He crossed the landing to slip one arm round my waist and pull me to him. He leaned in to kiss me, a long, smouldering, passionate kiss. Then he pulled back and said, 'God, I needed that. You look lovely Rosie, and you smell so good—vanilla and violet again?'

I nodded. We smiled sheepishly at each other for a few moments.

'Please come... in.' I grinned at him. 'Dinner is almost ready. Sit down, I'll get you a glass of wine. We'll start with the white,' I informed him.

'Yes ma-am,' he replied, looking around for somewhere to place the carrier in his hand.

'What's in the bag?' I enquired.

Nathan took out a bottle of Amaretto, a bottle of Drambuie, and a bottle of Connor's Gold, his family-produced Bourbon, along with several shot glasses, and placed them on the coffee table. I looked up at him questioningly.

'After dinner, we, my little songbird, are going to play a game. You up for that?'

'Well, it rather depends on what it is,' I began. 'Clearly it involves drinking shots. Isn't that a bit dangerous, given your rather clear designs on my body tonight? We wouldn't want to become incapacitated... again... now, would we?'

'Oh, it's a dangerous game alright,' he sizzled, 'It reveals a great deal about a person in a very short space of time.'

'What is it, then?' I asked him.

'Can't you guess?'

'Clearly not, otherwise I wouldn't be asking, would I?'

'I thought everyone played this game at college. It's called *Never have I ever*? Ring any bells?'

'Nope,' I said, 'I was a bit of a loner, Nathan, I didn't really get caught up in the social whirl of college or uni you know.'

His eyes twinkled at me. 'You have seriously never played *Never have I ever*? Well, this will be an eye-opener for you then,' he promised.

'Really?'

'Trust me,' he said. And there it was. Was I ready to trust him? His tone softened. 'I told you I wanted to know more about you Rosie, this game will help. And you'll find out more about me too—it's not one way.'

I realised I did trust him in this. For someone wanting a sex-only relationship, he seemed strangely hell-bent on getting to know me. But I didn't mind; I wanted to know about him too—he intrigued me. And there was something comforting in the idea of him knowing about my past—knowing and, hopefully, accepting who I am.

'Okay, okay. I'll serve dinner and you can tell me the rules.' I popped into the kitchen and brought him out a glass of well-chilled wine then went back in to finish preparing.

I brought the dishes in and served up.

'This looks great, Rosie, thank you,' he said. Gotta love a man who is so appreciative.

'So, what are the rules of this game then? How do we do this?' I asked.

'Right,' he began, 'we have a shot each in front of us and we take it in turns to make a statement that starts 'Never have I ever...' and you have to finish the statement with something like, 'peed in a public swimming pool'. If either of us has peed in a pool, we have to take a mouthful of the shot.'

'Right. So you say something you've never done but you think the other person might have, or something that you wanna find out if they have. Is that right?' I probed, starting to think this could actually be fun. I straight away knew a couple of questions I'd be wanting to ask.

'Well, sort of, but you don't have to only say things *you've* never done, you just have to own up and drink the shot too once you've found out what you wanna know. Oh and, when there's only two playing, you have to explain the circumstances too.'

'That sounds even more dangerous,' I ventured.

Nathan looked at me, narrowing his eyes for a few moments. 'How about you divulge as much, or as little, as you're comfortable with. You choose whether to go for the full disclosure or a brief headline—how would that be?'

'Okay, that sounds sensible,' I agreed.

We finished the course and I told Nathan I had vanilla ice-cream in for dessert. He laughed saying, very suggestively, 'You know, I think I might have just come up with an idea about vanilla sex that doesn't involve any missionary positions...'

My libido immediately kicked into overdrive and I glared at him, breathing hard and biting my lip in anticipation.

'Oh, baby,' he purred at me, 'all in good time. This game first, that game later.'

We left everything on the table—there would be no clearing up tonight.

We took up seats, Nathan on one couch, me on the other. He lined up the shot glasses in front of us. I chose Drambuie and he filled his to the lines with Bourbon.

'Who goes first?' I asked.

Nathan tossed a coin and he won, so he went first.

'Never have I ever… had sex in a car.' An easy one I guess he thought, to get it going.

'Define *had sex*,' I demanded.

'Okay, performed any sexual act in a car.'

I looked at him, smiled and reached for the shot. I took a swig, then he took a mouthful of his.

'So, why the need for clarification?' he asked me.

'I've given blow jobs in a car, I haven't *had sex*. Michael always wanted me to do that—well—insisted that I do that.'

'Michael?'

'He was my boyfriend when I was nineteen through to twenty-one,' I explained.

'Well, I can't say I blame him, Rosie, you do give amazingly good head,' he commented, softly.

'It wasn't like that, Nathan,' I snapped. 'It was nothing like you and me. Nothing has ever been like you and me.'

'You said it, Darlin', you ain't wrong there.' Nathan looked at me for a while, I think waiting for more, but I wasn't ready to give more yet. He let it go.

'Okay, so you've never fucked in a car. We'll have to put that right. One for the list of firsts, huh?' he said, gently. 'Your turn, Rosie.'

So now it was my opportunity to find out what his infuriatingly non-committal answer the other day had failed to reveal. 'Never have I ever… indulged in erotic-asphyxiation,' I challenged.

'Oh, clever girl. You catch on fast.'

He grinned. Neither of us moved.

'Okay, you got me. No, it's not something I've ever had the slightest interest in exploring,' he confessed. I breathed an internal sigh of relief.

The game continued.

'Never have I ever.... made out in the ocean,' was Nathan's second offering.

'Is this, like, gonna be an exploration of places to have sex?' I laughed at him, reaching for my glass and taking a smaller sip this time. If we got lots of questions in, I'd need to go a little bit carefully.

Nathan reached for his glass too. 'My family had a place in Naples, Florida for holidays. Lin and I would take off there for a couple of days every now and then, and we'd make out on the beach or in the sea when it was deserted. They were good times,' he said wistfully. 'And then, when I went travelling, there were a few episodes...'

'You said before her name is Linnea? That's quite an unusual name. I've only ever heard it on TV—someone in the old Stargate series was called Linea.'

'Yeah, it is quite unusual. Her family emigrated from Sweden—it's a Swedish name,' Nathan explained. I can't explain why but I felt something hard, heavy and rock-like forming in my chest. So, Linnea was Swedish and had been accepted into fashion modelling school; a picture formed in my mind and I had to fight to set it aside. Why should it bother me? She was an ex of some years now and his love-life, past or present, wasn't my concern.

Time to give *my* more detailed response.

'I'm assuming an estuary counts as 'in the ocean'? Michael and I went on holiday together to Cornwall. There was a natural rock pool—I think it was near Padstow. The tide would come in and cover it and when it went out again, it left a natural squarish-shaped pool. The day we visited, there was no-one around so Michael decided we would 'make out', as you call it, in the pool. That's it though, for me. Only the once. I scraped my back rather badly against the side, which was rough, natural rock. Luckily, it didn't become infected, I guess the salt water cleaned it quite effectively.

'It was enough to put me off going back there anyway, however insistent Michael was about it,' I said, all the while thinking, *not so good times*.

Nathan studied me for a couple of seconds then said, 'Your turn.'

I decided I would tell him about my first time and find out if he had ever done anything like it to anyone else. I swallowed hard, took a deep breath and said, 'Never have I ever… had sex with someone as the result of a bet, mine or theirs.'

Nathan didn't make a move but fixed his eyes on me. I reached forward, my hand shaking as I reached for my glass and emptied it. His eyes narrowed as a small frown settled on his brow.

'I was seventeen and still a sweet little virgin,' I layered sarcasm in my tone. 'His name was John and he was in the year above at sixth-form college. He was quite a well-liked guy, very sporty—you'd call him a *popular jock* in the States, I think.

'He started talking to me, which was a bit weird because I was a loner and kept myself to myself mostly. He was normally hanging around the barbie dolls so I couldn't understand what he wanted with a chubby little nobody like me. Anyway, he asked me out, several times, and eventually I said yes. He took me to the cinema, then on another day, he took me bowling.

'On our third date, he took me to his house to 'listen to some music'. His parents were out and we 'made out'. He'd been sweet to me and we were 'dating' so I thought: *Why not? It has to happen sometime. He's a nice guy and he really likes me.*

'Yeah right.

'He didn't force me or anything but, you know, he was as young as I was and not very experienced, although I couldn't tell at the time. He fucked me, came pretty quickly and that was that. His comment to me was, 'Oh dear. Missed the biscuit huh?' He left me lying on the floor of his living room and went into the kitchen.

'I pulled myself together and followed him but, before I went through the archway into the room, I could hear him on his mobile—he didn't waste any time. He was saying something like, 'Yeah—she finally put out. I win, and you owe me twenty quid, mate.' Then he said 'Nah. She lay there like a beached whale, about as much sex appeal as a cold fish.' And he was laughing, and I could hear whoever was at the other end laughing.

'He had the decency to look horrified when he realised that I had heard what he'd said but I just grabbed my things and ran.'

Tears stung my eyes but I blinked them away. I looked over at Nathan who looked appalled, his eyes full of concern. He moved, I think to take me in his arms, but I put my hand up. 'Please don't,' I implored him. 'Listen, as tragic stories go, Nathan, this isn't a patch on what you've been through. I'm a big girl. I don't let it get to me anymore. No one will ever use me like that again. They always say: *Make mistakes 'cos you learn by making them,* don't they? Well, that was my first fucking big mistake—that's all.

'So,' I continued, 'how about you? Anyone you made bets on?'

He shook his head. 'You know, high school boys can be real

jerks, right? They're full of themselves, and testosterone, and desperate to appear cool in front of their pals. No, Rosie, I never made a bet on a girl's virginity, either to take it or to goad someone else into it. But I did know guys who did and, for the most part, they were real jerks. There's nothing I can say, except this: that guy was the real loser. He missed out on what could have been a real nice teenage experience for both of you, maybe even a sweet relationship with a beautiful girl. And look at you now, I *would* bet that he'd give his right nut to be with you, now, Rosie.'

'Yeah, yeah. Like you said, there's nothing you can say. Anyway, not a chance. I have higher standards and expectations these days,' I said. 'I believe it's your turn.'

'You wanna continue this Rosie? Are you sure?'

'Yes, I'm sure. Nathan, I said I would tell you about my stuff. It seems this sort of works to let me. Let's see what else it dredges up.'

'Okay. Urmmmm, never have I ever.... been involved in a threesome,' he claimed, looking at me speculatively.

I reached out for my next shot. Nathan looked quite shocked for a second, then composed himself again as I withdrew my hand without taking it. Then he leant forward picked his up and slugged it back.

'Oh, I can't wait for this,' I said.

'Hey, what can I say? I'm a guy. When it's on offer, I'm not gonna be turning it down, you know? First time was when I was travelling. I was in a bar in Vienna, and there were these two sisters. We started shooting the breeze and—you know how it goes. Next thing I know they were arguing over who was gonna have me. I threw a suggestion out there and they went for it. I was younger then,' he added grinning all over his face.

'And recently?' I fished.

'Not in the last coupla years.'

He laughed. 'I'm getting on a bit now, you know.'

'Ha ha. Not so's you'd notice, Nathan. I don't doubt that you could keep two women *very* happy.'

He smirked at me, his eyes twinkling wickedly. Then his smile sort of faltered as the implications hit him.

'Why? What did you have in mind?' he asked, looking apprehensive.

I laughed at him. 'Don't you go worrying your pretty little head,' I reassured him. 'I want everything you've got all for me, thank you very much. So, we are only talking FFM... er MFF—whatever it is?'

'Er... too right we are.'

'Well, I have to say I am somewhat relieved. I had this image in my head of you and another guy with one girl... And what with you being quite clear that you don't share—'

'Oh no—that wasn't me,' he protested, 'I definitely have no desire to have any other guy's... tackle involved anywhere near me.'

Oh this was too good an opportunity to pass up.

'Pity...' I murmured, under my breath, as I reached out and picked up the shot, taking a swig.

'What did you say?' he demanded, looking shocked again.

'I said, 'Pity'.'

'Well?' he demanded. 'Why did you make like you weren't gonna take the shot?'

'Because I wanted to hear what stories *you* might have first,' I replied, giggling, 'so we couldn't be falling foul of double standards, huh?'

'More like you wouldn't be owning up if I hadn't,' he retorted. 'Well, let's hear it then. Are you into women as well as men?'

'Oh no. My threesome was MFM. Two guys all to myself.'

He looked horrified. I worried that I may have disclosed too much. But—what the hell? He'd just told me he'd had two women together, on more than one occasion.

'Only the once,' I said. 'I had made a date with Jam..., one of my FBuds and one of the others called to say he was at a loose end. He sounded a bit down. I told my first guy I was a bit concerned about him and he suggested inviting him over. I wasn't thinking about how it might go down, but we sat talking and drinking and... the first guy told us about a threesome he'd been involved in and it sort of went from there. No really kinky stuff— erm spit-roasting mainly...'

'Enough!' Nathan snapped. 'I definitely don't want any pictures in my head. So, when you say, 'Pity', does that mean you'd want to do it again?' He sounded pretty ruffled. I decided not to tease him, as had been my initial intention.

'No, Nathan. It's off my bucket list and, now I know the reality of it, I don't have any desire to reprise it. And I really have no desire to share me between you and someone else, male or female. You are, without a doubt, everything I want in bed and, like I said, I want *you* all to myself.'

He visibly relaxed. 'So, you were teasing me, huh? When you said, 'Pity', huh?'

'Maybe... A smidge,' I confessed.

'Hmmmm—about that spanking...' he said, his eyes flashing dangerously.

'Don't you even think about it.' I countered. 'Anyway, You're the one who brought it up. You obviously wanted to rattle my cage. You can't get all pissed off and bent out of shape because it backfired on you.

'It's my turn now,' I hurried on, wanting to get past the last disclosure. 'Never have I ever... had anal sex,' I stated all in a rush.

Neither of us moved initially then Nathan slowly reached out and took his next sip, all the while gazing intensely into my eyes.

'There have been occasions when a woman I'm with has expressed the desire. And I certainly wouldn't wanna disappoint—ever.' He was grinning at me now. 'And to be clear—we are talking about insertive anal sex with a woman here. Like I said before, I'm not into guys—or strap-ons.'

'Okay,' I squeaked, burning up with curiosity but embarrassed about asking more. Nathan could obviously see that.

'Go on Rosie, ask me. I can see that you want to. Never be embarrassed about asking me anything.'

'Is it very different? I mean, is it something you like doing a lot?'

'Yes, it is a bit different. Yes, I have liked doing it. But Rosie, I love everything *we* do. You said before that everything with me was different—it's the same for me. I guess there's some strong chemistry between us. This is—we together are—awesome. Seriously. I am happy to go at your pace and do what you like doing. Anything you wanna try—I'm your man. As long as it's only me,' he added, looking at me very pointedly.

'Moving on,' said Nathan. 'Never have I ever... been in an abusive relationship.'

'Oh, nice one, Nathan, straight to the point,' I observed.

We both picked up our glasses and downed their contents.

'You first, then,' I said.

'Well, you know my story now, Rosie.' Nathan sighed.

'Not the conventional idea of an abusive relationship but, Linnea was cheating on me, using me and then bullied and blackmailed me into going along with what she wanted. So, yeah, I would term that abusive. So, tell me about this Michael. I'm assuming it's him *you're* referring to.'

'Yep. I've thought long and hard about this, Nathan; that man destroyed any self-esteem I may have still had following the bet incident.

'He was older than me by fifteen years and he treated me like a child. I was given instructions and, if I did anything to displease him, he would punish me by staying away, or he would sulk. And I would run around trying to please him.

'It was Michael who insisted I give up Uni—that's College to you. He said he couldn't see any point in me carrying on as I didn't need the qualification and he wanted more time with me—he said.'

Nathan interrupted me. 'How does a nineteen-year old loner even meet and end up in a relationship with a thirty-five year old? Was he a tutor or lecturer or something when you were a student?' he asked.

I could feel the blush starting at my feet. I cast my eyes down. 'I just didn't see him coming, Nathan. I was so inexperienced and when he started paying me attention, I was flattered. I mean, after the John thing a couple of years earlier, I was more on my guard, but Michael was persistent and, at first, very good at being someone I would look up to. Kind, self-deprecating, so worldly and wise and so genuinely interested in me. He liked the same books, the same music even the same coffee drink. At first, anyway.'

'You still haven't said how you met.'

I closed my eyes visualising my favourite little coffee-shop-cum-vegan-cafe in Brighton. I loved the smell, the ambience, the *feel* of the place. It was quirky and fun—mismatched furniture and crockery, weird abstract art pictures all over the walls that had price tags, small chandeliers all over the ceiling—also with price tags. They had a wall of bookshelves with all sorts of books on it, there for the taking, with a little sign asking you to donate the last book you read that you really loved to share it with someone else.

'It was run by a heavily tattooed and pierced couple who made me feel at home the very first time I walked in through their door. I ordered a latte made with oat milk and sugar-free caramel syrup, and one of their vegan flapjacks then went to sit down. The smaller one brought my order over and looked at my Uni study books. She asked me what I was reading for fun and I told her I was between novels. She went over to the bookshelves and came back with a small paperback in her hands. 'This is the perfect book for you,' she announced and handed me Flowers for Algernon by Daniel Keyes…'

'I know it—read it in school. I'm pretty sure I've still got a copy of it at my apartment,' Nathan interjected.

'To this day, I have never cried over a book as much as I did reading that one,' I confessed. 'So much for 'reading for fun'. But it has remained one of my favourite stories. I even looked out the old film of it, *Charly*, with that lovely actor, Cliff Robertson. I know there's a newer version, but the old one resonated more for me.'

I paused, memories of reading that book for the first time, along with its subject matter, threatening to turn those tear-duct taps on again.

'And, Michael?' Nathan pressed, gently.

'So, I start going there regularly and there's a guy who is

often in there at the same time as me and this one time, we're both waiting at the counter to order. He's in front of me and he orders a latte made with oat milk. That captures my attention. And then he adds in, 'With sugar-free caramel, please.'

'I looked at him properly for the first time and noticed he was kinda nice-looking, in an older way. He looked back at me and smiled, and then went and sat down at the only empty table.

'I gave my order and looked around for where I could sit—he was still sorting his case out and saw me looking around so he gestured to the seat opposite, inviting me to share his table. Gratefully, I walked over and started pulling out some of my study books when, bugger me—he pulls out the very copy of Flowers for Algernon that I had handed back a couple of weeks before. I had bought my own copy by then.'

'Coincidence after coincidence,' Nathan observed. 'I'm thirsty and liquor ain't gonna cut it. You got any beers in, Rosie?'

'In the fridge. I've got some lagers. Peroni—will that do?'

'Perfect. Can I get you one too?'

'Yes please,' I said and started getting the rest of the story straight in my head while he was gone.

Ice cold lager. There's nothing quite like it when you've been talking too much. I gulped down a couple of mouthfuls, immediately soothing my throat, and gestured my appreciation to Nathan.

'So. He orders the same coffee as you and is reading the book you happened to have handed back a week ago. Was he in the café when you did?'

'What?' No. I have no idea. I don't remember. Why?'

'Just wondering. Go on.'

I took another swig of Peroni and continued. 'I asked him whether he was enjoying the book and it started us off talking about it and what a wonderful story it was.

'Anyway, to cut a long story short, we kept bumping into each other in the coffee shop and he eventually asked me out—he took me for Afternoon Tea in the Grand Hotel and then to the theatre to watch a play. And it went from there.

'At first, he was very kind and sweet to me. I had told him about my childhood, and he said he wanted to look after me. He moved in with me so he could better take care of me, he said.

'I told him about my awful experience with John and he was very patient with me at first. He explained that my orgasm would come with time and practice—that I needed to learn how to angle myself to make the most of penetrative sex...'

'You mean, like, it was *your* responsibility to move the right way so that you could come?' Nathan probed.

'Uh-huh. I know.' I felt the heated flush rise up again, my cheeks burning with shame and embarrassment.

'Anyway, it wasn't until I finally saw the light and thought back over it all that I realised he had, little by little, taken everything away from me that gave me independence and identity, making me wholly dependent upon him and desperately needing his approval to do anything. I was almost paralysed, not daring to make any decisions myself. It was almost like I *wanted* to be controlled—that I *needed* to be completely submissive. Not in a BDSM way—nothing like that.

'He used that approval as reward, or withdrawal of it as punishment. The sea pool incident I described earlier—when I put my foot down and refused to go back there because I'd hurt my back so badly when he fucked me against the pool wall, he threw such a strop, we had to pack up and leave, cutting our holiday short. Then he told me it was over—not for the first time by any means.

'I was so desperate to be loved, and he did tell me he loved me. So, I always ended up doing what he wanted me to do. And every time he discarded me, I would be devastated, terrified that no one else would ever love me. I was convinced that I had to make it work with him.'

I paused for a few moments, that awful sinking, anxious feeling I'd always felt in the pit of my stomach when I was with Michael trying to establish itself again. I took another swig of lager, although it threatened to come straight back up again this time.

'If—when—he snapped his fingers, I would always go running back. I was his yo-yo.' I continued.

'As I explained, he wasn't even a giving lover. I didn't know that because I'd never experienced a real give-and-take relationship. In fact, he was very boring, you know? One position and blow jobs—that was about the sum of it. The one being missionary—and none of it ever got me off. I guess that's one of the reasons it's not a favourite.

'I didn't see any of this until I found out he was screwing around. When I confronted him with it, he told me I was being 'childish' and 'petulant' and that I should grow up. He suggested that it was perfectly natural for a man who wasn't getting everything he needed from one woman to seek it elsewhere. When I countered that with, 'Fine but I want the freedom to do the same,' he hit me and told me no one else would want me because I was short and chubby and didn't even know how to fake it decently or give a proper blow-job.'

Nathan held his hand up saying, 'Jeez, Rosie, please tell me you dumped him then?'

'As a matter of fact, I did. Then it got worse to some extent.'

'Worse? How the fuck could it get any worse than that?'

'Well, after I dumped him, threw him out of my flat—I had to threaten to call the police to get him out—he came crawling back professing undying love for me, telling me he'd been a jerk and begging for forgiveness.'

'You didn't...' Nathan whispered, hoarsely.

'No, no—I'd finally come to my senses, found some dignity from somewhere. I told him, no way. I told him that if he'd really loved me, he'd have treated me a whole lot better, and that's when he dropped his bombshell on me, when he realised I had finally seen the light and there was no going back.

'He knew about my allowance, you see. He confessed that the only reason he'd ever been with me was because he didn't have to work if he was with me. He'd been cheating on me from the beginning. He told me he didn't ever fancy me. I had as much sex appeal as a beached whale—there's that whale again? Sex with me had been something to endure not enjoy.'

I had to move. I got up and paced. 'Two years! Two bloody years! He took two years of my life because he wanted access to my money. And when he couldn't get it, he tried to destroy me.

'Afterwards, I had a few one-night stands. I don't know why—maybe I felt the need to prove that someone would wanna fuck me even if I wasn't loveable and you know, the irony is that in those few encounters, I found more giving, more respect and equality, and more fun than I'd ever had before. I found I liked sex when it was reciprocal and that it could be two people simply having a nice time together. It didn't need to be any more complicated than that. As long as you don't allow it to become more complicated and as long as real trust doesn't have to be a part of it.

'And that's where I am now. And that, my gorgeous, sexy, Dixie Adonis is how we find ourselves in my flat with a night of mind-blowing, uncomplicated sex ahead of us.'

I stood in front of him, eyes locked with his.

'Now I know your story and you know mine. We can be two people, on an equal footing, having hot sex together. What do you say to that?'

Nathan continued gazing at me with those beautiful eyes that I still wanted to dive right into.

'Rosie, you have absolutely nothing—nothing—to be embarrassed about or ashamed of. He took total advantage of an inexperienced young woman who needed a little love and tenderness in her life. And you came through. Look at you now. You are so much more than my equal, Rosie Byrne, you are magnificent.'

As he sat looking at me, that slow, sultry smile crept across his face.

He stood, still holding me with his eyes. His warm, comforting hand cupped my cheek. 'Rosaleen Ciara Byrne, you are, beyond any shadow of a doubt, the smartest, most talented, most beautiful, sexiest and most fascinating woman it has ever been my pleasure to know. Did I mention hot as fuck? I'm not exaggerating when I say that sex with you has been awesome. You rock my world, baby.'

He pulled me into him, wrapping his strong arms around me.

I forced myself to speak. 'Then take me to bed, Nathan. And let's pick up that ice cream on the way? I'm intrigued about what you have in mind.'

Chapter Nineteen

Nathan

Leaving her that morning, knowing I wouldn't be seeing her again until I got back the next week, was one of the hardest things I'd ever done. The night before had been very productive. She managed to tell me her story—enough for me to start understanding where so much of her hang-up came from. And it explained her strange reaction the previous night when I jokingly suggested she might be after me for my money.

If I ever met this Michael, he wouldn't survive the introduction. The damage he'd done to my fragile elfin-faerie. More than ever, I wanted to wrap her up and take care of her—yep I had it that bad.

Only thing was, I hadn't managed to resolve *my* big hang-up, and it was tearing me up.

I spent some time in the morning with Mason, my PA—my right-hand man in the organisation. The business would be the last thing I needed to think about while I was away, unless something entirely unforeseen reared its head, and I knew Mason would keep me in the loop if that were the case and I was needed; he would keep everything ticking along nicely. As I said before, my talent was finding the right people, empowering them and then delegating.

I spent some time with Rhys in the afternoon. He was another of my incredibly lucky finds. I hit the jackpot when fate brought us together. He definitely knew his stuff and, from the way he ran the bars, you could tell he was exceptional. And he and I together made a great team at finding great people and then training them up the C&M way. That was the only reason we now felt confident enough to contemplate opening a second Café Paradiso.

This template wasn't something you could replicate in the same city—there needed to be only one to keep it unique. However, opening a replica in another big city—that was a good bet but only if we could find the right people to run it the way we wanted it to be run. The Nathan Connor/Rhys Evans method made that a distinct possibility and that was what we were working on, and what I would be presenting to my daddy during my visit home.

I went back to my place, got my things packed up then paced the floor. I couldn't settle, and I knew my night would be sleepless—probably my week if this was anything to go by. We'd agreed not to spend the night together but I realised I had to see her. I had to lay my cards on the table. My fear was that she'd have too much time to over-think stuff without me there to distract her. There was nothing for it—I had to try or I'd self-destruct.

Everything was ready to pick up and get to the airport in the morning; if I got back late, I'd still make it easily.

I hailed a cab and it pulled up outside her apartment. I had a sudden terrible thought that she might already have my replacement for the week up there.

Turned out she didn't. She wasn't home at all. I wandered down the street thinking about returning home. I got to Soho Square Gardens at the end, walked all the way around it then headed back up the street again. I saw her in the distance, arriving at the flat—she must have come from the Shaftsbury Avenue end. She was alone. I breathed a sigh of relief.

Rosie

As always, Josh lifted my spirits and helped me to get things into perspective.

'Wow, Rosie. He sounds like ideal Fuck Buddy material. Fantastic in the sack, makes you laugh, cooks and is exclusive to you. What more could you want? I mean, what more could you want, full stop?'

He held his hand up before I could respond. 'I know. I know. But you say he also wants a for-sex relationship. So, in your world, that makes him even more ideal, if there is such a thing. But there's something you're not saying, Baby Girl? Something that's making you feel uneasy. Spill. Gimme the juice.'

The couple next to us at the bar left so Josh grabbed the vacant seat and pulled it closer. We were now both perched on stainless steel and black PVC bar stools facing a bare-brick wall adorned with lit shelves displaying collections of spirit bottles. The green marble lamp stands at each end of the bar topped with Tiffany lampshades should have looked out of place but somehow blended into the décor beautifully.

I stared at my fingernails tracing the geometric indents in the stainless-steel bar counter.

'I don't know Josh. Why was I so desperate for him to agree? Why do I feel so empty that he's going to be away for a week?'

'Is that it? You're worried about going without for a whole week?' He waggled his eyebrows and then grinned at me, ruefully.

I snorted—it seems to be a feature of my conversations with Josh; he says something that makes me react just as I've taken a slug—this time of beer. At least it sprayed out of my mouth this time—not down my nose.

'No. That's just it,' I said, mopping up the spillage with a tissue pulled out of my bag. 'I don't mind at all as long as I know he's coming back.'

I put my hand up to catch the server's attention and indicate another couple of beers. I mused for a few seconds that I was thinking in American. Beers? Lager, surely.

Josh swivelled his seat to face me directly.

'You do like him Baby Girl, don't you? Is that what's spooking you? And you know what I mean...' Josh's eyes bored into me.

'I don't know how I feel, Josh. All I know is that he's different and he makes me feel different. And I need to be careful—keep this whole thing in perspective. I'm not in the market for anything complicated. And, more to the point, neither is he.'

'He has stated that? Like, outright?'

Our bottles arrived, lime segments duly squashed into the neck. We picked them up and clinked them together—one of our little rituals.

'He's been very clear and I quote, "I'm in this for the sex, Rosie, and I expect you to keep your end of the deal." I'd say that's pretty clear, wouldn't you? But then he goes and introduces me as his *girlfriend*. What's that about?'

Josh went still for a few moments. I could almost hear the cogs whirring. 'My guess would be that he believes you and he are going to be in this… this—whatever it is—for a while and he needs to give you some sort of label to explain your relationship. *Girlfriend* sounds more like a CEO-style relationship than Fuck Buddy—wouldn't you say?'

'When you put it like that,' I laughed, a weight lifting from my shoulders.

'But, Baby Girl, this is more than your usual Fuck Buddy relationship anyway isn't it? I mean, you've been out together for dinner twice, and you've spent pretty much every night, the whole night, together since you met. He hardly rates the same as Curly, Larry or Mo—guys you might individually see once a week—or fortnight—for a session of hot sex and then a home delivery pizza at home at most.'

I snorted again. My seat was getting uncomfortable and I was shuffling about on it. 'Mmm hmm.'

'Look, let's work out the pros and cons.' Josh grabbed a serviette and got a pen out and started writing. We both contributed to the process and ended up with this:

Upside:

1 getting plenty – when he's in the country

2 great sex

3 not going beyond what's going on now

4 enjoying dinners and staying over

5 exclusive arrangement – could get rid of condoms

Downside:

1 exclusive arrangement – leaves other guys high and dry

2 feeling threatened by unwelcome feelings

We both looked it over a few times then Josh piped up with, 'If it's bothering you that you're having feelings, you could always hook up with one or two of the guys while he's away. He'd never know and you could get your perspective back.'

'No!' I cried out, batting his shoulder. '*I* would know, Josh. I've committed to keeping us exclusive while it lasts and agreed to talk to him if I'm feeling things are getting too close.'

'And are things getting too close?'

'Not for him, I don't think. I guess I'm a bit smitten, honeymoon period and all that. But I'm sure it will wear off and I can keep it under control in the meantime.'

'You do know it's not inconceivable that he'd fall for you, don't you?'

I huffed—well more like a dry snort as in no beer or other drink involved, thankfully.

'I don't see that happening, Josh. Like I said, he's been very clear.'

'So, there's no problem then?'

'I guess.'

'Chill Baby Girl, go with the flow and see where it takes you. And look who's here...'

Josh's eyes lit up and I followed them to see a guy through the window heading towards the door. I would have known it was Fabrizio, not only because I knew he was due to arrive, but he looked so Italian. Dark-haired, he reminded me of a young Al Pacino but with a slightly squarer jawline, more masculine and handsome. And definitely taller.

The Godfather was one of our go-to movies—I knew immediately why Josh had been attracted.

He leapt up from the barstool, his face a picture. Fabrizio looked our way and I saw that same look of delight mirrored in his features. He made his way over, extending his hand out to Josh who took it in a two-handed grasp.

Then he turned his gaze toward me and immediately captured me with warm, dark-amber eyes and a gorgeous smile.

'Fabri, this is Rosie. Rosie meet Fabri,' said Josh.

Fabrizio, Fabri, let go of Josh's hand and took mine. A smooth, firm grasp enveloped my hand and pulled me slightly towards him to brush a gentle kiss on my cheek.

'Ciao. Piacere,' said a rich, warm voice that had me melting on the spot. Italian has to be the dreamiest language in the world to listen to. 'Josh has told me much about you Rosie, I feel as if I know you already.' His English was perfect and the accent drool-worthy.

'The pleasure is definitely all mine,' I responded, flirting with him a little—I was allowed. 'And Josh has told me a lot about you too.'

Josh had told me that Fabri was an actor and a classically trained singer. He'd had several parts in West End musicals and ran drama workshops between parts—as he was then.

'He hasn't told me where in Italy you are from, though, or what brought you to London…'

Josh put his arms around my shoulders and gave them a little squeeze as Fabri told us about his home-town, his eyes shining and his hands assisting in his descriptions and explanations.

Well, I come from Genova,' he started, 'a very old and auspicious historical city in Northern Italy, the doorway to Europe and the birthplace of Christopher Columbus…'

I could tell this was a practised speech—he was obviously asked often.

'Oh. I thought that was Genoa,' I interrupted and Fabri went on to explain that it was indeed, but that they call it Genova at home. 'And I came to London because it is the world capital for shows and theatre—and I am an actor so this is where I need to be.'

I could definitely have listened to Fabri talking for hours, his gorgeous accent and the way he made everything sound fascinating. But this was only his and Josh's third date, and Josh was disappearing for a few weeks the next day, so I stayed a polite length of time then decided I had to rush, 'So much to do.'

Fabri and I arranged to meet up for a coffee later in the week so we could allay Josh's anxieties and check up on each other. Fabri was amused by all this but we did hit it off and a coffee together would certainly not be onerous.

We said our farewells and Fabri's 'Ciao,' had me insisting that he teach me some Italian phrases the next time we met.

A big hug from Josh and I left to find my way back to my flat, this time via tube—the Northern Line would get me to my nearest tube station, Tottenham Court Road.

Pretty much as soon as I got in my door, the buzzer sounded and I answered. A gruff, impatient voice spoke.

'Rosie?'

'Nathan, what are you doing here? You're not supposed to—'

He cut me off. 'Just let me up, Rosie.'

I knew something was wrong, I'd never heard the slightest hint of impatience in Nathan's voice; he was so laid back when he wasn't being searingly intense.

I pushed the release button and heard the door open through the intercom. He didn't use the lift, and I heard him coming up all the flights two stairs at a time; he was in some hurry.

He got to the top where I was waiting for him outside my front door. He stopped dead and looked at me, dark eyes in a dark face.

'You'd better come in,' I said and walked in leaving him to follow. I stood in my living room, waiting for him to explain why he was there.

He paced the floor like a panther in a cage. He kept looking at me like he was trying to find words. There was such anguish in his eyes, I thought something must be terribly wrong.

'Nathan, tell me what this is all about,' I asked him gently. He strode across the floor, took me in his arms and kissed me hard, crushing my lips with his mouth and grazing my skin with his stubble.

I whimpered and he immediately lifted his face away from mine looking at me, searching my eyes.

'Nathan, Baby, you are hurting me,' I whispered. He stepped back slightly, not letting go of me, but his grip did ease.

He was in such turmoil. I reached my face up and kissed him gently on the lips. 'Tell me,' I murmured.

'Where have you been, Rosie?'

'Wh—what?'

'Where have you been?' Who have you been with?' His tone was harsh now, his eyes cold.

This couldn't be happening. My heart pounded and drawing breath became an effort.

I summoned all my resolve, moved out of his arms and grated the words out between gritted teeth.

'I think you should leave. Now.'

I glared at him.

'Have you been with one of your Fuck Buddies?'

I was alone with this large, powerful man, but I tried to assert the force of my will.

'You don't get to ask me that Nathan. You don't get to tell me what I can and can't do or who I can or can't see. And you don't get to call my integrity into question. You just get to leave. Now.'

For a few moments, he stared back at me. My neck started prickling as butterflies formed in my stomach. I was vulnerable here. How had I let this happen?

His gaze softened and suddenly his eyes widened.

'Rosie. No. No. I don't mean to... Christ! What the fuck am I doing? I'm sorry, Rosie. I'm sorry I'm frightening you. I never want to hurt you. I...

'You have nothing to fear from me, I promise you. I would never hurt you. I don't know what came over me. Jealousy? I don't know. I haven't felt anything like that in...

'It took me by surprise. I didn't know how to deal with it and I fucked up, Rosie, and I'm truly sorry.

'Look, I'm gonna leave now.'

He reached up as if to stroke my cheek but seemed to think better of touching me and pulled his hand back. He gazed at me, looking completely shattered, full of remorse.

My breathing was rapid and shallow. I needed to slow it down or risk going into full panic attack mode. I didn't try to speak, I concentrated on my breathing, trying to slow my heart rate.

Nathan appeared to be waiting for me to say something, but I simply couldn't speak. Not yet.

He nodded then turned on his heel and headed towards the door.

I wanted him to leave.

I didn't want him to leave.

I can't explain it. Alarm bells were going off in my head. But he had pulled back. He appeared as shocked by his behaviour as I was. If I let him go now, and part of me was saying I should, I believed I wouldn't see him again.

He got to the door. If I didn't say something now, he'd be gone. But I couldn't speak. My heart rate had increased again and I was panting now. My head was full of fog and sparks.

Then, he hesitated before reaching up for the latch.

He turned back to face me.

'I am so sorry, Rosie. You are absolutely right. I have no right to demand anything from you. You are under no obligation to explain anything at all to me.

'I've got something I need to say but I can't seem to find the words.'

He sounded almost scared, but scared of what?

'I don't want to leave like this. If I leave now, it feels like it would be over—that *we* would be over and I don't want that. You have every right to send me away and tell me not to come back. I was totally out of order. But…

'Rosie?

'Rosie?

'Shit!'

He rushed across the room and took me into his arms as grey mush filled my head. I let myself collapse into him.

Nathan

I recognised what was happening to her. I've seen panic attacks before.

Setting aside the fact that I was the cause of this—that I had somehow pushed her into it—I knew enough to help her now.

I gently sat her down on her three-seater, head on a cushion and talked to her.

'I think this is a panic attack, Rosie. Have you had one before? Don't try and talk, squeeze my hand if you have.'

She squeezed. That was good. She would know that it wasn't as devastating as it felt, that she'd get through it.

'Let's get your breathing under control. Gently now. In through your nose and out through your mouth, as slowly as you can. With me.'

I breathed deliberately, in and out giving her the chance to synchronise with me. She still had hold of my hand where she'd squeezed and, after a few breaths, her eyelids fluttered open and she gazed at me, alarm written in her eyes.

'Don't try and speak just yet, Darlin'. I'm here until we get you sorted.'

Her other hand reached out and grasped my free hand. She held on to my hands tightly while I talked her through slowing her breathing. When she was taking longer, more even breaths and her colour coming back to normal, I said to her, 'I'm going to go and get some water for you, Sweetheart. I'll be right back.'

I tried to take my hands from hers but she held them in a vice-like grip, her eyes widening again.

'Oh, Rosie. I'm not going anywhere. I'm here—I'm staying here until you're fine again, Okay? I'm only going into the kitchen to get you some water and a sweet cup of tea. I will be straight back.'

She nodded and released her grip.

When I came back in and helped her take a couple of sips of water, she managed, 'Thank you,' and a rueful little smile.

I went back into the kitchen and finished making her a cup of sweet tea. It was one of my momma's cure-all's—whenever we were poorly or upset over something as older kids, she would make us a cup of *English* tea with plenty of sugar in it.

I took the steaming mug in to her and she wrapped her hands around it as though it were the most comforting thing in the world.

'I—I haven't made any… plans for while you are away, Nathan. I was always going to wait for you to get back. I don't want us to be over either but…'

Jeez. She was coming out the other side of a panic attack and her first words were to try and allay my fears.

'I know, Rosie. It's a big 'but'. Just, please don't make a final decision until I'm back—until we've had time to talk.'

'You have trust issues, Nathan. It's hardly surprising.'

'Well—I haven't had trust issues since Linnea, but that's probably because I haven't needed to trust. I haven't allowed myself to be in a position of needing to trust anyone. The whole thing took me by surprise. But it's no excuse. To lose control like that….'

'Nathan. It's none of your business, and I didn't want to tell you after you demanded to know like that, but I was out with friends tonight—gay friends, to be precise. I was so mad at you for accusing me. Don't do it again.'

I nodded. 'I promise,' I whispered to her.

She reached her hand up and stroked my cheek. 'Let's put it

behind us. This week will give us both space, and when you return we can get back to…' She struggled for words.

'Hot as hell sex,' I finished for her.

'Yeah. That,' she agreed, even managing a little smile.

She finished the glass of water and had drunk half of the tea I'd brought in for her. Her eyelids drooped and her movements were sluggish.

'Right, young lady. I'm putting you to bed.'

Her eyes widened at me.

'Not like that, Darlin'. You're exhausted. I want to make sure you're okay. I'll get you to bed and stay with you, okay? No funny stuff, I promise.' I grinned at her while I crossed my heart with my finger. She smiled, and then her eyes grew heavy again.

'My stuff is all packed and ready to go. I'll get Duncan to pick me up earlier from here first. It'll be fine. Is that okay with you? For me to stay?'

She was already almost asleep but nodded her head groggily. I picked her up and carried her through to her bedroom, undressed her and tucked her in.

I made a couple of calls, brushed my teeth, then stripped and crawled in beside her. I gathered her up in my arms in our spooning position and kissed her ear and the back of her neck. She sighed—contentedly I'd say. Relieved, I closed my eyes and tried to get some sleep.

This woman! I don't know what I did to deserve her, but whatever it was, I'm fucking glad I did it. She somehow fixes me.

In the little time I have known her, she has filled that gaping, aching hole in my heart and restarted it, even dealing with my fuck up today.

I cannot, will not let that happen again. She's got enough of her own demons to deal with. She doesn't need mine muddying the water.

I know now that I am ready for what's ahead this week.

My sister's wedding is in a few weeks' time and while I'm home this time, we are having a pre-wedding get-together for family and key people. Of course, my sister's best friend will be one of those key people. That would be Linnea. Apparently now separated and getting divorced.

The family still have no idea what went on between us—they believe we drifted apart and then I lost my way a bit. I have successfully managed to avoid any contact over the years in my visits home. This time, it's not feasible, unfortunately, unless I stay away for the wedding and pre-wedding gathering. That would hurt my baby sister – I'm not about to do that. At least, everybody's perception of the past means that no-one will be scrutinising me, watching for my response to seeing her again.

How do I feel about seeing her again? A week ago I was dreading it. Not because I still have feelings for her—all that well and truly died a long time ago. In the early weeks, maybe even months, I do believe I would have gone back to her if she'd crooked her little finger, but that's because I thought I was still in love with her. That passed.

No, I was dreading it because I was still so full of pain and anger at what she, and my supposed best friend, did to me. I had been unsure of my ability to keep that all under wraps for the duration.

Now, I'm no less angry, but my life is so full of joy right this minute because of a certain wonderful little songbird. I was in so much pain at the thought of Rosie being with someone else—that eclipsed everything. And now I know I was being stupid and am pretty damn sure that my elfin-faerie isn't capable of deceit, I don't believe anything can touch me.

There is still hope for me, that I can earn her trust so that she will let me love her.

Chapter Twenty

Rosie

I sat in a Heathrow Terminal 5 coffee shop with my oat milk Caramel Latte, waiting for Nathan's flight to disembark. I hadn't let him know I was going to be there; I was hoping he would be pleased to see me.

I thought about the events of the last week—there was a lot to process.

I had been in touch with Matt, Liam and Jamie. Jamie was all loved up with a new girlfriend and loving life—he deserved it, he was a lovely guy—they all were. Anyway, they all knew that, at least for the time-being, I wouldn't be seeing any of them.

Matt, sweet, surprising Matt said that he envied the lucky guy who had persuaded me to go all monogamous. Go figure! Liam asked me to please, please get in touch if anything changed.

Interestingly, I wasn't devastated at the idea of not seeing any of them. If anything proved that my Rules worked for me, I'd say it was that. I really liked each one of them, and they me, but the Rules had kept us all focused on what the relationships were all about—sex and fun, not emotional investment and inevitable heartache. My Rules truly had enabled a kind of freedom. Now, it seemed they were being whittled away. I'd better watch out then if I wanted to retain that freedom.

Fabrizio and I had a lovely evening together on the Thursday. He was off up to Edinburgh at the weekend. He was so excited about seeing Josh, it warmed my heart. He couldn't stop talking about him. I have such great hopes that Josh has finally found his happy-ever-after. He is so loving and giving; he deserves to have someone to share his life with who adores him.

The band had two gigs, Friday and Saturday. Sid announced that he had secured us more bookings at Café Paradiso, starting in three months' time, unless there were any other cancellations in the meantime. That was great news. Apparently, the management wanted to discuss the possibility of a regular slot. Sid didn't need to check with us that we'd want that. I was somewhat surprised that they hadn't made themselves known to us at the gig, but I guess I had been a bit preoccupied with Nathan at the time and should maybe have sought them out. Ah well, it hadn't stopped them from booking us, so all was well.

We'd got a bit of a lean period coming up in a couple of weeks' time, but all three of the trio had managed to get other bookings with other ensembles to cover their income. It's not so critical for me—I've got my trust fund to live off.

The Big Band open rehearsal on Sunday had been fun. Many of the numbers I did with them, I did other versions of with my band, so it made learning the lyrics easier. The difference was, it was the same every time with the Big Band—when you've got twenty musicians playing together, it has to be from the same hymn sheet, so they'd have scores in front of them. Nothing so easy for me though. The bandleader liked to put me on the spot. I was allowed to remind him of my song list from which to choose numbers, but, in the rehearsals, I would never find out what I was singing until he announced it to the audience. I did get a head's up in advance for actual gigs.

Some of the numbers I did with the Big Band weren't really transferrable because they needed a bigger sound and beat. Having four trombones, four trumpets and five saxophones as well as a piano, double bass and guitar—not to mention drums *and* a percussionist to back you, made it possible to do some fantastic songs. That Sunday, the bandleader picked one of my favourites and it made me smile—Blacksmith Blues, originally sung by Ella Mae Morse—it starts *Down in old Kentucky, Where horseshoes are lucky...* I'd have to ask Nathan if horseshoes are still considered lucky.

Nathan.

The morning he left, he'd been like a cat on a hot tin roof. Not the so-laid-back-he's-almost-horizontal Nathan I was used to. He fussed over me, making sure I was fully recovered. He didn't want to leave me, but this trip was important—a pre-wedding family gathering. His sister was getting married in a few weeks' time and this would be his last trip home before it. In the end, I virtually had to chase him out.

He even asked for permission to text and call me while he was away. I told him he better had or there'd be hell to pay.

I thought over the night before he left. The thing is, I totally understood how unfamiliar emotions could knock someone out of kilter and I did believe that is what had happened with Nathan. It would seem I wasn't the only one dealing with unwanted emotion creeping in. We would both have to be vigilant to keep the lid on that.

His final word was to tell me that his PA, a guy called Mason, was at my disposal. I could call him and ask for anything I needed. A card pressed into my hand gave me his contact details.

The same day, my front door buzzer had sounded in the middle of the afternoon. I strained to look down at the doorway to see a motorcyclist bearing a large bunch of flowers. Intrigued, I went down.

He handed me a beautiful arrangement of pale pink and white lisianthus, already in a vase, pointing at the note that was attached. I opened it.

Rosie,

I wanted you to have something to make you think of me while I'm away.

N x

As if I needed anything to make me think about him.

He texted several times a day, to find out what I was doing, how I was, was I missing him? We had several lengthy interchanges, some of them extremely naughty, that had me giggling and gasping in my gym during an early morning workout, in the supermarket when I was doing some grocery shopping, in the deli queue, picking up a lunch-time sandwich. These had me longing for him to be home.

He made one audio phone call to ask me if I would consider being his *Plus One* at his sister's wedding in Kentucky. I couldn't believe that it was scheduled for one of our gig-less weekends. I said yes—I've done the *Plus One* thing before with

Matt. I was a little concerned about meeting his incredibly close family, but Nathan reassured me that we would only be there for the day of the wedding and would have to leave the next day; he had to get straight back.

He would be throwing himself into work when he got back this time, but he went to some pains to reassure me that our 'liaisons' were top priority in his downtime. It seemed the right moment, so I suggested the tests to him. I was on the pill—I wasn't taking any chances—so if we were having a totally exclusive relationship, as Josh and I had noted on the Pros and Cons list, we could dispense with the condoms once we were both cleared. He was very up for that. What a surprise.

Then he made the Facetime call. He was alone and, because he'd misplaced his phone for a few hours, this was the first chance he'd had to make face-to-face contact, without possible interruption, when the time difference allowed. It was kind of awkward at first, getting naked and masturbating for him, but it turned into kind of nice, especially when he got naked for me too. And being able to gaze at his gorgeous face and watch the effect I was having on him was incredibly hot, not to mention watching him pumping himself to synchronise our climaxes.

That had been two days ago and now I was waiting to look directly into those beautiful eyes again.

I checked the Arrivals screens that told me his flight was now in the baggage hall. I made my way to the exit doors in the Arrivals Hall where the passengers would emerge looking for their families, their drivers or for signs to where they could get a taxi, coach, bus or a rail link. I waited and waited. The doors kept opening, and I would scan the travel-weary faces coming through, desperately seeking a sighting.

The stream of people seemed to go on forever. I was beginning to lose hope, thinking all sorts of things: he'd missed the flight, he'd decided not to come back, he'd come on an earlier flight, he'd decided on a later flight.

And then I spotted him, all crumpled, stubbly and sleepy-looking with bed-hair barely smoothed down. He looked up and saw me beaming away at him, and his face lit up like a beacon, filling the arrivals hall with sunshine so bright, I was nearly blinded by it. My God, he looked edible: those shoulders to die for, those hips begging to be straddled and those eyes, those eyes... melting chocolate—dreamy and gorgeous.

As soon as he cleared the barrier, I couldn't help it, I ran and threw myself into his arms, showering him with kisses all over his face. He stumbled back, nearly falling, then righted us both, buried his face in my neck and clung to me so tightly, I thought he was going to suffocate me.

'Oh my God, Rosie, you are a sight for sore, sleepy eyes. I didn't think I'd see you until later tonight. This is just the best, Darlin'. I'm home.'

I loosened my leg grip and he lowered me until my feet were on the ground then he took my face in his hands and kissed me long and passionately.

'I take it you didn't miss me much then?'

'Nah!' I said, 'You hardly entered my thoughts all week. I happen to be here waiting for me mate and you popped through those doors—what a surprise.'

'So, you won't be needing a lift back into town then, huh? I'll go find my driver—and see y'around?'

'Funny man!' I exclaimed. 'If you think I'm letting you out of my sight, Nathaniel James Connor, for even ten seconds...'

'I do happen to have a set of handcuffs in my case,' he said, menacingly, piercing me with darkening eyes, 'we could be fastened at the wrist if you like? Might prove a bit tricky though when I head through that door over there,' he said pointing to the men's toilets. 'I tell you what—you look after my case here while I make a visit and we'll save christening the handcuffs til we get back to my place. Wha'dya say?'

I was blushing madly, my heart hammering in my chest. There are times when I just didn't know if he was pulling my chain or being serious. *But you know what?* I thought, *it will be fun finding out.*

Well... that is... it would be fun, eventually. I had forgotten to mention before he left that my period was due the very day he was due to arrive back. I am regular as clockwork which meant that I would be coming on mid to late afternoon.

'Erm... look, about that. Christening your place, that is. Nathan, I'm sort of due on. I can't... I might start before... or during...' I stammered out.

He cupped my head in his hand and brushed my cheek with his thumb, his eyes softening. It made me go weak every time he did that. He gazed into my eyes and murmured, 'That's not a problem for me, Rosie. Only if you're up for that though. I can wait if it would freak you out. We can do other stuff—as long as I can hear those incredible sounds you make and watch you as you come.'

I was mortified. It seemed Nathan obviously was no stranger to period sex—but I was. At the same time, though, I wanted him desperately. I didn't think I could wait five days to feel him inside me again.

Once again, Nathan came to my rescue. 'How about we christen my shower first, huh? Whatever you want, Rosie.'

Nathan

After my welcome home, I was thinking I should keep going away and coming back. The sight of her in the Arrivals hall made my heart leap in my chest. I had missed her so much that it felt like I could breathe again when I held her in my arms.

Duncan, my go-to driver, had spotted me earlier when Rosie had thrown herself at me and was loitering in the background, waiting for me to signal him over. I didn't keep a permanent driver and car in London—I didn't mind getting cabs as a rule. For specific, scheduled journeys, I had a contracted Private Car and Chauffeur Firm; they knew Duncan was my first choice and to keep him for me whenever Mason booked. We would pay for his whole day to make sure he was at my disposal.

He greeted me with his usual deference, referring to me as *Mr Connor*. I could see out of the corner of my eye, that Rosie was sizing him up, trying to work it out in her head.

On the journey home, I told Rosie all about presenting the details of the new venue and how my daddy had been so impressed. I didn't mention that he had observed I looked somehow different, like someone had switched my interior lights on. He'd asked if it was this project, or was there something else I hadn't mentioned. He's pretty shrewd, my daddy.

I told him a little about Rosie, said we were getting pretty close but that she was wary of being in a committed relationship—a sort of half-truth. He suggested I bring her to the wedding. I think he was intrigued and wanted to check her out. She is, after all, the first woman I have shown even a flicker of interest in since Linnea—seven years ago now.

I told Rosie about the gathering, about how happy my baby sister had looked and about her best friend being there. She looked into my eyes, searching, I think, for how I felt about that. I told her it was cool, that I'd felt nothing seeing Linnea again. She took my hand and kissed it.

I didn't tell her that Linnea was acting as the liaison between the wedding planner and the out-of-state friends and relations, me being one of those, and that would mean her contacting me directly with updates and information. To that end, she was now a contact in my cell phone. I don't know why I didn't say. Maybe I thought Rosie might feel a bit threatened.

The thing is, Linnea had been pretty obvious about wanting me to take her to bed, a situation I found both distasteful and easy to resist, but probably the reason I didn't feel inclined to mention her further to Rosie. The whole episode threatened to pull a load of unwanted emotion to the surface for me, and I didn't want anything to spoil the euphoria of seeing Rosie waiting for me at the airport.

I didn't realise at the time that decision was going to come back and bite me in the ass.

We got to my place and I introduced her to the guy on reception, making sure they had her name and took a photo of her to make sure she wouldn't have any trouble getting in when she turned up on her own.

I showed her into my apartment for the first time. As soon as we got into my hallway, I grabbed her up into my arms again and just kissed her and kissed her. I wanted to take her there and then, on the floor, against the wall, and sink into her any way I could, but I had to take it slower—wait until we were in the shower, assuming she was up for it. I could see when we'd had the conversation that she was embarrassed about the idea of having sex while she was menstruating. I had to let her decide whether it was something she could be comfortable with.

I told her I would unpack then have that shower to give her the chance to decide whether, or not, she wanted to join me in there.

She wandered off checking my apartment out while I unpacked and turned up in my bedroom as I was emptying the last few things out of my case. I gave her the small package I had brought home with me. 'This is for you—I owe you these,' I said, grinning. She carefully opened up the tissue paper to find a set of pretty, lacy lingerie, black with little pink ribbons and bows. I explained they had been chosen with the help of my sister.

'These are so lovely,' she said. 'How did you know what size to get me?'

'Well, I took the liberty of checking your bra size before I went. An' you've already mentioned your dress size, remember? You said you were a six or eight depending on brand? I told my sister and she said the US equivalent is two or four—these panties are apparently four but small so she thought that would be a safe bet. She put in two pairs to match the bra, just in case,' I told her, grinning again. 'And, by the way, she said great cup size, but you must be tiny everywhere else.'

Rosie blushed and looked close to tears. 'Thank you, Nathan, they're gorgeous. I'm... I don't know what to say. Thank you. And please thank your sister for me too.' She clearly felt uncomfortable and appeared to search for a distraction.

'So, where are these handcuffs then?' she challenged but

gasped in horror as I pulled them out of a pocket in the lining of the case. I pinned her with my eyes, watching and waiting to see what she would do or say. This was fun. I could see a whole range of emotions cross her face, could see that she wanted to please me but that the thought of being somehow forcibly restrained terrified her. Eventually, I relented and smiled the best reassuring smile I could summon.

'I had these at home—' I started.

'Did you use these with Linnea?' she demanded looking horrified.

'No,' I protested. I've had these since I was a kid. They're real enough, a cop gave them to me—well an ex-cop who worked security for my daddy. No, Rosie, I thought it would be fun to see your reaction when I brought them out.' I laughed.

'You! You bastard!' she threw at me. I tossed the cuffs on the bed, grabbed her and tickled her. She couldn't get away from me and was squealing with laughter. Then she started that adorable, 'Stop! Stop! I'll wee! I'll wee!' One of these days I'll have to put that one to the test.

I relented, and let her go scampering off to the bathroom. I dropped the cuffs over the bedpost at the foot of my bed and finished up sorting my stuff. Then I realised she was standing in my bedroom doorway, buck-naked.

'Jeez, Rosie, you're gonna give me a heart attack.' I said, drinking in the glorious lines and curves of her beautiful little body.

'I thought you'd be jumping into that huge shower of yours any minute to freshen up and might like a bit of company?' she purred at me, sticking her chin out, trying to look so brave and unfazed. I had to know she wanted this.

'Are you sure, Darlin'? God, I've missed you. I want you so

much but please don't feel you *have* to do this.'

'I'm sure, Nathan. I want you, too, and if you really are comfortable…'

I didn't need any further prompting. I immediately picked her up and she snuggled into me as I strode to the bathroom. I put her down on her feet and we both stripped my clothes off. I turned the shower on and waited until it was at temperature then pulled her in with me.

I loved having her in the shower with me. I loved running my hands all over her body, lathering her up and then rinsing her down. And I loved the feel of her hands running all over me, the way she took her time over my chest and abs, revering me. Then she looked up into my eyes, hers full of wonder. She made me feel like a fucking god. I loved watching water cascade over her hair and her skin until she was glistening and twinkling.

When we had finished worshipping each other's bodies, I cupped her head in both hands and kissed her gently. Still looking into her eyes, I told her my news, smiling. 'I'm clean, Rosie, it's official.'

She grinned back at me. 'Me too,' she breathed.

'I am so gonna own you.' I didn't wait another minute. I reached down to find she was already wet for me. Lifting her up and bracing her against the tiles, her legs wrapped around me, I plunged into her free of any obstruction. This was where I wanted to be, where I felt like we were made for each other and where every movement was ecstasy.

She let me know she was okay, and I pushed further into her. I was learning her triggers, beginning to know how to angle into her to hit her sweet spots and I soon had her crying out at each thrust. Then I lost all conscious thought, crashing into her, hard, like I could fuck away my pain. She had become my anchor, my lifeline and she felt so damned good that fucking her hard could make everything else go away.

Her cries pulled me back. Worried that I may be hurting her, I spoke her name softly into her ear, and that's when she exploded on me, crying out *my* name. I let go and came hard, shooting my seed deep inside her for the first time, marking her properly as mine.

How in hell could I have missed her so much when I'd only known her for a couple of weeks? How did being without her make me feel so empty when I hadn't even realised I might be lonely before her?

'You are mine, Rosaleen, Ciara Byrne,' I whispered in her ear, *and I want you to be mine for a long, long time.*

Chapter Twenty-One

Rosie

'Stay with me tonight, Rosie? I've missed you so much, and I wanna wake up and find you next to me.' Nathan had dried me down with one of his huge, fluffy bath towels and was brushing out my wet hair.

For a moment, I found myself feeling overly emotional. My dad used to brush out my hair when I was little and no one, apart from hairdressers, has done that since. It made me feel so cherished at the same moment that Nathan was asking me to stay. I gritted my teeth and spoke through it.

'I've missed you too, Nathan. Really missed you.' My voice came out gruff and shaky.

It was ridiculous. It was only two weeks since we'd met and he'd been away for one of those.

He stopped brushing my hair and turned me around to face him, gazing intently into my eyes. His eyes wandered over my face, eventually settling back on my eyes with something going on behind his, but I couldn't tell what. 'What?' I asked him. 'Is something wrong?'

'Not a goddam thing,' he replied, 'I just love looking at you, and I haven't had a chance lately.'

'But my hair is wet and all my make-up has washed off.' I protested. I was blushing but underneath I was elated. He still made me feel so desired and wanted. It hadn't all been in my imagination—something I had considered a few times since he'd gone away. Hell, what had just happened in the shower had made it very clear that *I* owned *him.* It was *me* in his head, *me* he was seeing with his eyes closed, even when he had done that thing he does when we're fucking hard like that—it was almost as though he was somewhere else in his head for a few moments. As it got to the point where pain was mingling with intense pleasure, he came back with *my* name on his lips. And the sound of his voice speaking my name like that was what took me over into that breathtaking, exhilarating free-fall.

What was it he'd said after? *You are mine, Rosaleen, Ciara Byrne.* Possessive? Territorial? A bit of a caveman? Actually, I discovered I liked it, being the subject of Nathan's alpha male attention.

I had picked up some sandwiches at the airport for a bite of lunch—I guessed we might want something quick and easy so that we could spend the first couple of hours of our time otherwise engaged.

We were going out to dinner later with Rhys and his wife, Caroline. Nathan had assured me that I would really like Caroline; I had confided to him that I rarely get on well with other women. I don't know why, I seem to rub them up the wrong way. I have difficulty staying engaged in conversation if they start talking about clothes, make-up celebrities or things domestic, and they usually spot that I have zoned out and get offended. I know I should try harder. I got on well with Annie because we had a love of music, and specifically Jazz, in common but, interestingly, we had never met up outside of things to do with the band.

Anyway, Caroline was apparently a career woman, also in the hospitality business but working for a different company—a hotel chain. Interesting to talk to and lots of fun on a night out, she 'doesn't seem to take herself too seriously'—Nathan's words. I had liked Rhys very much and so I was determined to try hard that night to be friendly to Caroline.

Nathan was still drying off, so I wrapped a towel around myself, clipped my wet hair up and wandered off to find his kitchen again. I had only taken a cursory look around the apartment earlier. I had been too distracted by my euphoria at having Nathan back to take too much notice.

I wandered agape around his huge kitchen spotting pretty much every gadget going—a full-sized light-grey Kitchen-Aid mixer and matching food processor, slow-cookers, pressure cookers, pots and pans and utensils of all shapes and sizes hanging from a central grid above a huge island, a massive six-ring hob on one side, two ovens, a huge microwave, a steamer oven and a café style coffee maker. It was gorgeous—all muted greys, white and silver, glass and stainless steel and highly polished doors and surfaces.

I walked over to the massive American fridge-freezer—one of those that have the ice and water dispensers on the doors—that stood next to a floor-to-ceiling wine cabinet and a sizeable beer fridge. I pulled it open to retrieve the sandwiches I assumed Nathan had shot in there earlier, to find it completely stocked with obviously fresh foods.

He appeared in the doorway, a towel wrapped around his hips, low-slung giving me the most provocative view of his incredibly sexy torso. As my eyes scraped their way up his body to his dreamy, liquid chocolate eyes, he smirked that lazy, crotch-tightening half grin. 'Like the view, huh?' He was so arrogant. But honestly? I loved his cocky self-assurance—it was so sexy.

I threw one of the sandwich packs at him in response. 'Nathan, this fridge is fully stocked—there's even a huge dish of something prepared, ready to cook here. If I'd known, I wouldn't have bought you a pathetic sandwich. Where did this all come from? And all this stuff in your kitchen? Don't tell me you use all this?'

'Okay. Working in reverse. As a matter of fact, I do, on occasion, use all this stuff. I told you I like to cook. In fact, I'm looking forward to cooking for two in this kitchen—there's usually only me and I freeze the rest. Secondly, it was very thoughtful of you, buying some sandwiches for us, Sweetheart. And, finally, I have a housekeeper, Rosie. Carmen. She stocked the fridge up ready for me and left me something to throw in the oven. She often does that. She's the one who keeps this place looking like this. She's a miracle worker and I wouldn't be without her.'

I felt a pang of jealousy as I pictured the woman bearing that exotic name in common with the sexy Opera heroine. Needless to say, she was a dusky, Latin firecracker with a rose between her teeth. Well, at least that was a departure from the tall, willowy blondes I usually pictured him with—although, of course, Carmen would be tall and beautiful.

I also realised how little I *still* actually knew about my Dixie Adonis. I mean, I now knew he worked in hospitality for his family's business and that his daddy had sent him travelling around the world for as long as he wanted. I knew a little bit about his role in the family business and I knew he wasn't short of a bob or two. But it was only wandering around this magnificent apartment earlier that gave me some idea of how he lived.

I had imagined him renting a flat not dissimilar to mine, but this was in another league altogether. The lounge was at least twice the size of my lounge/diner and beautifully decorated: the walls matte black with silver-grey silk-slub curtains and furniture scattered with black, silver-grey and pale taupe cushions—the black ones with an amazing geometric pattern in pale taupe; a magnificent pewter candelabra with a matching five-candle standard lamp and a huge mirror framed in what looked like white waxed driftwood. The whole scene looked like something from the Ideal Homes Exhibition—breathtaking.

There was a separate, equally impressive dining room in dark maroon and cream with crushed velvet curtains and sumptuous dark-wood furniture, two lovely guest rooms with en-suites and the master bedroom, which was adorned in the same colours and style as the lounge.

Then there was the art on the walls – oil paintings, acrylics and Indian ink drawings that all looked like originals.

The huge bathroom, the shower of which we had christened that afternoon (there was a massive free-standing bathtub waiting for our attention too), was en-suite to the master bedroom and there was also a separate dressing room. What with the fabulously equipped utility room, this was already one of the most luxurious apartments I had ever seen. And there were two doors I hadn't even got to yet—I was very curious to know what was behind them.

We sat, still wrapped in our towels, on bar stools at the

dining end of the kitchen island. Nathan had grabbed a couple of plates, two wine glasses and a bottle of white from his wine cooler—a Californian Sauvignon Blanc. Sandwiches and a good white wine—can't beat it for a quick lunch.

'This apartment is amazing,' I gushed. 'The décor in the lounge and your bedroom is fabulous —I love it.'

He grinned that lazy, sexy smirk. 'Well, I'm glad it meets with your approval, Rosie. I fully intend for you to spend a lot of time here, much of that in my bedroom.' He sat looking at me with that smoulder in his eyes liquifying my insides. He knocked back the last of the wine in his glass, and his expression darkened to a deep shade of serious.

'C'mere, Rosie,' he growled at me.

I couldn't tear my eyes from his; I couldn't resist his command. I slid off my stool and moved to stand in front of him. He opened his knees and pulled me in between them. Loosening my towel, he let it drop to the floor, stood me back, devoured my body with his eyes then lifted them back up to mine. He took hold of the back of my neck with one huge hand, my waist held firmly in the other. I loved the feel of his hands on my body. Then he spoke, low and quietly commanding. 'Rosie Byrne, you are mine. All. Mine,' he growled at me.

I felt a frisson of apprehension snake down my spine, but I was spellbound; I couldn't move.

He took his hand from my waist and cupped the side of my face, his thumb gently tracing my lips. 'These lips,' he growled, 'mine. This mouth,' pushing his thumb in and watching as I duly sucked on it. 'Mine.' His hand moved down to gently encircle my throat, 'Mine.' Despite the gentleness of his touch, that frisson blossomed into a knot of fear in my chest. It was becoming harder to breathe.

Stroking gently up and down the side of my neck, leaving sparks on my skin, he moved his hand down to cup my breast and rub his thumb over my hardening nipple. Whatever fear I was feeling didn't stop my body from responding to his touch as I felt heat flood my sex. He moved his head in to lick and nip my other nipple. 'These magnificent tits, Rosie,' he continued, squeezing the breast in his hand almost, but not quite, to the point of pain, 'they are most definitely all mine.'

His hand trailed to my waist, his other hand moving from the back of my neck to splay over my belly then feather over to my hip. 'Oh God, Rosie, your amazing curves, so beautiful. All mine.'

He was worshipping my body while claiming it.

The knot in my chest loosened a little as my apprehension very slowly dissipated.

Nathan moved one hand down, his fingers seeking first my clitoris, then my entrance. His eyes closed as he sighed and bit his lower lip. 'Jeez, Rosie, always so wet for me. What you do to me. This fucking tight, pretty little pussy—this is mine. All. Mine.'

His hands moved to cup my buttocks. 'And this delicious butt? Mine.' One finger stroked between my bum cheeks to brush ever so gently over my anus. 'And if you decide you wanna try it, I'd like to claim this too—be your first. Only if it's what you want though, Rosie.'

His expression softened for the first time as his eyes crinkled in the corners and a slight smile formed on his lips. 'And those luscious legs and pretty little feet? It's me and only me they wrap around, my beautiful Rosie, because you are all mine. Every. Fucking. Inch. Of you.'

My fear had almost drained away by now, but my chest was

still heaving, my heart beating wildly. Nathan's eyes suddenly filled with concern. 'Oh no, baby,' he breathed, pulling me into him, wrapping his arms around me, his lips next to my ear. 'Never, ever be afraid of me,' he whispered. 'Don't you know? I… I… Rosie, I'm yours too. All. Yours. You *own* me, Rosie.'

Chapter Twenty-Two

'I'm yours too. All. Yours. You *own* me Rosie.'

I was overwhelmed by the emotion welling up inside of me, hearing those words. That, combined with tension draining out of me all in a rush, had me gulping for breath. Nathan pulled me in closer to him. 'You're okay—I gotcha.' Then I was aware of movement and found myself lifted, held to his chest and cradled in his arms as he walked us out of the kitchen and down the wide hallway.

We entered his bedroom and he laid me gently on top of his bed, immediately lying down next to me. He turned me on my side and pulled me back into him, his arms enveloping me. He nuzzled my neck and murmured into my ear until my breathing had calmed and I was mewling in pleasure, his breath on my neck and in my ear making me tingle all over.

As I realised I was lying naked on top of his beautiful quilt, I tensed and protested, 'Nathan, I might… I'll… We shouldn't,' I urged him.

He slid off the bed and disappeared into the bathroom, returning with a large dark blue bath towel. Asking me with his eyes, I shifted over, he placed it on top of the duvet, and I rolled back over onto it. He lay back down with me, pulled me into him again and whispered in my ear, 'I wanna be with you, inside you, Rosie. Nothing else matters in the whole damn world.'

Once again, I felt all the tension drain out of me and I melted back into him, revelling in the shelter of his body and arms and wanting nothing more than to be there and be joined with him.

He gently lifted my leg and draped it over his, guiding himself into me. As he entered me, we both moaned in pleasure. He moved, slowly, gently, stroking my walls with his beautiful cock. He kept up that dreamlike rhythm, stoking me inexorably, but oh so slowly, towards my climax until my breath started hitching at the sensations emanating from the heat we were generating deep inside me. It was then he reached down and found my swollen, sensitive clitoris with his fingers again, gently swirling them around and around as his pushes into me became thrusts.

I felt him harden and expand even more inside me as his breathing became rapid and ragged. Then he whispered into my ear, 'Come for me, Rosie. Let go now, I'm with you,' and the sensations took over; wave upon wave of gentle ecstasy flowed through my body as I sighed aloud over and over. Nathan tensed as his breathing faltered and he let out a low moan.

He lay behind me, holding me tightly, as if he were afraid to let go. I turned my head towards him. 'I *am* yours Nathan. I'm all yours.'

He let out what sounded like a long sigh of relief. 'Oh, thank God. And I'm all yours, my sweet, sweet Rosie.'

Was it affirmation he'd been looking for? It almost hinted at insecurity.

He'd told me I *owned* him. What did that even mean? Was it another way of telling me he was mine while we were together, that he wouldn't cheat while we were a thing? He'd made it very clear that wasn't his style and I believed him. So… I *owned* him for as long as we were a thing, then. I would take that, happily.

I slipped out of his arms and into his bathroom where I'd left my bag earlier. I fished out a tampon to have at the ready and jumped back into the cavernous shower.

I was starting to believe I'd get the full three months. Two to three months Nathan had said his relationships usually lasted before he moved on; I found myself fervently wishing he'd stay the full course with me. I was already dreading the thought of being without him, but I buried it deep in its compartment; I would deal with all that when the time came and make the most of now.

I dried off and hurried back to find Nathan asleep and gently snoring. Of course, he'd be exhausted. An eleven-hour journey starting at 4.30 pm, he wouldn't have been able to sleep for the first six hours, and then, if he's anything like me, he wouldn't have got much anyway in the short window left, even when his body was telling him it was time.

I gazed down at him, this beautiful, complicated man who had stumbled into my life and changed everything in two short weeks. I looked up realising I had missed the huge mirror on the ceiling over his bed. I giggled peering up at myself in it.

I looked up at the gorgeous form laid out naked and pictured the women he had shared this bed with. Needless to say, they were all beautiful, tall, willowy and perfectly made up and coiffed. I imagined Nathan watching them in the mirror as their perfect bodies writhed about over and under him.

As I stood looking up at him, his phone, which he'd put on the bedside cabinet, buzzed to indicate a text message had arrived. I had a quick look while it was still displayed on the screen in case it was something urgent.

My heart nearly stopped. It was from Linnea.

>>Hi Honey. Call me when you've got a minute 😘

I gasped. Nathan must have been sleeping more lightly than I realised because his eyes snapped open. He looked hard at me for a few moments. 'Rosie? What? What is it?'

Honey? Blown kiss emoji?

'You got a text.' I managed to snarl out.

He grabbed his phone and checked. He sighed and closed his eyes, running his hand over his face. 'C'mere.'

Rooted to the spot, I shook my head. Nathan leapt up and grabbed me, wrapping me in his arms so that I couldn't move, couldn't get away from him.

'Listen to me, Darlin'. She is only in my contacts because she is my sister's damned Maid of Honour and is in charge of communicating and updating far-flung wedding guests. And that is the goddamn only reason. And when this wedding is over, I'll be blocking and deleting her—believe me. I've just left. What the fuck does she want?'

Did I believe him? Should I believe him? Did I know enough about him to follow my gut, which was telling me it was the truth? I had seen the pain and hurt in his eyes when he'd told me about her. And he'd been so proud of himself that he'd been able to deal with the pre-wedding gathering and her being there. Why he hadn't told me this when he had recounted everything in the car, I couldn't figure. But I wanted this to be the truth, I needed it to be. I nodded.

Nathan obviously felt the change in my tension and pulled away to look me in the eye. He smiled ruefully at me and, when I managed a little smile back at him, he kissed me, tenderly, then murmured, 'I told you I won't let you down, Rosie. I meant it. I wouldn't say it if I didn't—I wouldn't say, you know? An' I meant every word today. I *am* yours. You *own* me. Please don't let her get into your head.'

I nodded. 'I'm so sorry I woke you. You must be exhausted,' I told him.

'Oh, I'm fine. Look, let's get dressed then we can head to yours and you can get ready and put some stuff together for staying over. We'll stop and buy you some bathroom stuff and a toothbrush, and you should pack some clothes to bring. Then I can keep you here with me as often as I want,' he said, smirking at me.

Nathan had contacted Duncan who, apparently, was at his disposal for the whole day, and he'd texted to let us know he was waiting outside. As we reached the car, Nathan suddenly piped up with, 'Duncan, I didn't introduce you two earlier. Rosie, this is Duncan McAllister, chauffeur extraordinaire. Duncan, this is Rosie Byrne, my girlfriend.'

Duncan's face said it all. He was clearly shocked. He looked from me to Nathan and then back to me. He took my hand in his, grinning all over his face. 'Rosie, I cannae tell you how surprised and *delighted* I am to meet you,' he said in a soft Scottish lilt. He looked back at Nathan. 'Well, you take your time ol' man, but you certainly know how to pick 'em. Gorgeous. I thought so earlier when I picked you both up at the airport—but you didnae choose to introduce me then.

'Rosie,' he aimed back at me. 'You make sure he looks after you. And you tell me if he doesnae. I'll sort him out.' He gave me a conspiratorial wink.

That wink was so cute—actually, Duncan was pretty cute. In his late thirties, I'd say, sandy coloured hair, piercing blue eyes—he reminded me of a young Kurt Russell when he was in the film Stargate, cute but with a hard streak. I could see Duncan in uniform… I realised Nathan was watching me size him up.

He growled. 'Back off, Duncan. She's all mine,' he snarled, but with a grin on his face. Clearly, these two were on bantering terms.

Again, Nathan had introduced me as his girlfriend. And, again, something shifted in my chest when he did, leaving me a little breathless as we climbed into the car. It went to my head even more than the first time:

Nathan Connor is my *boyfriend*!

Nathan Connor is *my* boyfriend!

Nathan Connor is my boyfriend!

This is my *boyfriend*, Nathan Connor.

I'd like you to meet my *boyfriend*, Nathan Connor.

See that dreamy, gorgeous hunk of a guy over there—he's *my* boyfriend!

Hmmm. The thing was, I didn't have that many people to introduce him to. There was Sid and the band—they'd already met him and, boy, was I going to have *some* explaining to do. There was Josh and Fabri. Oh, I couldn't wait to see Josh's face when he got a load of Nathan—*my* boyfriend.

We arrived at Café Paradiso, promptly at seven pm. Duncan dropped us off, offering to pick us all up and deliver us home or wherever else we wanted to go later in the evening. Nathan explained we might be quite late, but Duncan grinned at him and said he'd appreciated his rare lie in that morning and was only too happy to finish his day late—besides, he was already smitten with Nathan's *girlfriend* and wanted to see her again. He said the latter while winking at me. Nathan snarled at him, throwing his arm possessively around my neck. I could take a lot of this being fought over.

The hostess greeted us. 'Good evening, Mr Connor. I do hope you enjoy your evening with us.' Wow. He was known here. I remembered that last time we'd been here and smiled.

We were shown straight to our table and Rhys arrived with Caroline very shortly after. Rhys greeted me warmly, leaning in to kiss my cheek. *Wow. So we're on cheek kissing terms already.* It made me feel all warm and fuzzy. Caroline was very friendly towards me. She did that weird looking back and forth thing that everyone seems to do when Nathan tells them I'm his girlfriend.

Caroline was really pretty, early thirties, I reckon, strawberry blonde and blue/green eyes—the sort that change colour depending upon what you are wearing—that night they looked more blue than green. We ordered our meals and Nathan and Rhys mulled over what wines to order. Then Nathan downloaded his meeting with his *daddy*, going through all the questions he'd asked and praising Rhys for preparing him so well. As he was talking, the first bottle arrived—Champagne. It was opened and poured and Rhys proposed a toast: 'To Café Paradiso's new and up-coming resident band, Rosie Byrne and her Trio.'

I looked questioningly at Nathan. What was this about? What did they know that I didn't?

'He hasn't told you, has he,' Rhys stated, rolling his eyes at Nathan who was grinning sheepishly.

'Café Paradiso is one of Connor and McQueen's bars and restaurants, Rosie. I wasn't there the night you played—but the big boss was, and he was very impressed.'

OMG—I'd been sitting with the management all along that night. 'But, what does that mean? Resident band?' I asked, my heart hammering in my chest.'

Rhys continued as Nathan smiled at me. 'We'll start you off in about three months' time with a regular slot on a Monday or Tuesday night. We'll gauge how it goes and look to increase that if all goes well and you attract the numbers. We'll sort the promotion with Sid—we'll build up some hype and advertising. Assuming, of course, that you and the band are happy with all of this.'

I was speechless. This was exactly what we'd hoped for, to get this sort of regular deal with the exposure that would put us in front of influential jazz promoters.

'You didn't say a word!' I fired at Nathan. He grinned at me, shaking his head.

'Hey, I didn't want to steal Rhys's thunder. I can recommend, but it's ultimately his decision—he's the Ops guy.'

'But you didn't say a word about Café Paradiso being one of your places, all the time we were in there—in the dressing room...'

Rhys coughed, Caroline giggled, and I blushed—bright red, I'm sure.

'Maybe shouldn't mention the extra-curricular activity, eh?' said Rhys grinning widely. 'Some might think... well, best not to say…' the three of them were laughing now, but I was horrified.

Nathan took my hand. 'Look at me Rosie,' he insisted. I did. He was serious now. 'The band are being offered the contract because they are the best jazz band we've had perform in a long time, not to mention they have a phenomenal singer. They're going to make a name for themselves, and we want Café Paradiso to be associated with that. Understand?'

The laughter had died now, and Rhys piped up with, 'I'm sorry, Rosie. I was only joking. Nathan is right. We're trialling this, not only because Nathan has recommended you but because we've had some terrific feedback from the customers who were there when you performed.'

I nodded, found my smile again and we all clinked glasses a second time. Everyone relaxed.

As we ate our meals, the conversation was easy and engaging. Caroline is lovely, Nathan was right—very easy company. They both were. Chatty and entertaining, they both had us laughing throughout the meal.

Caroline questioned me about my singing and the band. She told me that she couldn't promise anything until after she'd seen us herself, but if what we did turned out to be suitable, she might also be able to put some bookings our way. She announced that they were coming to see us on Friday and, when I looked surprised, berated Nathan for not telling me. He explained that we'd had one or two 'other things' to talk about since he'd arrived home only that afternoon. I blushed, again, and everyone chuckled knowingly. I found I was enjoying this—it felt good.

Before dessert arrived, Caroline announced she had to go to the 'little room' and I leapt up to find out where it was too.

Once in the *Ladies,* she turned to me.

'I don't know how you've done it Rosie, but my God, are you good for that man. I have never seen him this relaxed and happy. Laid back and languid, yes—that's the whole Kentuckian thing isn't it? But his eyes are shining, he's smiling all the time. He looks... really alive, somehow.'

She stood in front of the basins checking herself out in the mirror. Only a little bit taller than me, Caroline had a fuller figure, the classic hour-glass shape.

'Have you met previous girlfriends of his?' I asked her.

She looked at me sideways. 'Nathan hasn't had previous *girlfriends* Rosie, this is a first, along with double dating, I might add. No, Nathan has had women he's 'having a thing with'. He's never referred to any of them as his *girlfriend,* though. To be honest, I haven't seen that many of his women.' She fumbled in her bag and pulled out a lipstick.

'My impression was always that he was either a bit of a serial dater or only in it for the sex, you know? That sounds terrible doesn't it—and he is so lovely. He just never seemed to take any of the women he was with that seriously. And they certainly didn't last very long.'

'I know, I know,' I jumped in. 'He told me two to three months has been the longest in years. I'm sort of hoping I get the full three months before he gets bored and moves on.'

Caroline finished touching up her lips and turned, looking at me bemused. 'Rosie, I doubt very much he sees you like the others. Like I said, he's *never* introduced anyone as his *girlfriend*—he usually only gives their name if he introduces them at all. Besides, have you seen the way he looks at you? The man is smitten. He's not letting go of you any time soon, I'd hazard a guess.'

'So, you *have* seen him with *some* other women, then?'

I turned and studiously checked over my make-up to cover up the way my heart was yammering in my chest, waiting for Caroline's response.

'Yes, a few. Mostly at the Copper Pipe when he's picked someone up, either there or wherever he was before arriving there.' She chuckled, 'He doesn't exactly have to work hard at picking up women in bars.' She rolled her eyes.

'They don't look like me, do they? The other women he's... dated,' I probed. Caroline took a breath as though she was going to say something then changed her mind. 'I know, Caroline, I know of one or two—tall, thin, blonde?'

She turned full on to look at me squarely, realisation dawning on her face.

''Well, yes—I'd say that describes most of the ones I've seen. Blondes or redheads. But I would add not as young as you, not as pretty as you by a long shot, and the ones I've actually met? Nowhere near as nice as you—you're lovely you know.'

She rubbed my arm in a reassuring gesture that touched me.

'I'm so excited! We'll surely have lots of double dates—we'll have you both to dinner in the next week or so. And, maybe you can persuade Nathan to invite us to his for dinner. I'm *dying* to see this fabulous apartment of his. Rhys has waxed lyrical about it every time he's been there.'

Caroline continued chatting away, gaily. She was one of those people who carries on talking even when they're in the cubicle. She was irrepressible. I liked her very much and felt the same way about double dates and dinners together.

We got back to the table to find Nathan missing. He'd apparently misplaced his phone—thought he might have left it in the restroom, he'd told Rhys.

We had a laugh when he got back to the table, phone safely in hand. 'Well, that's restored my faith in human nature—it was handed in at the bar. This is becoming a bit of a habit,' he told us. 'Second time in a week I've managed to put it down somewhere without realising.'

'Old-age, old man,' Rhys teased him. 'Losing things is only the first step, you'll be turning up at the office in your pyjamas next.'

Chapter Twenty-Three

Nathan

My girl was an absolute delight. I hadn't enjoyed an evening in company like I did that night for a lot of years. The food was excellent. The wine was great. The company was entertaining; Rhys and Caroline were so easy to relax around. But best of all was having my Rosie with me. Just being able to look at her across the table, hear her tinkling laughter or her dirty giggle, touch her hand, her cheek, rub my foot up her shin under the table and see what was written in her eyes when she looked at me.

When we got back to the apartment, I took her in the shower again. We would be having a lot of shower sex over the next couple of days if it was the only place she felt comfortable. Period sex was a first for me too, but, with Rosie, I wanted her any way and every way I could have her.

As we lay snuggling up in bed, she looked up at the ceiling mirror and met my eyes in it. Before she could ask the question, I sucked in a breath. And announced, 'One.'

'One what?' she asked sounding perplexed. 'The answer is I've watched one woman in *that* mirror and she's beside me right now. I've had one woman in this bed, Rosie, and that's you.'

She shot up into a kneeling position and looked directly at me, laughing. 'Well, thank you for sharing,' she grinned at me, 'although I would point out that I didn't actually ask. I don't get it, though. You've slept with lots of other women, Nathan. Where do you usually go?'

'Well, technically, I've *slept* with a small number of women—mostly by accident, you know? Too much to drink. Too tired to bother moving. I can count them on the fingers of one hand—and that would include you, who, I would add, I sleep deliriously happily with by choice. Your *No overnighters* rule? Well, that was pretty much *my* rule too. Until you.' I smiled ruefully at her.

I could see she was quite taken aback. 'Where?' she pressed. 'I didn't have Gabrielle Harris down for a quick fumble in the pub loo type of girl,' she said, laughing at me.

'Very funny. There are hotel rooms, you know. Or their place. And... there is a small apartment attached to my offices. I set it up when I first bought this place and was having it done up. It has a second, external entrance so I don't have to walk through the offices to get to it. Which is handy late at night so I don't set all the lights and alarms off. That's my go-to pad, Rosie. Well, it's been my go-to pad.'

'Why...?' she asked me, her eyes searching my face. I knew the next answer would make me seem like a real asshole, but it felt right to be honest with her.

'This is my home, my space. This is where I can relax and be me. I guess I never wanted to let any of them into my space. I never wanted any of them to see who I am. The office apartment is very functional, it hasn't got my personality stamped all over it. All I was really interested in was sex.'

'No, Nathan, I got that. I meant why am *I* here? Why have you brought *me* here?'

'I guess I *want* you to know me, Rosie. Hell, you've already gotten further in than anyone in the last seven years.' I smiled at her.

She smiled back at me. 'So that's what it was then? In the kitchen earlier? You were feeling vulnerable. Exposed because I was seeing you in your home environment. You weren't marking your territory, putting me in my place. You were looking for affirmation to ease your anxiety?'

Christ. How can someone so young see so much? It's like, when she's looking into my eyes, she can really see me—who I am. And yet I sense she doesn't see what I feel for her. Maybe that's because she doesn't want to see it. I still need to tread carefully here. I think she's still poised to fly if she feels things are getting too close.

'You scared me a bit, Nathan,' she said, very quietly. I pulled her off her knees to lay next to me, her head on my chest, and stroked her silky soft hair.

'I know, Darlin'. I'm sorry. That wasn't my intention. I know how sensitive you are to bein'... well, to the idea of someone trying to control you. I should know better. I'll be more careful in future, I promise.'

I thought about the shower earlier. 'Rosie, I don't scare you or hurt you when I'm... we're... you know, fuckin' hard, do I? You don't think I'm tryin' to control you when I order you about in the bedroom?'

She pulled back to look directly into my eyes. 'Nathan, nothing you do scares or hurts me in the bedroom—wherever we're having sex. I love every minute, seriously. I kind of really like it when you're dominating; it's not the same as trying to control me. And I love it when you let *me* take control and order *you* about too—I think it's all the more exciting because it's usually the other way around. And I particularly like the hard fucking. It can get a bit painful when you do that thing where you get lost in your head for a couple of minutes and really crash into me, but the pain sort of adds to the pleasure, and I absolutely adore that moment when you come back and say my name. In that moment, it's like I'm the air you breathe.'

'You know, that's all new to me too, Rosie. Don't get me wrong, I like reasonably rough sex—a lot—but losing myself completely like that is something that's only ever happened with you. Fucking you hard is like getting a fix to an addiction. I would stop, though, if I was hurting you.'

'No—I don't want you to. When you come, crying out my name? It's intoxicating—a real high, Nathan. I guess I'm addicted too.'

She frowned for a second, thinking, then giggled. 'Do you think they do patches that help cure that type of addiction?' She giggled harder, 'Come get your Sexual-High Patches here—never need another man again.' Her giggling was infectious, and I was laughing too.

'Man, I hope they never come up with that one. I'd hate to be redundant.'

'Oh Nathan,' she laughed, 'you'll never be redundant, Baby. Lifelong job with me and that's a fact.' She continued laughing, then choked, I think when she realised what she had said. Her face fell a bit as she coloured up. 'I mean, I mean—you've got a job with me for as long as you want it is… is… what I meant.'

She slipped out of my arms and off the bed. 'I've got to pay a visit… all that giggling….' and she ran off to the bathroom as fast as her legs would carry her.

I love those British idioms—paying a visit. I smiled. And then, my smile widened as I played over, in my head, what she had said. 'Lifelong job. Lifelong! She didn't say a job for as long as she wanted me; she said, for as long as I wanted it. I fist-pumped. 'Yesssssss!' What is it they say? Softly, softly, catchee monkey.

Rosie

I slid down the door as soon as it closed behind me, my arms wrapped around myself. The conversation in my head went something like:

Well, I think you got away with it this time—you need to be more careful.

More careful about what? We were talking about sex. If he did hear what I said, he'll assume that's what I meant.

And was that what you meant? You were simply talking about sex?

Of course. What else could it mean?

Face it. You're falling for him, girl. And if you're not careful, you're going to give the game away and he'll disappear faster than a speeding bullet. Just because he's let you in, he's brought you here, he looks at you differently to how he's looked at other women—none of that means he wants more than sex, primarily. Cool it, okay?

Okay.

I'm falling for him?

Yeah, I think I am.

Oh bugger!

Chapter Twenty-Four

The next morning, we showered together, yet again.

We both dressed and finished making ourselves presentable to the world. Oh my. In a dark, beautifully tailored suit, this time with a crisp, bright white shirt, Nathan looked edible—as always. He spotted me staring at him and did that head to one side, eyebrow arching thing that now had a direct line to my lady-bits. 'Such crude thoughts you naughty girl,' he chided, then promptly turned me round and planted a smack on my bum.

I was rendered speechless, my mouth open and my eyes almost bulging out of their sockets.

'Fuck! Your ass in those tight jeans looks so inviting. Next time, though, I'm having me some bare butt cheek,' he announced, grinning madly with a mischievous glint in his eye.

'OW!' I roared. 'That bloody hurt! And you most certainly are not. Don't you dare. Don't you bloody dare do that to me again,' I spluttered, furiously. He grabbed me around the waist again and pinned me to him. However, much I struggled, it was hopeless, I was never going to be able to wriggle out of his grasp.

'Let go! Let me go!' I shouted at him. The bastard was

laughing. Eventually, I stopped trying and stood, panting in his arms.

He murmured in my ear, 'It didn't hurt that much.'

Okay, so it hadn't hurt that much, but I wasn't admitting that.

'And part of you liked it,' he claimed.

Had I?—Liked it? Is that why I was so mad?

'I told you, Rosie, I will never *hurt* you, hurt you. Trust me. Do you trust me?'

I thought about it. Did I? Of course I did. I put myself at his mercy constantly, let him do whatever he wanted to my body, never fearing that he would knowingly do anything that might hurt me.

'Yes,' I sighed, 'I do trust you, Nathan.' I relaxed into his arms. He kissed me, a soft, sensuous meeting of lips and caressing with tongues. Then he looked at me.

'Good. Now we gotta finish your tour of this apartment then get some food down us and start the working day. Do you like sourdough bread?'

'Erm... yeah, I do.'

'Poached eggs? Avocado? Cherry tomatoes? Trendy brunch?'

'Sounds delicious,' I replied, 'If you've got all the makings in, I'll make a start...' I began.

He interrupted, 'No you won't. *My* kitchen, *I* say who makes brunch—and this mornin' it's me.'

'You won't hear me arguing. Well except—Nathan it's arse not ass. An ass is a type of donkey or a stupid person. There's an r in the word: a.R.s.e. You Americans insist on getting it wrong all the time.'

Nathan had scheduled his work meetings for the afternoon

so we could take our time in the morning before he had to dive full-time back to work. I had band rehearsals booked for the afternoon and for Friday afternoon and my vocal coaching session on Thursday. I had been trying to plan out my time but, thinking about trying to fit in lots of Nathan, movies, quiet reading time and the gym had been looking a bit difficult. That is until Nathan showed me what was behind the two doors I hadn't ventured through yet.

The first door took us into an incredibly well-equipped home gym with an industrial quality treadmill, a multi gym contraption with interesting looking pulleys and handles, a weights bench beside two rails of dumbbells—some definitely good for me—and a high bar for doing chin-ups—immediately my thoughts flashed to watching Nathan's back while he worked that one. When I managed to steady my heart rate again, I also saw that there were mats, various other bits of equipment about the room and mirrors all along one wall. This was simply perfect. I looked inquiringly at Nathan.

'Of course, Sweetheart—any time—*all* the time. Bring your gear here so you can dive in whenever you get the chance. And speaking of diving in, bring some swimwear; there's a pool downstairs. Unfortunately, it's monitored by CCTV otherwise I'd be suggesting you don't bring any swimwear…' He was smirking at me again.

The last door opened into a larger room, almost the same size as the lounge and I gasped as I walked in.

In one corner was an office set-up—a desk with a state-of-the-art PC on it and a dock for a laptop. In the centre of the room, there were half a dozen home cinema seats—the ones with cupholders and side trays and that recline. I couldn't see a screen on the wall because all the walls were lined in bookshelves, occasionally broken up with statues or other art objects, but mostly full of books and a couple of wide columns of DVDs.

Nathan walked over to one wall, pushed on a button and two whole sections of shelves moved forward, then slid apart, revealing a huge screen above a unit housing black boxes in various sizes. His eyes twinkling, he was grinning from ear to ear at my expression. 'Cool, huh?' he chuckled. 'I've also got automatic blackout blinds at the windows.'

I wandered around the room scanning the books—so many books. 'Have you seriously read all these books or are they for show?' I asked him.

'I have definitely read every book in this room—some of them more than once. Of course, I tend to use my Kindle a lot these days, especially when I'm travellin', but I do still like the comfortin' feel of a real book in my hands—and these chairs work equally well for readin' as for watchin',' he told me.

I was gobsmacked. He'd read *all* of these books.

It took me a few minutes to work out the organisation, but I could soon see that they were set out in specific genres then in alphabetical order by author. I could see a whole section of British classics—Austen, Brontë (all of them), Dickens, Lawrence, Hardy to name but a tiny few—and next to it, shelves of American classics. But what caught my eye was a huge section on Science Fiction and Fantasy.

'Oh my God, Nathan. Aldiss. Asimov. Clarke. Philip K. Dick, Heinlein… you know about Science Fiction… wait a minute…' I raced to the DVD section and, sure enough, there were loads of Sci-Fi films including, of course, Blade Runner and Blade Runner 2049.

'But you didn't say a word when I was rabbiting on the other night,' I spluttered. 'You let me lecture you as though you knew nothing.'

He treated me to a heart-melting smile. 'Oh, Rosie, there is nothing I love more than hearing you talk about something you love and are passionate about. Well… maybe there are a couple of things I might love more…' He grinned at me. 'But that was the first time you were really openin' up about somethin' that interests you. I wanted to let you talk and talk. I could have listened to you all night.'

He strode over to me and threw an arm around my waist, the other hand tucking a stray strand of hair behind my ear before he planted a gentle, chaste kiss on my lips.

'And, yes, Blade Runner is one of my favourite films too. Not to mention one of my favourite soundtracks. Alexa,' he called out, 'play the Love Theme from Blade Runner.'

'Playing the Love Theme from Blade Runner,' came the response.

Tinkling chimes sounded, opening one of the smokiest, most sensual pieces of music I know. Nathan cupped my head in his hands and looked intensely into my eyes, his shining. Then he kissed me softly, tenderly, and time seemed to stand still as we were bathed in music that sent its haunting tendrils snaking through my senses, making me feel utterly exposed to this man.

After what seemed like an eternity, he ended the kiss and took me in his arms, tucking my head under his chin. He rested his cheek on my crown, delivering the softest kisses on my hair, and we stood, swaying gently to the hypnotic sound.

I was fighting tears back. I wanted this moment to never end. I felt safe, secure, cherished, and with those feelings came the realisation of how empty my life had been to this point—and would be again when this was over, when Nathan moved on. I had to be careful, to make sure he'd stay in my life for as long as possible.

For the first time, I imagined the possibility of this lasting beyond Nathan's usual three-month limit. And I wanted that. I really wanted that. Did he? Was that why I was here, in his private and personal space?

The music ended and we stood there, seemingly neither one of us wanting to break the spell it had cast over us. I felt emotions welling up; I had to shatter the moment. I pulled back, 'God—it's fabulous isn't it? It always gets to me like this,' I told him, by way of an explanation for my tear-filled eyes.

His intense gaze held me for a few moments more, then he broke away. 'Yeah, me too,' he rasped.

'Right. Brunch.' he announced, gruffly. 'What would you like to do while I'm preparing it?'

I laughed. 'I'll stay here, have a good look at what you've got. See what I can borrow to read.'

I pinched my thigh. I was sure I must be dreaming. Nothing could feel this good, surely. There had to be a catch….

Nathan

So much had happened since I had found her waiting for me at the airport, it hardly seemed possible that that was less than twenty-four hours ago. I was more convinced than ever that she was falling for me—her attempt to cover up her reaction during the Blade Runner music didn't fool me for a minute. She had been as emotionally affected by our embrace as I had.

Now, I had to play a waiting game and let her come to

that realisation in her own time. There was no need to rush anything. I knew how *I* felt and I was pretty sure I knew how she felt. I truly believed that we would get there. The feeling was so strong, how could we not?

I made us brunch and then got a cab to detour and drop her off at her place on the way to my offices. I'll be picking her back up on my way home. It'll be my place for the next few nights—my shower is bigger.

Friday night arrived before we knew it. Rosie's band were playing a pub in Chiswick. Rhys, Caroline and I met up and headed out that way together.

The band had commenced their first set when we got to the place, so we snuck in and hovered around the corner. It was a bit of a weird set-up for live music: the bar was L shaped so, while everyone in the long part of the L could see the band, those of us in the shorter part couldn't. But we could hear clearly enough, thanks to the decent speakers set in the corner point and aimed in both directions. Rosie was on form, her hypnotic voice enthralling everyone. I heard her scat singing for the first time. She had told me she was trying it out with her singing coach. She was terrific at it—This Can't Be Love—it sounded great. Rhys was clearly impressed, giving me the thumbs up as the band opened up their fourth number.

Caroline was equally impressed. She was there, partly to check the band out for bookings at some of the venues in the hotel chain she worked for as Entertainments Manager. She told me, as we were listening to the last number of the first set, that she could definitely put a fair amount of work their way. Rosie would be over the moon.

As soon as they finished their set, I popped my head around the corner and made my presence known to her. I pointed to the bar and we met there, me giving her a polite kiss on the cheek by way of a greeting. She was being scrutinised at gigs so I held onto her hand and brushed my thumb over her knuckles to let her know I wanted to do so much more. She kept looking around.

'How long have you been here?' she asked me.

'We arrived pretty much as soon as you'd started. We stayed out of the way so as not to distract you,' I explained to her. 'What's up, Sweetheart, you seem a little spooked?'

'That must be it.' Relief smoothed her features. 'It must have been you—maybe I'm so attuned to you, my body knows when you're near.' She smiled.

'What must have been me?' I probed.

'Well, when I was going through my first few numbers, I got this weird feeling that I was being watched, not watched like someone in the audience. It was more intense than that somehow—you know, prickles at the base of my skull and goosebumps up and down my arms,' she said. 'It was obviously my senses picking up your wavelength,' she insisted. 'I'm so glad you are here; I was missing you.'

'I miss you all the time I'm not with you, Darlin',' I assured her.

Rhys and Caroline had made their way over to the bar by this time and, after they had waxed lyrical about how good Rosie and the band were, Caroline told Rosie she would be contacting her about some bookings. The other band members popped over to say, 'Hi' and I introduced them to Rhys and Caroline too. They were delighted to hear that Caroline was interested in booking them.

What with Café Paradiso and Caroline's bookings, Rosie and the band were looking at some regular, well-paid work in the very near future. This would, in turn, enable them to maybe expand the line-up and invest and concentrate on producing some good promotional videos to help punt for more work and more exposure where it counts: Ronnie Scott's, The Nightjar, Boisdale's for example. Things were beginning to move for Rosie Byrne and her Trio. I was happy for them; they deserved it—she deserved it.

The guys started their second set. This one had a few more modern and contemporary songs in it but given a jazz rhythm or timing. We managed to carve ourselves some space out at the bar in the long section this time so we could watch as well as hear. I smiled to myself a little when Rosie sang a beautiful Bossa Nova version of I'm Not In Love, glancing at me a few times to see if I was getting the message, and grinning at me. But it was when she put her heart and soul into their version of the Chris Isaak song, Wicked Game, that she kept eye contact with me, telling me she didn't want to fall in love with me, that it was a wicked thing to do to make her dream of me. That hit me hard. I'd never dreamed I'd meet someone like her either and I was damned if I was gonna lose her now.

We all had a drink together at the bar before everyone went their separate ways home. Rosie and I grabbed a cab back to mine. My phone started buzzing while we were on our way. It was Linnea again. I rejected the call and rolled my eyes at Rosie.

Neither of us gave any more thought to Rosie's *weird* feeling.

Chapter Twenty-Five

Rosie

The next couple of weeks went by in something of a blur. Nathan was working hard at his offices during the daytime and at his home desk some of the evenings. I spent time rehearsing and learning new songs, having vocal coaching sessions, gigging, spending time in Nathan's fabulous gym or library.

I met Carmen. She went to Nathan's apartment nearly every weekday morning so it was inevitable that I would meet her eventually. She's a short, stocky woman in her fifties who clearly likes to mother Nathan—and now me too. She was lovely and I adored her already.

We spent one evening at Rhys and Caroline's; true to her word, she invited us for dinner. I can't remember ever spending an evening with a boyfriend and friends before this, and now it's starting to happen regularly. If this is *normal* I'll take it. It makes me feel warm and contented. We chatted about superficial things—favourite foods, favourite films, travel destinations. We laughed at silly jokes and stories each of us recounted; Caroline was definitely the funniest storyteller and Rhys the best joke teller—his timing was perfect.

Persuading Nathan to invite them back to his for dinner was a cinch; he was more than happy to have a bunch of people to cook for and show off his culinary prowess, not to mention his wine stock. He cooked up the most delicious beef hotpot, having made his own sourdough bread to dip in the gravy.

He only kept a live yeast culture starter in his fridge that he religiously fed once a week! He called it *Dave*.

During dinner, Caroline, gravy dripping down her chin, piped up with, 'Oh God, Rosie. You *have* to keep this man. He cooks like my nan. And I have to tell you that's the compliment of the century.' We all laughed, but a knowing look passed between Nathan and me. I guess he was letting me know not to take that comment to heart. I guess....

Something constricted in my chest. For that split-second, I wanted to take it to heart, wanted to think in terms of *keeping* him. Not an option—I knew that.

We spent almost every single night together, at his place or mine, the intensity of our physical relationship showing no signs of easing. I wanted him all the time and it seemed he wanted me as badly. He never tired of telling me I was beautiful and that my body was perfect. He delighted in 'eating out my pretty little cunt' as he called it. God, he had a filthy mouth and I loved it—I loved it when he talked dirty to me, which was pretty much every time we had sex. When I called him out on using the 'C' word, he delighted in telling me, 'If it's good enough for your D. H. Lawrence, it's good enough for me. You do know how lovely that scene is in *Lady Chatterley's Lover*, don't you? How beautiful Lawrence makes Oliver's use of that word?'

And he was so inventive when it came to finding angles and places for me to be so he could enter me from yet another position, although, we'd always end up sleeping, either in our lovely spooning snuggle with Nathan wrapped around me from behind, or with his head buried between my breasts and my arms wrapped around him.

I was eating more regularly when he was around. I'd stopped losing weight but, right then I didn't mind. I loved that he looked at my body with such longing and obvious wanting, that he delighted in touching me, in running his hands over my skin.

One day, true to his word, he hired a car, a beautiful Maserati GT. It was black with gorgeous black and red leather upholstery, simply breathtaking. Nathan said if we were going for my first experience of real sex in a car, we should do it in style. He said there was no other car with the sheer style and beauty of this one and as there was no one with the sheer style and beauty of one Rosie Byrne, we were a perfect match. He'd misjudged a bit though. He'd forgotten all about the central column in both the front and the back seats.

We toured around the beautiful, wooded areas of Sussex and Surrey and had lunch in a lovely country pub. I finally told Nathan all about Josh. I wanted them to meet soon, the two people who meant the most to me. Nathan agreed that as soon as Josh was back from touring, we would arrange a foursome dinner date.

After lunch, we found a secluded spot where we weren't in much danger of being discovered. Nathan set up his iPhone to play through the sound system and soon had Led Zep booming. Starting with Black Dog. How appropriate—he soon had this 'Mama' sweating and grooving.

Then we explored ways of having sex in such a confined space. What worked the best involved me giving him head kneeling one side of the column, him sitting the other and then me being straddled across his lap with my head pressed against the roof at an unnatural angle. We laughed, we sang along with Robert Plant—loudly, we panted, we growled, we shouted out each other's names. My Dixie Adonis made it all a wonderful, beautiful experience that I will never forget.

Can you fall in love with a car? If so, I have.

The only thing that marred the day was a call coming to Nathan's phone. When he took it out of his pocket, I was on his lap so couldn't have avoided seeing who it was if I'd tried. He rejected the call, cursing her again.

He took me to the National Gallery, particularly to see the paintings of Monet displayed there. Any painting I pointed to because I liked it, he told me all about it. He is such a dark horse, this man. He knows about a lot more than he lets on. First the extensive library of books he has and his pretty in-depth knowledge of the Classics and now, Art. He promised to take me to the Guggenheim Museum in New York to see the largest collection of Kandinski paintings anywhere in the world, so he tells me, including the original of one of the prints I had on a wall in my flat. I'd never been to New York—that would be another first for me.

That night, he was taking me to a concert in the Barbican. A cellist he particularly liked, Nathan was clearly excited about taking me to see him. Afterwards, we'd be spending the night at his place.

Sharing his love of the cello with me, promising to take me to New York to visit the Guggenheim Museum, particularly wanting to meet my best friend, Josh, not to mention spending every moment of his spare time with me, can I believe that he is seeing 'us' as more? Am I setting myself up for a massive fall even thinking it is possible?

Nathan

I can honestly say that it was the best evening of my life. I had told Rosie we should dress up some—it's not an absolute requirement when attending a concert at The Barbican but many people do. Rosie, as always, looked breathtakingly beautiful in an off-the-shoulder, figure-hugging little number, dark blue lace over a pale pink lining and a pair of pale pink stilettos to match.

There was only one hiccup; my phone rang in the car on the way, and when I took it out of my pocket with Rosie sitting next to me, she could see the caller's name as clearly as I could. It was Linnea. Again.

This was getting extremely uncomfortable. I would be glad when the wedding was over and I could block her calls. Rosie looked at me, her eyes searching mine for—I don't know what. I immediately explained that she was probably checking for the final details of our travel to make sure everything was going according to plan. I wished to God I had told her about Linnea's role in the wedding planning right back at the beginning; it was beginning to sound pretty lame now, but I tried to be as nonchalant as I could. I rejected the call. It could wait. If it was something important to do with the wedding, she could damn well text.

We arrived, and I took her arm and led her into the theatre and our seats, slap bang in the centre of the front row. I had a standing instruction with Mason that whenever this guy was performing in the UK, he'd get me two tickets. I could always sort out a date to take near the time.

I couldn't have timed this one better. Rosie's eyes lit up and her mouth formed a big O. I grinned at her and told her I wanted her to have the full experience. She hadn't heard a lot of cello music, she'd previously told me, and I'd held off playing all my favourites when she was around, wanting this to be her first real experience of the instrument I loved so much, played by this guy with such passion, fire and sensitivity.

The theatre filled then hushed. Rosie looked at me, eyes shining with anticipation, and the strings opened one of my favourite pieces, Benedictus—it's beautiful. I watched Rosie, couldn't take my eyes off her. The cellist played his opening bars and her mouth fell open. I reached across and stroked her cheek. She closed her mouth, looked at me again and grinned, then her eyes darted straight back to him. She was completely entranced. As he moved on to the second part of the melody, I saw her chest heave and her breathing hitch; she was fighting back tears. *Oh Darlin', it gets me like that too.* I took her hand; she looked down at mine, raised it to her lips, and then lifted her face back to gaze in awe at the soloist and the orchestra as they reprised the first section.

When the choir opened up, her eyes widened, and tears rolled down her cheeks. By the time the soloist came in for the final refrain, her chest was heaving, and her eyes were closed, a look of pure ecstasy on her face. The house fell silent and then she was frantically rubbing the tears from her face with the back of her hand as the audience completely erupted into rapturous applause. She scrambled in her bag. I handed her the pack of tissues I'd brought with me; I kinda thought they might come in handy.

'God, that was exhausting. You might have warned me,' she hissed at me, laughing and clapping with the rest of the audience.

'You might have hated it,' I said. 'It gets me like that but there was no guarantee you'd feel it too.'

'Oh Nathan,' she said, 'I think it's one of the most beautiful things I've ever heard.'

'Then you're in for a treat, Honey, there's more of that to come.'

The rest of the concert was simply amazing, watching the range of emotions coursing through Rosie as she watched the cellist. She was hooked, there was no doubt, and I was overjoyed; I'd have a wonderful time introducing her to all my other favourite pieces.

When the final piece finished, the audience were applauding and whistling and calling out for what seemed an age. The star of the show bowed, the conductor bowed, they both bowed together. Then, the soloist, ever the ladies' man, blew kisses to the audience. He looked directly at Rosie, smiling, and wiped an imaginary tear from his eye before blowing a kiss directly to her and nodding to me. It was such a lovely gesture, but then, looking at Rosie, who wouldn't be moved?

I took her into the members' bar for a drink while the crowd dispersed. She was full of it. She'd loved it. She described all her favourite parts, '... and when the huge drums sounded, it was ....', '.... and then when the guitarist played that twiddly bit I just ....', '... and then I couldn't help but cry when ....' I sat listening to her babble away, utterly entranced by her infectious enthusiasm and the incandescent light that always shone from her beautiful eyes when she was passionate.

Chapter Twenty-Six

We got back to my place. I took off my jacket and tie and poured us both a glass of wine. 'More?' I asked her.

'Oh yes, please.'

I issued the instruction, 'Alexa, play 2Cellos Benedictus. Here's more of the same but with a different twist,' I said to her, still hypnotised by her reaction when the music opened again.

She gazed at me, calculating. Then she took my hand and led me into my bedroom, the music now issuing from the speakers I have in there. She reached up and kissed me lightly on the lips, then walked over to the bedpost, lifted the handcuffs off it, walked back to me and offered them to me, her eyes a mixture of adoration and apprehension.

'For me?' I asked her. 'You'd do this for me?' She nodded, almost imperceptibly.

'If it's what you want,' she whispered.

I was so moved I could barely speak. 'Take your dress off,' I commanded her, my voice a hoarse whisper. She complied, leaning down to take it by the hem and then raising it slowly up and over her head. She was wearing a tiny pair of silky panties. I moaned at the sight of her bare tits. They were so goddamn perfect; my cock reacted every time I saw them bared.

I took a few moments to adore that exquisite body then I put my glass down and knelt in front of her. I slid her panties down and under her shoes. I indicated that she should raise one foot. She held onto my shoulder for support as she did so and I slid one shoe off, kissing her foot before placing it back on the ground. I did the same with the other. Then I buried my face in her belly, kissing the cute mole on her hip and her delicious little triangle of dark curls. I ran my hand up the inside of her thigh and lightly brushed her slit with my finger. She gasped and bit her lip.

I stood up and led her by the hand to the bed. 'Lie on your back, head on the pillow,' I whispered in her ear. Then I knelt over her and took her hands above her head. I placed a wrist into one cuff, looped the second around one of the bed rails, and then fastened it onto her other wrist, hanging the key over the next rail.

She was completely mine, had surrendered herself to me, trusting me implicitly.

I fell on her like a ravening wolf, biting, licking, sucking, nipping. I wanted to devour her—but oh so gently. Hurting her was never going to be on my agenda. I covered her shoulders, her breasts, her thighs and her belly with my tongue, my lips and my teeth. She gasped and wriggled and squealed, but not once did she protest.

I was still fully clothed and it was time to rectify that. Never taking my eyes from hers, I stood up, disrobed, dropping everything on the floor—I was in a hurry to be back with her. Once naked, I climbed back on the bed to kneel between her legs. I parted her thighs further, bending her knees up either side of her body and moved in to take her as close to heaven as it is in my power to do with my tongue, my mouth and my fingers.

When she had been bucking and crying out for some time, I stopped and waited while her body relaxed and she sighed. I lifted my head to look at her. Her eyes were closed, and she looked at peace—no fear, no anxiety. Slowly, she opened her eyes and found mine. She smiled, still no words, no protestations.

I moved up the bed, grasped her thighs and pulled her onto me, easing into her. God, she felt so good around my cock, so tight and so wet. I moved rhythmically, pushing further and further into her.

As she moaned again, I was seized by a sudden compulsion; I knew it was barred in the Rules, but I had her in my power, and I wanted to hold her to me, feel her whole body under me. I lay forward pinning her to the bed.

Missionary position.

I rested on my elbows, my hands supporting her back, so I could watch her face as I started moving again. She wrapped her legs around me, and a small moan escaped from her lips every time I pushed deeper into her. I thrust more urgently, feeling the tension building in her body, as it was in mine.

Something was missing.

'Fuck this Rosie, I want your arms around me,' I said as I hitched us both up the bed, still joined, loathe to leave the warmth of her core. I grabbed the key and unlocked the handcuffs. I moved us back down the bed as she smiled up at me and took my face in her hands.

'Oh my Nathan,' she whispered, 'my beautiful Dixie Adonis.' And she started kissing me softly, lovingly and then urgently as I resumed moving inside her again.

She gripped my shoulders, clinging to me as tension built in both of us again. I pushed deeper, wanting to lose myself in her. She tensed, froze. I pushed again and again, so close now but holding back, willing her over the edge. When she cried out and was suddenly writhing frantically under me, calling out my name, I let go, poured everything into her and found myself falling, falling into her. I collapsed into her arms, as she nuzzled her face in my neck.

As we lay there, bathed in sweat, wrapped up in each other, I couldn't hold back any longer. I had to tell her how I felt.

I pulled back to look at her. I cupped her sweet, sweet face in my hand. 'Rosie, oh Darlin'...'

I was stopped short by the tears forming in her eyes. A huge teardrop spilled out of one eye and slid down the side of her face. Then one the other side. Then they were streaming as her chest hitched, wracked with sobs.

'Nathan, I'm so sorry. I'm so sorry.'

What the fuck was this? What was going on? I felt the world around me crumbling.

'Rosie? What is it? What's going on?' I pleaded with her, as gently as I could, not really wanting to hear what she was going to say, terrified she was about to tear my world apart. I held my breath, waiting.

'I can't help it, Nathan. I can't stop it. I'm falling in love with you. Hopelessly. I want to stay here, you holding me like this forever. I tried not to let it happen. I know this isn't what you want from me...'

I closed my eyes and took a deep gulp of air as I started breathing again. When I opened them I must have had the biggest grin on my face. She looked at me quizzically, her sobs halting.

'About time,' I sighed. 'What do you mean it isn't what I want from you? It's everything I want from you. You must know you're playing *Catch Up* here, Darlin'?'

'Wh-wh-what?' she whispered, her eyes searching mine.

'You know, Rosie. You've known for a while.'

She gazed at me for what seemed like an eternity. Then she said, 'Nathan, I think I've been in love with you since you first whispered in my ear. Remember what you said?'

'You're okay—I gotcha.' She nodded, smiling.

'I guess if you believe in love, and I didn't, not for a long time, but if you do, then you probably believe in love at first sight too. 'But, it was when you whispered that in my ear, that's when something shifted inside. I think that's when it happened for me. You know, if you hadn't turned up at the gig, I was gonna go back to the offices the next day and track down who you were.'

'Me too,' I laughed.

'Really?' she asked, almost incredulously.

'Are you kidding me? Remember, I was on a promise—from the hottest, most gorgeous girl I'd ever seen. You're damn right I was coming to find you.'

'I do love you, Nathan,' she said, smiling, her eyes shining. 'You told me when you were drunk, you know? I told myself that I hadn't heard properly or that you were drunk and didn't mean it…'

A tune suddenly came into my head, and I just had to… 'Rosie, oh Rosie, I'd like to paint your face up in the sky,' I sang to her.

I stopped in horror as I watched her face crumple, tears filled her eyes and she started hitching and gasping again. In seconds, she was sobbing uncontrollably. I wrapped her tightly in my arms, not knowing what to say or do, as she wept into my chest, clinging to me.

'Oh Rosie, Darlin', tell me. Please tell me what's wrong,' I pleaded with her.

Between heaving sobs, she got the words out.

'My dad… Nathan… My dad… used to… sing that… to me. He loved me… I know it… He did love me,' she protested. 'Why did he leave me, Nathan? What did I do wrong?'

'Sweetheart, you didn't do anything wrong,' I told her. 'He didn't leave you, he died, didn't he?'

'He disappeared,' she whispered, as sobs took her again. Between her sobs, she stammered out her story. 'He left the house one day and never came back. There was never any trace of him found, they never even found his car. Eventually, he was presumed dead. My mother always maintained that he left us—she was convinced there was a suitcase of money. She told me he didn't want either of us enough to stay. That he had a *fancy woman* and had left us for her, that I had been a burden to him.

'The thing is, Nathan, there *was* a woman. I remember meeting a woman my dad introduced to me as Maria. I don't remember what we were doing or much else about it really, just that I'd been with him when he picked her up in his car. I was too young to draw any conclusions. It's funny though—without being told, I never mentioned her to my mum. I never saw her again after my dad disappeared. Did he run off with her and start a completely new life somewhere? Without the complication of a kid? I guess I'll never know.

'He did provide for us before he vanished. He set up trust funds for both me and mum a couple of years before any of this happened. He ran an investment company and they made huge amounts during the dot com explosion. My mum's was for enough money to live on for the rest of her life, including paying for expensive private clinic fees. I have no idea what mine is worth—my dad stipulated that I wasn't to get control of it until I was twenty-five. He wanted me to be able to live a reasonably normal life before I took on the responsibility of managing the money. That's why Martin has looked after me all this time.

'I'll never want for anything financially, Nathan, but I'd rather have my dad...'

I had naively thought that the two guys who had mistreated her were responsible for her lack of self-worth, for her believing she couldn't trust or love anyone and be loved right back. Devastating as their actions had been, those two had only fed her deepest fears: that her father, the only person she believed ever truly loved her, had deserted her and that she was somehow to blame. I stroked her hair.

'And your mom, Baby, I guess she deserted you too in a way?'

'I'm not sure if she was ever capable of loving anyone,' Rosie told me. 'She was pretty self-obsessed and already an alcoholic even before my dad went.' She lifted her head up to look me in the eye.

'You know I came pretty close to trying my mother's way out. After Michael. But I am so horrified by what it has done to her, I couldn't keep it up. I'd get rat-faced, then feel so bad for the next couple of days, I couldn't face it again. I'd think about where it would lead, the vomiting, the incontinence, sores down the legs, looking like a corpse. After about the fourth attempt, I stopped. I like a drink, I might even get a bit drunk sometimes, but I have no interest in losing myself in a bottle. I guess that's one life's lesson she taught me, huh?

'I haven't seen her for five years. I think she's in the States somewhere, in and out of re-hab facilities. I think that's the only reason she's still alive.'

'Jeez, that's tough,' I said. 'You know, I would say that that makes you stronger than you realise. I can't take any of that away for you, Rosie, believe me I would if I could. But I can promise you this: I will be with you for as long as you'll let me—and beyond.

'I will never desert you.'

She snuggled into my arms, soothed by my words, for that night anyway. I kissed her hair, her eyes and her lips. Then I held her tightly to me.

Her breathing softened, evened, and she drifted off peacefully to sleep.

And I drifted into the most contented sleep I've had for years.

Chapter Twenty-Seven

As I drift back into consciousness, my arm is draped across a still-sleeping Rosie and her leg is draped across mine. And I know that I want to wake every morning from now on like this, to find her beside me. We haven't spent many nights apart since we met just a few short weeks ago but this is the proper start of our life together. I am hers and she is mine and I never want to be apart from her again.

My phone buzzes. Another fucking text from Linnea. I don't even bother to read it before deleting it. I can't wait now for this wedding to be over, to delete her from my contacts list, once and for all.

I can't wait for the wedding for another reason now though. I want to introduce Rosie as my girl to my family. I want to see my momma's face when she sees how happy I am and how much I love this woman. I know they're going to love her, and I know she will love them.

It occurs to me that Linnea actually did me a favour all those years ago. If she hadn't dumped me, I'd have married her. And I may even have been superficially happy. But the fact is, we'd never shared the depth of feeling I am experiencing now with Rosie. Linnea had never shared my love of music, or literature, or art.

Was Linnea an inevitable step along this road, a step designed to put me on hold until I found Rosie at the point at which she was ready to find me? And for Rosie—was it inevitable that she had to go through all that she did to be ready to find me just at that precise moment?

I wonder what it is that tells a man and a woman, in those first few moments of eyes meeting eyes, those first whispered words, that they belong together. Because I am pretty sure that was when I knew, and Rosie says the same. Was it purely the chance meeting of a chemistry with its exact complement? Or was it something more than chance? Was it her I was seeking all along? All I know for sure is that she is *it* for me, the one, and I intend to do everything in my power to make *her* happy.

I meant every word I said to her before we slept. My life's mission now is to make my beautiful, fragile elfin-faerie feel safe, secure and loved, really loved, every single day, help her build the confidence to unfurl those wings... and watch her fly...

Rosie

I awake in the morning to find Nathan gone from the bed, already up and about. I pick up his shirt from the floor, pull it on and pad out to find him. The events of the night before are playing through my mind. While it ended very emotionally for me, elation still holds me firmly in its grip, lifting my feet inches off the floor.

I told my beautiful, wonderful man that I love him, terrified that it would chase him off but unable to stop. And he told me it was everything he wanted.

He loves me. I can hardly believe it—part of me still doesn't, but I'm shutting that voice down. He loves me—yeah, yeah, yeah!

And soon, he'll be taking me to his home for his sister's wedding. And introducing me to his family as his genuine girlfriend. Scared? You bet. This is a real family. Will they think me good enough for their son and brother?

I am good enough for Nathan, and that is enough for me. I *will* look forward to this trip. I can do this.

I find him in the kitchen preparing coffee and crumpets, singing along in his wonderful, rich baritone voice, to something familiar. It's an Elvis Presley song, 'Can't Help Falling in Love', but I don't recognise the version.

He looks up as I come in and does that thing where he tilts his head slightly forward and to one side as his eyebrows shoot up and everything inside me melts. 'I was gonna bring you breakfast in bed. You okay this morning, Darlin'?' he asks me, tentatively.

'How could I not be?' I answer him. 'Who is this? I haven't heard this version before.'

'My brother was into Pearl Jam in his early teens,' he tells me, 'and this was something he played a lot. Kinda appropriate, huh?'

We both sing along to each other, telling each other that we can't help falling in love.

I grin at him. 'I want to tell you again this morning, Nathan.'

'Honey, you can tell me any goddam time you like.'

'Nathan?'

'Uh-huh?'

'I love you.'

'Okay,' he responds, grinning at me.

I glare at him. 'Oh, you're asking for it,' I menace.

'Well, why don't you come on over here and give it to me then?'

I sprint across the kitchen and leap into his arms. He kisses me then says in my ear, 'I've waited to hear that, Rosie. You have made this old man so very happy.'

He puts me down. 'Oh and by the way, you look hot as hell in that shirt—it'll give me perfect access to your ass.

'Oh God, Americans. How many times? The word is arse, Nathan—there's an 'r' in it. As I've mentioned before? An ass is a type of donkey or a stupid person,' I tell him, for what must be the tenth time. 'This,' I say flashing my bare bum at him, 'is called an aRse.'

'No,' he says, 'that, there, is called *Nathan's* aRse. It belongs to me.'

He leaps forward as if to grab me, but I am too quick for him and pad back to the bathroom to freshen up.

I am positively euphoric.

He loves me, he really does love me. I'm not imagining this. And as long as I can see myself reflected in his beautiful eyes, I can face anything the world might throw at me.

Oh… and Rosie's Rules? Consigned to the bin.

I don't need them any more. I'm free…

Epilogue

The blonde woman in headphones looked down at the notes she was writing:

- *Handcuffs from home*
- *I'm all yours*
- *You own me*
- *Mirror above bed - only woman he's watched - only woman in apartment*
- *Gabrielle Harris – check out*
- *You're everything I want*
- *Father disappeared - left for another woman*
- *Mother alcoholic*
- *Sings to her*

Who knew modern surveillance technology could be so… useful? It had been so easy to lift Nathan's phone and install the App.

Who knew eavesdropping could be so much fun—and so productive? She was going to have a field day with this lot…

The End…

Thank you for reading Rosie's Rules. *I do hope you have enjoyed reading it as much as I have enjoyed writing it.*

If you did, please leave a review—or, at the very least a rating, on Amazon and Goodreads. Let other readers know how much you enjoyed the book and help this author get her work out there….

To find out what happens when Rosie and Nathan attend the Wedding in Kentucky you'll need to read the next book in the series, Rosie's Rival. (Get a sneak preview of Chapter One under Read More.)

Musical Note

A special thank you to all of the artistes, musicians and songwriters featured or hinted at. You are here because I think your talent is awesome. All music, songs, song titles and lyrics mentioned in the novel, Rosie's Rules are the property of the respective composers, songwriters and copyright holders.

The following playlist includes all the songs and pieces of music mentioned in the book and/or are the versions I listened to while writing it:

Strangers in the Night – Frank Sinatra : Music by Bert Kaempfert with English lyrics by Eddie Snyder
Bye, Bye Blackbird – Julie London : Music: Ray Henderson Lyrics: Mort Dixon
Fever – Peggy Lee : Eddie Cooley and Otis Blackwell
Cheek to Cheek – Eva Cassidy : Irving Berlin
Moondance – Van Morrison : Van Morrison
Every Step You Take – Karen Souza : Sting
At Last – Etta James : Mac Gordon and Henry Warren
I Put a Spell On You – Nina Simone :Jalacy "Screamin' Jay" Hawkins
Angel Eyes – Sting : Music Matt Dennis Lyrics Earl Brent
The Girl From Ipanema – Astrud Gilberto : Antonio Carlos Jobim – English Lyrics: Norman Gimbel

Creep – PostmodernJukebox feat. Haley Reinhart : Radiohead Albert Hammond Mike Hazlewood
Seven Nation Army – The White Stripes : Jack White
Blacksmith Blues – Ella Mae Morse : Jack Holmes
This Can't Be Love – Ella Fitzgerald : Rogers and Hart
I'm Not in Love – Karen Souza : Eric Stewart and Graham Gouldman
Wicked Game – Daisy Gray : Chris Isaak
Benedictus for Cello – 2Cellos : Karl Jenkins
Benedictus for Cello Live at Arena Zagreb – Stjepan Hauser : Karl Jenkins
Fix You – Coldplay : Coldplay
Soave sia il vento – A Trio from Cosi Fan Tutte by Wolfgang Amadeus Mozart
Au fond du temple saint also known as The Pearl Fishers' Duet – from Les Pêcheurs de Perles by Georges Bizet
Smooth – Santana feat. Rob Thomas : Itaal Shur and Rob Thomas
The Game of Love – Santana feat. Michelle Branch : Gregg Alexander and Rick Nowels
The Love Theme from Blade Runner Vangelis feat. D. Morissey on Tenor Sax : Vangelis
Black Dog – Led Zeppelin : Led Zeppelin
She Loves You – The Beatles : John Lennon and Paul McCartney
Rosie – Don Partridge : Don Partridge
Can't Help Falling In Love – Pearl Jam : Hugo Peretti, Luigi Creatore, and George David Weiss

Find a version of all of these on Spotify: Rosie's Playlist Rules

Read More

Now that you've followed Rosie and Nathan's journey discovering their love for each other, do you want to know what happens next?

Rosie's Rival

Stunning, vivacious and talented young jazz vocalist Rosie Byrne has met her match, the love of her life, Kentuckian Nathan Connor, owner of London's prestigious Café Paradiso—bar, restaurant, premium live music venue. The heat is rising as their undeniable chemistry binds them together. But his ex, Linnea, with technology resources at her fingertips to play very dirty, embarks upon a determined campaign to tear them apart.

When traumatic events reveal that there are even more sinister forces at play, can this fledgeling relationship weather the barrage of perilous storms heading its way and see this pair navigate a path to calmer waters.

From the opening sentence, this sequel to Rosie's Rules, takes the reader on a roller-coaster ride of emotions and thrills. If you like your romances with feisty characters, a strong storyline and explosive level steam, this is a must for you.

Read the first chapter on the next page...

Rosie's Rival will be published in June 2023

Book Two: Rosie's Rival

Chapter One

Nathan

What the fuck?

Where the hell was Rosie? I called out her name. Her hat was on the bed, but no other sign of her. There were no cosmetics in the bathroom, no clothes in the wardrobe, and no bag.

I'd gone up to our room to find out what was holding Rosie up. My sister's wedding ceremony was starting soon, and the guests were already making their way out to the rows of seats facing the beautiful wedding pavilion erected on the grounds of my family's home in Lexington, Kentucky.

I'd sensed something was off earlier, but she kept saying she was okay, so I'd assumed she was just a bit overwhelmed. I didn't have the chance to probe any further; it was easier to accept her assurances and assume she had a good reason for wanting to return to the bedroom.

I was going to regret that.

I spotted my phone on the bed. As I flicked the screen on, I saw that there was yet another text I'd missed from Linnea, my sister's best friend and Maid of Honour—and my ex—but I didn't have time for that, and besides, my strategy with her was to ignore everything.

I tried Rosie's phone. It transferred to voicemail. I left a message and tried again. Voicemail again. Was she rejecting my calls?

I raced down the stairs and dashed outside, where one of the gardeners was doing something at one side of the house.

'Hey Jim, have you seen a young woman? Dark-haired, this high?' I yelled at him.

'Uh-huh, Nathan. I saw one just like that get into a limo. The driver put a small case in the back.'

'When? How long ago?' I frantically demanded.

'Not long. Five minutes or so....'

My first instinct was to take one of the cars and go after them. I decided to wing off a quick text first.

<<Rosie. I don't know what happened, but I know you are in a car and headed away. I'm coming after you. I love you. N

She responded, but I wished she hadn't:

>>Please don't. I'm safe and will get home okay. This is your sister's wedding, and I don't want to be the reason you miss it. Take care. Goodbye Nathan.

Goodbye? Was that like a definitive Goodbye? *What the fuck?*

<<Rosie. What's going on? What's happened? N

As I waited for a response, I took a few minutes to think things through. My immediate problem was that this was my sister's wedding, and I had to see it through. Rosie was safe, and I knew where she was going. I guessed that her trustee, Martin, had arranged everything for her, including flights back to the UK and transport to London and that he would ensure she was looked after.

I needed to stay, and I wracked my brain for something to explain her disappearance.

I sought out my momma.

'What's wrong, Nathan?'

'Rosie got a call from home and had to rush back, Momma. She was bitterly disappointed about having to leave and miss the wedding. She sends her apologies. We called for a car, and she's on her way to the airport. *I'm* staying for my baby sister's wedding, but she won't miss Rosie being here, having never met her.'

'Okay, Honey. That's such a shame. I do hope everything is all right with Rosie. I'll tell your father while you get yourself calmed down and smartened up again.' She hugged me. 'I do appreciate you staying, son. I know your sister would be devastated if you weren't here.'

For what seemed the longest hours of my life, I had to make like I was enjoying my beautiful sister's wedding, not wanting to ruin her big day. I had to make polite conversation with my family and their friends. My only respite was getting to spend a little time with my niece, Lily-May, and my nephew, Bowen. My brother's children were always a delight to me;

that day, they were a godsend.

All the while, I was desperately trying to work out what had happened to Rosie. Why the fuck had she run?

And then there was Linnea.

After the ceremony, she was hovering around me, trying to get me to pay attention to her. I remembered there had been a message from her on my phone. I thought I'd quickly look at that and then shut her down completely. I'd had enough of the suggestive texts and constant calls, none of which I'd answered.

>>So, my sexy Stud Muffin. Can't wait to see you, Babe 😘

I was horrified, remembering that the phone had been in our bedroom, on the bed. Had Rosie seen it? I scraped my hand through my hair, gritting my teeth. Shit! I could hardly blame her for jumping to conclusions if she *had* seen this, but surely, she would have come and said something.

Sensing Linnea had become my shadow, I headed into the empty library. I closed the door behind us and turned on her brandishing my cell phone.

'What the fuck was this supposed to be, Lin?' I demanded. 'When have you ever called me Stud Muffin? And… just… what the fuck?'

She grinned, a mischievous child caught in some cute misdemeanour, and tried to put her arms around my waist. I stepped back out of her reach. She closed the gap and tried again.

'Oh Baby,' she purred at me, 'stop fightin' this. You know you want me.'

I firmly gripped her upper arms, and held her away from me.

In a tone laced with incredulity, I fired back at her, 'Stop fightin' what exactly? In what world could you possibly believe that I'd want *you*? After everythin' that happened seven years ago, Linnea, you must be delusional.'

'Oh Baby, come on. I made a huge mistake leavin' you for Ethan. It's time for you to forgive me, and let's get back to where we were.'

She looked at me through her eyelashes. *Ugh!*

'Forget your little distraction. I see you sent her packin'. I mean, she's hardly your type, Baby. Talk about cradle-snatchin'. Come back to the grown-ups. You know we were so good together.'

Letting go of her arms, I put my hand up to stop her from closing in again and stepped back, trying to widen the gap between us.

'Let me start by sayin' that hell will surely freeze over before I ever want anythin' to do with you, *Baby*. And for the record, *Baby*, Rosie is the most beautiful *woman* I have ever known. And I mean *ever*.'

She faltered and stopped trying to get close to me. She stood gazing into my eyes.

Good. I had her attention. 'And you wanna talk about good together? What we had all those years ago? It doesn't come close to what I've found in Rosie.'

Her eyes flickered.

'And what makes her *so* special, *Baby*, is that beautiful as she is, she's even more beautiful on the inside, unlike others I could mention, who are ugly and bitter and twisted.'

It was a cruel thing to say, brutal but true, and it seemed

to hit the mark. Her face fell, and I saw defeat in her eyes. I almost felt sorry for her. Almost. But shit! Had she seriously believed we could go back?

I'd had enough and turned to open the door. 'So, *Baby*, are we clear? I think we're done here.'

I walked away from her and out of the library, seething. It would seem she got the message—she didn't approach me again for the rest of the day.

With no overnight flights available, I left early the following morning. I had to get to Rosie and find out why she'd run. I loved her, and she loved me. Whatever was wrong, we could fix it. Even if she had seen the text from Linnea, I could explain that.

I just had to get to her.

About the Author

Love Parker is a new contemporary romance author, who loves to create strong, if flawed, engaging characters destined to fall hard when they meet, and then let them dictate the story they tell. Well that's what she says now because she actually set out to write a standalone story with a planned plotline until her two main characters took over, decided where the plot was going and dictated that there had to be sequels. If it sounds crazy—that's because it is—but true!

A forces child and then married to an executive in the airline industry, she is well travelled, having lived in far-flung places—Singapore, Libya, Germany, Scotland, New York in the USA, as well as all over the UK. An ex-English Teacher and Chartered Company Director, she now lives in the North-East of England with her husband and dog, a Jackawawa called Bobby, where she is indulging her desire to be a jazz singer and author—oh and part of a folk band too!

In her spare time, she likes reading, keeping fit, watching TV and Movies, and going to concerts and gigs—from Pubs and Jazz Cafes to The O2, Wembley Stadium and Madison Square Garden.

She really enjoys great food, in wonderful restaurants or home cooked. She will always feature some of her favourite foods in her stories.

Most of all, she loves spending time with close friends, particularly her real-life hero, her rock and the gorgeous man who makes everything possible—Mr Parker.

You can connect with me on:

- http://www.moonstormbooks.com/love-parker
- https://twitter.com/LovePar90985849
- https://www.facebook.com/love.parker.88
- https://www.instagram.com/love.parker.88
- https://www.tiktok.com/@loveparker29?lang=en

Subscribe to my newsletter:

- https://forms.gle/RhFQ6MA7r9sdUDmT9

Printed in Great Britain
by Amazon